The
Dilemma

BOOKS BY JULIA ROBERTS

My Mother's Secret

The Woman on the Beach

THE LIBERTY SANDS TRILOGY

Life's a Beach and Then...

If He Really Loved Me...

It's Never Too Late to Say...

Christmas at Carol's

Carol's Singing

Alice in Theatreland

Time for a Short Story

One Hundred Lengths of the Pool

As J.G. Roberts

THE DETECTIVE RACHEL HART SERIES

1. Little Girl Missing

2. What He Did

3. Why She Died

The Dilemma

JULIA ROBERTS

Bookouture

Published by Bookouture in 2022

An imprint of Storyfire Ltd.
Carmelite House
50 Victoria Embankment
London EC4Y 0DZ

www.bookouture.com

ISBN: 978-1-80314-527-3
eBook ISBN: 978-1-80314-528-0

This book is dedicated to my friend David, whose son, Jude, had kidney failure after suffering Meconium Aspiration Syndrome at birth. It's been a long road, but I hope you are both recovering well after transplant surgery xxx

PART ONE

ONE

Charlotte

The deafening sound of music recedes as the door to the ladies' loo swings closed behind me, but I can still feel the heavy bass vibrating through my body, beating in time with the miniature drummer in my head. A few years ago, I could have put it down to a dozen or more gin and tonics and the start of the inevitable hangover, but I barely drink these days.

I lay my hands on my flat stomach and offer up a silent prayer, hoping that maybe this month it will be answered. I'm six days late with my period, but that's not unusual for me. I made a promise to myself a couple of years ago that I would wait until I was a week late before doing a pregnancy test after suffering the crushing disappointment of so many negative results. I must admit I feel somehow different this month. I can't exactly put my finger on it, but it's as though my body has a secret that it's not ready to share with me yet. For the briefest of moments, I picture myself opening my eyes to look at the window in the white plastic stick and blinking hard to make sure there is no mistake and that it really does say pregnant. I've waited so long for that elated feeling... surely if I wish hard enough, it will eventually happen.

It feels unfair that some women can fall pregnant easily and yet it just won't happen for me and my partner, Zack. I long to hold my newborn son or daughter in my arms. I'm desperate for our baby, conceived and carried with love, to be showered with everything Zack and I have to offer. But each month my body lets me down.

I've had all the tests, and there's no physical reason why I can't become pregnant, so maybe the experts are right that it could be my desperation for a baby that is the problem. I've tried to follow their advice to relax and enjoy my relationship with Zack. I've charted the best days of the month to try to conceive and taken all the recommended supplements. But all to no avail.

The volume of the music suddenly increases, accompanied by the sound of female voices as the door starts to open. I duck into a vacant toilet cubicle even though I don't need a wee. I can't face the question 'Are you okay?' from someone fifteen years my junior if they should notice the tears trickling down my cheeks. And what would I say in response? I'm not okay. My maternal clock has been ticking for most of the ten years Zack and I have been together, but despite neither of us taking precautions, those two little words 'not pregnant' appear to crush my hopes each time I allow them to be raised.

Trying not to think about the germs as I rest my cheek against the cool tiles of the cubicle wall, I reach into my handbag for a tissue to mop my tears before my supposedly waterproof mascara starts to run. The last thing I want is for Zack to know I've been crying when tonight is supposed to be a celebration.

It was his idea to come out to Paradise, the nightclub where we first met ten years ago. The decor hasn't changed much, even down to the fake palm trees illuminated by fairy lights. Apparently, the owner had been inspired by a club he had visited on the party island of Ibiza, but the effect isn't quite the same when the heat is generated by radiators rather than a balmy July evening in the Balearics.

Ten years ago, it was after gazing up at the dark ceiling, punctuated by twinkling lights that were meant to represent stars, that I noticed Zack staring at me. He was up on the stage, slapping out the bass riffs in an eighties tribute band. Until that moment, I'd always thought people were exaggerating when they spoke about being struck by a bolt of lightning when they first locked eyes with their future partner, but I felt the sizzle of excitement immediately.

When his set had finished, he came and found me at the bar and insisted on buying me a drink even though my glass was full. I can still remember my heart thumping in my chest when he asked for my number. I left before he finished playing the final set. I didn't want to be just another groupie falling into bed with him, no matter how much I fancied him.

I deliberately turned my phone off before getting into bed that night, because I didn't want to lie awake wondering if he was going to call, and if he didn't, wondering why not. When I woke the next morning and switched my phone on, there was a voice message asking me to meet for dinner that night, and despite my best intentions to play it cool, I agreed.

If I'm honest, I would have preferred to celebrate our anniversary with a candlelit dinner in the restaurant where we had our first date, or even just had a romantic night in, but Zack was so pleased with himself for remembering our special date and suggesting a night in Paradise that I hadn't the heart to say that I didn't really fancy it. He paid extra for the VIP area and ordered champagne, which I toasted him with but have only sipped at throughout the evening. If he's noticed, he hasn't commented.

'Are you going to be much longer?' an urgent female voice asks. 'Only I'm desperate and you've been in there for ages.'

'Just coming,' I say, pressing the flush on the toilet and unlocking the door. 'Sorry, I wasn't feeling too good,' I mumble by way of explanation, but it's lost on the blonde teenager who rushes past me.

I quickly check my eye make-up in my urgency to leave without further engagement with the girl or any of her group of friends who are giving me sideways glances. The heat and sound greet me as I open the door and make my way back to the roped-off VIP area.

'There you are,' Zack says, as I slide into the booth next to him. 'I was about to send out a search party. Are you okay?'

'Yes, fine. I've just got a bit of a headache,' I say, hoping that Zack will take the hint and suggest an early exit.

'That explains it,' he replies.

'Explains what?'

'Why you've barely touched your champagne.' He did notice, then. 'I guess we've got out of the habit of hanging out in nightclubs with the music on full volume. Does that mean we're getting old?' he asks, pulling a face.

'You speak for yourself,' I say, lifting his arm and draping it around my shoulder while I snuggle against his chest. He might be five years older than me, but he is still a very handsome man and attracts a lot of female attention.

'Maybe this wasn't such a good idea after all,' he says, dropping a kiss onto the top of my head. 'I thought it would be good fun taking a trip down memory lane, but the drinks are overpriced, the clientele makes me feel like a grandad and the band is nowhere near as good as Go East.'

Go East was the band Zack used to play with before he decided it was time for him to make use of his qualifications and get a "proper" job teaching music in a school. He still gets the occasional call to do gigs, mostly weddings or big birthdays.

'On second thoughts, I agree about feeling old,' I say, thinking back to the group of girls in the loos. If I'd had a daughter when I was in my teens, she would have been around the same age as them. The thought only serves to underline the fact that I didn't have a child when I was in my teens, and I'm now in my mid-thirties and I've still not been blessed. 'It was a nice idea, but I do feel a bit out of place.'

'Come on then,' Zack says, knocking back the rest of his champagne. 'There are other more enjoyable ways to celebrate our tenth anniversary.'

He pulls me into an embrace and kisses me with a passion that still leaves me weak at the knees even after all these years together. We both get to our feet and Zack guides me towards the exit of the VIP area while softly singing along with Rod Stewart.

The lyrics of *Have I Told You Lately That I Love You* are still running through my mind when we climb into a taxi a few minutes later. I know how lucky I am to have a relationship that is so close to perfect. Am I asking too much for it to be made complete?

TWO

THURSDAY 1 FEBRUARY

According to the digital readout on the Echo Dot on my bedside table, it's shortly after 3 a.m. when I eventually concede defeat. Sliding out of bed in an attempt to not disturb a gently snoring Zack, I feel my way across the bedroom to the en-suite bathroom, only putting the light on when the door is safely closed behind me. I glance in the mirrored cabinet before opening it to retrieve the ibuprofen tablets and I'm met with raccoon eyes and a tousled mane of hair that bears a striking resemblance to a bird's nest. I'm usually very good at removing my make-up before bed, but there was an urgency to Zack's desire tonight after the disappointment of our night out. A smile plays across my lipstick-smudged mouth. We might be too old to enjoy Paradise nightclub as much as we used to, but we certainly still enjoy each other, I think, while swallowing two pills.

Although they're the fast-working ones, I know it'll still take a few minutes before the throbbing in my head is dulled sufficiently for me to get back to sleep. As I put the packet back in the cabinet, I spot the pregnancy test. Technically it's a new day, so my period is now a week late and I'm pretty sure a few hours won't affect the result. I tear the packaging on the test open, as I must have done fifty or more times over the past few years, and close my eyes in silent prayer as I pee on the stick. Afterwards, I sit down on the fluffy mat, leaning against the bath and hugging my knees to my chest while I wait for the result.

Zack finds me there three hours later. He's by my side in an instant.

'What are you doing in here?' he asks, taking hold of my hand. 'You're freezing cold. Aren't you feeling well? It can't be the alcohol, you hardly touched a drop...' His voice trails off when I raise my head and he notices my tear-stained face. 'What is it, Charlotte? What's wrong?'

My eyes flick sideways to the pregnancy test, and then back to meet his. For a moment, I can't read his expression. Still holding my hand, he sinks down onto the bathmat beside me as tears overwhelm me again. Stupidly, I allowed myself to believe that I felt different, that this time I was pregnant with Zack's baby, but those two words couldn't be any clearer. Zack is silent while I cry the pain out of me.

As the sobs subside, he places a hand on each side of my face and looks into my eyes as though searching for something. 'We can't go on like this. This obsession with having a baby is destroying you. No, I take that back, it's destroying us.'

I start to speak, but he gently places his fingers on my lips.

'What if you never become pregnant? What if it's just not meant to be?'

It's the start of a conversation we've had many times before, which always leads to me begging him to go for fertility tests and him pointing out that he already has two boys from a previous relationship. His point-blank refusal to even consider that his sperm count might have diminished as he's got older is always hurtful and adds to my guilt at not being able to conceive. This morning, though, there is something different about his expression that suggests he doesn't want to talk about it. It could be because it's a school morning and he has his routine timed to the minute, or maybe his patience with me has finally run out. I can see how my desperation to be a mother might have worn him down to such an extent that it's starting to erode the love he feels for me.

His hands are still cupping my face and his eyes hold mine. He seems to be struggling with what he is about to say. A terrible thought occurs to me. What if he asks me to make a choice? Zack is my world; he has been since that first meeting ten years ago. I can't imagine my life without him, but it would be so wonderful to complete our family with a child.

'Am I not enough for you, Charlotte?' he eventually asks.

There's a slight quiver in his voice and my heart aches that he could believe such a thing to be true.

'Don't say that,' I reply. 'Of course, you are, it's just that—'

He quietens me again. 'What if I told you that you and I will never have a baby?'

As his words start to sink in, I feel the blood drain from my cheeks.

'I... I don't understand,' I stammer. 'Did you go for fertility tests without me knowing? What did they say?'

My heart is pounding thunderously in my chest. Why didn't Zack tell me he'd had tests? And when did he have them? How long has he known that he couldn't father our child and why on earth didn't he tell me? There are so many questions I need answers to.

'No, I didn't go for tests,' he says, his eyes still searching mine. 'I didn't need to.'

'Then how can you be so sure?' I ask, my mouth so dry that I can barely speak.

'I've wanted to tell you so many times, but I was afraid of

what it might do to you,' he says, dropping his gaze for a moment. 'I thought you would eventually accept that we weren't destined to be parents. I was waiting for the right moment to suggest we go to the dog rescue shelter and get a puppy...' His voice trails away.

I'm concentrating on his words, trying to make sense of them, but my head is in a jumble.

He raises his eyes back to mine. 'After Paula and I split up, she took our boys back to Australia with her. I didn't fight it because I knew it was the best thing for them, but it almost broke me. It's bad enough if you only get to have your kids on alternate weekends, but my boys weren't even in the same country. I couldn't face the possibility of that ever happening again. I had a vasectomy,' he finishes, in a voice little more than a whisper.

The room starts to spin. I'm grateful to be sitting down or I suspect I would have fainted. All these months, no, years, I've been peeing on plastic sticks, praying for a positive result, and suffering gut-wrenching hurt as I received its cruel message minutes later, were futile. It was never going to be a positive result and Zack knew that, yet still he let me continue with the charade. I'm winded, as though he's punched me in the stomach, but if he had, I'd be in less pain. I'm struggling to believe that Zack, my kind, caring thoughtful Zack, could have let me hope every month, all the time knowing that it was in vain.

'I'm sorry,' he says. 'I should have been honest with you when you first started talking about us having a baby, but I didn't want to lose you. I thought, well, hoped that I'd be enough for you...'

I want to tell Zack that it's okay, that I understand. But it's not okay and I don't think I'll ever understand. I can't find my voice. It seems to have been swallowed up in the shock of finding out that he has been keeping something so momentous from me. I want to feel angry with him, or upset, or just feel anything, but I'm numb.

'We can get past this, can't we?' Zack asks. 'We love each other and we're good together. Once you've got used to the idea, we can dream about different things for our future.'

'Stop talking,' I finally manage to say, releasing my hands from his and resting my head in them. I'm trying to make sense of what Zack's just told me and for that I need quiet. Quiet and space. I don't want to be in our bathroom with him. In fact, I don't want him anywhere near me.

'You have to understand, Charlotte. I was terrified of losing you. Can we talk about it?'

'Not now,' I say, my voice sounding far calmer than I feel. 'You need to get in the shower, or you'll be late for work.'

'You're right,' he says. 'But we're okay, aren't we? We can work this out?'

I nod, pushing myself up using the side of the bath for support. Zack scrambles up too and holds me close for a few seconds before reaching past me to turn on the shower.

My legs are like jelly as I head towards the kitchen to make coffee. I just need to hold everything together until Zack leaves for work.

The twenty minutes it takes for Zack to shower, dress and have his coffee and toast seem like an eternity. Normally, we laugh and chat about what the day ahead might hold for him at school and me at the shop, but there is nothing normal about today. He's been talking to me because I could see his lips moving, but nothing he said seemed to register, so I just nodded and smiled.

Usually, we have a long lingering kiss at the front door, neither of us wanting to break the embrace, but I stay seated at the table as he makes a big show of putting on his coat and hat and gloves ready for the freezing temperature outside. When I don't go over to him, he comes back to the table and drops a kiss on the top of my head.

'I know you're angry with me, but I did it for us. I couldn't bear the thought of there not being an *us* because we couldn't have children. You do understand, don't you?' When I don't answer, he adds, 'And you do know that I love you more than anything in the world?'

He places his hands on my cheeks to lift my face so that he can make eye contact, the rough texture of his gloves against my skin making me recoil slightly. The eyes that I've always trusted to reveal the truth are filled with concern.

'I know,' I manage to say, but can't find it within myself to reciprocate his declaration of love. I just want him to leave. I need space.

'We'll sit down and talk it through tonight,' he says, letting me go and heading towards the door. 'I've got private lessons until six, so I'll stop off on the way home and get a pizza.'

And then he's gone, leaving behind the silence I've been craving since he dropped his bombshell. It only lasts a few moments before it is shattered by huge wracking sobs as realisation dawns that Zack is not the man I thought he was and my life with him has been built on dishonesty. That's what really hurts. All my hopes and dreams for us as a family have gone up in smoke, and while it's distressing to know that I'll never be a mother to Zack's children, it's the lie of allowing me hope that is so utterly devastating.

When I think every last tear has been wrung from my body, I sit very still, gazing around the space I've shared with Zack for the past ten years. The memories of our life together flood my mind. Passionate lovemaking on the sofa, tearing each other's clothes off, such was our urgency. Quietly listening to music or watching Saturday night television on that same sofa, indulging in a stuffed-crust pizza and a bottle of Italian red before my desire to get pregnant dramatically reduced my alcohol intake.

One final tear escapes the corner of my eye. Zack is going to stop off on his way home to bring me my favourite takeaway.

But I won't be here.

I can't live another moment with someone I no longer trust.

THREE

SUNDAY 25 FEBRUARY

Through the fog of sleep, I can hear a ringing sound. I reach from beneath the warm duvet to turn off my alarm and shiver as my hand comes into contact with the cold air. I need to speak to the landlord about fixing the heating, which gave up the ghost on Friday evening a couple of hours after he would have arrived at a remote cottage in Wales with no internet and no phone signal. While the weekend away sounds idyllic, the timing of his trip couldn't have been worse from my point of view, as yesterday was the coldest day of the year so far. And temperatures are set to tumble even further today, according to the weather forecaster, who delivered his news with what could only be described as a smirk. He should try living in a Victorian cottage with single-glazed windows and no heating. That would soon wipe the smile from his face.

After fumbling with the top of my ancient alarm clock for a few seconds, wondering why I can't turn the ringing off, it dawns on me that it's Sunday morning. The ringing noise is my phone, which I pick up off the bedside table. I peer bleary-eyed at the screen, trying to figure out who could be calling me so early. I'm shocked to see that it's almost half past eleven. For the first time since I walked out of my life with Zack almost a month ago, I've slept through a whole night and almost a whole morning too.

I hit the green button to answer the call.

'Hello,' I croak.

'Please tell me you're not still in bed,' Annabel says in a voice far too loud and cheerful to deal with. 'It's a gorgeous morning,' she continues. 'Perfect for a walk around the nature reserve, followed by a pub lunch at The Old Packhorse. Their Yorkshire puddings are to die for.'

My stomach rumbles at the mere mention of food. I can't actually remember the last time I had a proper meal, but I could hazard a guess and say three weeks ago, when Annabel insisted I accompanied her to her parents' house for Sunday lunch, three days after I packed up my belongings and moved into the spare bedroom of the riverside apartment she shares with her boyfriend, Finn. Her parents didn't seem to mind having an extra guest at their table. It's not as though there wasn't enough food to go around, particularly as a sparrow has a bigger appetite than I currently do. But looking back, they must have thought I was pretty antisocial as I barely uttered half a dozen words the whole time we were there.

My loss of appetite means that I'm no longer carrying the comfort weight of a stable relationship, but I wouldn't recommend it as a diet plan. I'm now virtually the same size I was in my modelling days, which is where Annabel and I first met. She and Tiffany, another of the more experienced girls at Faces Model Agency, took me under their wing after I was signed at sixteen. Tiff and I speak on the phone sometimes and occasionally meet for a coffee and a catch-up, when she can squeeze me in to her hectic life running around after her two teenage daughters.

Annabel and I have kept in much closer contact, which might be because we have more in common. There are only two years between us in age and neither of us has children. If I ever broach the subject, she insists that it's her choice not to be a mum. *Why would anyone willingly subject themselves to stretchmarks, saggy boobs and sleepless nights?* she always says.

'What do you think?' Annabel asks, breaking into my thoughts. 'We're due a proper natter, we haven't really talked since... well, since... you know.'

I do know. I was so devastated by Zack's deception that I haven't even been able to talk about it to my best friend in all the world. She's been here for me, helping me through the practicalities of moving out of Zack's in a hurry and letting me stay at her place for a few nights. It was Annabel who suggested trying to find somewhere local to her to rent so that she could keep an eye on me. She spotted the advert for Myrtle Cottage in the estate agent's window and came with me to view it. She was all too aware of how broken I was but didn't bombard me with questions or try to change my mind as some people might have done. She knew that I would open up to her when I felt ready.

I wriggle into an upright position, pulling the duvet cover around me and observe my breath hanging in the icy air as I exhale. Maybe the time has come to talk. Maybe sleeping through a whole night is a sign that I'm finally starting to come to terms with Zack's appalling betrayal. I remember my new landlord mentioning The Old Packhorse and its open fire the day I moved in. I'm sure the heating will get fixed as soon as I'm able to tell him about it, but in the meantime the thought of warming my bones in front of a roaring log fire is very appealing.

'Okay,' I say. 'Give me half an hour to get myself up and showered.'

There's an element of surprise in Annabel's voice, as though she expected to have to try harder to persuade me to venture out, when she says, 'I'll pick you up at midday then.'

She ends the call quickly, presumably not wanting to give me time to change my mind.

I'm just finishing rough drying my hair when I notice Annabel's bright blue Mercedes pull up outside on the double yellow lines. The only drawback to renting Myrtle Cottage is that there's no parking space for my battered old Mini, but, fortunately, the village hall is close by and there are always spaces in its car park.

Myrtle Cottage is in the middle of a Victorian terrace near the centre of Bray, a historic Berkshire village which is probably best known for its film studios. I suspect the cottages were originally built to house farm labourers, although as the nearby town of Maidenhead has grown there isn't much farming land now. Since Annabel moved in with Finn a little over a year ago, she has fallen in love with the area.

I allow myself the briefest of smiles as I grab my gloves, keys and coat and pull my bobble hat on over my almost dry hair. Until I moved here, I've always been a city girl. I couldn't comprehend why anyone would want to live in the sticks. Throughout my modelling career, I shared a flat near Clapham North tube station with some of the other girls from the agency, before moving into Zack's flat in Earlsfield. I always enjoyed the hustle and bustle, the delicious aromas coming from the street food stalls and the ability to be in the West End of London in around twenty minutes.

I did sometimes contemplate moving to a bigger place with its own little garden further out of London to raise our family, but there wasn't any point discussing it with Zack until we had a family to consider. I swallow hard. That's a conversation that I'll never be having with Zack now. My hopes of having children with the man I've loved since I first laid eyes on him have evaporated and with them the likelihood of me ever becoming a mother. Pulling the sage green front door of Myrtle Cottage closed behind me only serves to underline that the part of my life I've spent with Zack is over. It will be a long time before I'll be able to trust another man.

Annabel was spot on with her assessment of the Yorkshire puddings at The Old Packhorse pub. I'm not usually their biggest fan as the ones I remember from my childhood were stodgy and greasy. My mum was good at a lot of things, but, unfortunately, cooking wasn't one of them. However, the one I'm currently savouring my last mouthful of is a complete contrast. It's as light as a feather and crispy without being crunchy. I haven't managed to finish all the potatoes and beef because my stomach feels fit to burst, but there's no way I'm going to leave any of the Yorkshire pud.

'I told you they were good,' Annabel says as I finally lay my knife and fork side by side on my plate.

'Good is an understatement,' I reply, relaxing back in the leather club chair that has most likely been polished by thousands of backsides over the years.

It was quite late by the time we arrived at The Old Packhorse after our walk around the nature reserve, but luck was on our side as a table had just become free right in front of the roaring fire. By the time we'd placed our order and chinked glasses of red wine together, my fingers had thawed out and I was getting some feeling back in my toes.

The waitress is hovering now.

'Shall I clear your plates away?' she asks, clearly unsure whether we have finished or not.

'Yes please,' Annabel says.

'Was everything all right?' the waitress says anxiously, glancing down at the amount of food still on my plate.

'Delicious,' I reply. 'There was just too much for me.'

'That'll be why you're so slim,' she says. 'I wish I had your self-restraint.'

Annabel and I lock eyes across the table. We both know that portion control has nothing to do with me dropping over a stone in four weeks, but neither of us says anything until the waitress is out of earshot.

'You are starting to look a bit scrawny, if I'm honest,' Annabel says.

She's always honest. It's one of the things that I love about my best friend. That and her loyalty.

'Is that why you brought me here? Are you trying to fatten me up?' I ask, trying to keep the conversation light.

'You know why I suggested lunch. You can't carry this whole break-up on your own. You're going to have to talk to me about it eventually and I figured a couple of glasses of Malbec would loosen your tongue. Speaking of which, do you want a top-up? I'm driving, so I won't have anymore.'

Thinking of all the Sunday drives into the country for a pub lunch, where I volunteered to be the designated driver because I couldn't be sure that I wasn't pregnant, causes an unexpected feeling. Instead of the sadness that has been weighing me down, I feel a bubble of anger for all the years I've wasted hoping for something that I now know could never have happened.

Annabel is already pouring the wine into my glass. I place my hand over hers and tip the bottle to drain the last drop.

'No point wasting it,' I say. And then in response to her expression, I add, 'Don't worry, I haven't turned to drink to drown my sorrows. I just fancy getting a bit tipsy.'

I take a generous sip of wine, enjoying the warm feeling that floods my chest. I'm aware that Annabel is watching me, waiting for me to unburden myself, but I'm not quite ready yet. I keep my gaze averted and make a big deal of twizzling the stem of my glass between thumb and forefinger.

Prior to taking our plates away, the waitress dropped a

couple of large logs onto what appeared to be the dying embers of the fire. As she did, Annabel looked across at me with her eyebrows raised, clearly believing that the fire was too far gone to recover. Now, as I concentrate on the contents of my glass, I notice the flash of a spark, followed by another before a small flame darts out from beneath one of the new logs. I watch, mesmerised, as more flames appear, licking the gnarly logs with their darting tongues. Another shower of sparks disappears up the chimney, accompanied by much hissing and spitting from the wood, almost in protest that the fire is being dragged back to life.

'I thought she'd left it too late,' Annabel says.

'Me too,' I reply.

'Just goes to show that even the direst situation is not beyond help.'

I turn to look at her as she gazes into the fire. I know she's alluding to me and my current difficulty, that she's letting me know she wants to help me rise from the ashes of my relationship.

I down the rest of my wine.

'Let's go back to mine,' I say. 'We can't talk here.'

FOUR

Annabel and I arrive back at Myrtle Cottage around 4 p.m. We're barely through the door before I open another bottle of red for the Dutch courage I need to tell her the whole truth of why I ended my ten-year relationship with Zack. It's nowhere near the quality of the Malbec at the pub, which is hardly surprising since it was under a fiver from the bargain bin in the local convenience store. I've already had enough wine for the taste to go unnoticed. But judging by the grimace on Annabel's face as she takes her first sip, it's less smooth full-bodied fruitiness, more paint stripper.

We carry our glasses through to the lounge and settle opposite each other, me in the generously stuffed armchair and her on the two-seater sofa, each huddled beneath a fleecy throw to combat the cold. There are no flickering flames to gaze into, so no excuse to avoid eye contact. By the end of the first glass of barely palatable red, I have started to talk.

It soon becomes clear that Annabel must have assumed Zack was having an affair for me to take the drastic action I did. Even when she knows what actually lies behind me packing my bags and leaving, she struggles to understand why I would throw away all the good things Zack and I had going for us just because we would never have a baby together.

'Lots of couples can't have children, Charlotte,' she says, refilling her glass for the third time and emptying the remainder of the bottle into mine. 'They still live a full and happy life.'

I can see it's going to be difficult for me to make Annabel understand why I did what I did. She's never shown any maternal instinct in all the years I've known her. In fact, the opposite is true. She's always been dead set against having babies of her own.

'And what about using donor sperm?' she continues, taking a big swig of the wine, which clearly isn't improving even after the two glasses she's already had. 'Didn't you give that any thought before you just walked away from the love of your life? Zack can't father his own children, but you could still have had a child together.'

I'm starting to wonder if opening up to her was the right thing to do, after all. And it seems she hasn't finished yet.

'Not forgetting adoption, of course. I know Zack is older and you are borderline age-wise, but there are so many children needing a home.'

Finally, she pauses, maybe realising that she's given me no opportunity to respond to any of her suggestions, not that I want to while she's completely missing the point.

'What?' she says. She drains her glass with a look of distaste and places it on the coffee table. 'That really wasn't nice. I need something to take the taste away.'

'I've got a bottle of gin that Hayley at Ring o' Roses bought me for Christmas,' I say. 'I can crack that open if you want to stay over?'

'Sounds like a plan,' Annabel agrees. 'I'm already over the limit, so would have called a cab, but can you imagine being done for drink-driving when I might as well have been drinking vinegar. I take it you have tonic water?'

'I'll check.'

I gather up the wine glasses and head into the kitchen. It gives me a chance to formulate the best explanation of why I'm so upset by what Zack has done to me. Although Annabel and I have never been on the same page when it comes to wanting children, I hoped she would be more understanding of why I could no longer stay in a relationship with Zack.

A few minutes later, when I've worked out what I'm going to say, I return to the lounge. 'Not only tonic water, I even managed to find a couple of strawberries,' I say, handing Annabel a large glass of clear liquid with the cheerful red fruit bobbing around in it.

'No ice though?' she says, chinking her glass against mine.

'I didn't think we needed it. It's so cold in the kitchen, I've got goosebumps on my goosebumps.'

'Fair point. You need to get the heating fixed ASAP.'

I settle back into my armchair, pulling the tartan throw back around me, and take a sip of my drink, savouring the warm feeling the spirit gives me as it descends towards my stomach. It's a long time since I've consumed so much alcohol in such a short space of time. I'm pretty sure I'm going to regret it in the morning, but it's helping me talk things through with Annabel, even if she's still struggling to understand what truly devastated me.

'What will you do if Finn tells you he wants children?' I say, speaking the words I rehearsed in my head while I was making the drinks.

'Hold on a minute. You're jumping the gun a bit there. We've only been together two years, we're not that serious yet,' she responds.

'Oh, come on, Annabel. This is the most serious you've ever been about anyone. You and Finn are made for each other.'

She gives a slight shrug. 'Well, not serious enough to talk

about babies. The subject has never cropped up because we're having too much fun with just the two of us.'

'But it will. And when it does, what if Finn feels the same way that I do about them. How will you react? Will you pretend that you want them too, while all the time continuing to take your birth control pills?'

She frowns. 'No, of course not. We'd have an adult conversation where we talk about what's important to each of us and how we could reach common ground if we disagreed.'

'And that's exactly my point, Annabel. I'm heartbroken that I'll never be a mother to Zack's baby, but that pales into insignificance next to the great big lie he's been living for years. He knew how much motherhood meant to me, how incomplete I felt without it, and yet each month he allowed me to hope. How could he do that to someone he is supposed to love?' I say, my voice faltering.

'Oh, Charlotte,' Annabel says, putting her glass down and moving mine so that she can wrap her arms around me in a hug. 'I hadn't thought about it like that. I just thought you were hasty to throw away your happiness without discussing all the options in terms of having a family together. But you're right. Whatever his reasons for not being honest with you, how could he watch someone he loves suffer time and time again? For what it's worth, I think you've done the right thing.'

The floodgates open then. Maybe it's the relief of finally telling someone the whole story or the reassurance from my best friend that I've done the right thing. Either way, the tears and the gin flow until both are done and we finally stumble to bed after midnight.

FIVE

MONDAY 26 FEBRUARY

It's been a slow morning at Stems, the florist in Maidenhead where I managed to get a job the day after moving into Myrtle Cottage. A quick phone call to Ring o' Roses in Earlsfield where I used to work was all the reference Michaela, the owner, needed. Either my former employer was hugely enthusiastic about my ability and work ethic or Michaela was desperate. I started work the day after my interview and it has been an absolute blessing to be kept busy so my mind can't keep dwelling on what might have been.

I've been the first one into work every day, using the code to unlock the key box and open the shop at precisely 7.30 to catch the morning commuters. It was a struggle this morning after the emotion and overindulgence in booze last night. I crept out of the house as quietly as I could at 7 a.m., leaving Annabel in the spare room to sleep off the alcohol and head home when she feels sober enough to drive.

It promises to be a long old day as we don't shut up shop until 7.30 p.m. so that the flowers ordered in the morning can be picked up on the way home. While it's a great idea for the customers, it's probably the reason that Michaela has such a swift turnover of staff. Apparently, my predecessor only lasted for ten weeks, but in fairness that included the busy Christmas period and the rush of Valentine's Day. Maybe that was the final straw. Perhaps she couldn't face the thought of Mother's Day, which, in my experience, is the busiest time of the year. I'm dreading Mother's Day too, but for entirely different reasons. This will be the first time in several years that I won't be harbouring a tiny hope of cradling a newborn in my arms before the next Mother's Day comes around.

Glancing down at my watch, I can't believe it's still an hour to lunchtime. Michaela doesn't work Mondays as it is the quietest day of the week. Last week, I brought in soup so that I could stay behind the counter for as much of the day as possible. Despite Michaela instructing me to take an hour for lunch, I only flick the sign on the door to 'closed' when I need the loo.

I'm on my way back from the loo when I notice a shadowy outline behind the glass shop door.

'Coming,' I call out, hurrying across the tiled floor and releasing the lock. 'Sorry, I was just—'

'Hello, Charlotte.'

It feels like my heart stops momentarily.

'Zack! What are you doing here?'

Even as I say the words, I think I know the answer to my question. Annabel must have woken up this morning and decided that Zack needed to be given a chance to explain. Maybe she has a point. After he left for work on the day after our tenth anniversary, I didn't waste any time packing my clothes, toiletries and a few favourite books and pictures into a suitcase and a couple of holdalls, before loading them into my Mini and driving to a local supermarket where I parked and called Annabel as I had no idea what to do next. I thought she had understood why I was so devastated when I explained things to her last night, but I've obviously overestimated her loyalty to me. How could she betray my trust and tell Zack where to find me?

'I probably shouldn't have come,' Zack says. 'But I wanted to make sure you're all right.'

There is a slight tremor in his voice. For the first time, I consider how he must have felt on arriving home from work to find me gone, with no explanation and no forwarding address. Although Annabel didn't say that he'd been in touch with her, I suppose he might have been. He knows she's my best friend and the person I'd turn to in a crisis.

'I'm fine,' I say, my voice as tightly controlled as the emotions I'm struggling with. My depth of feeling has caught me by surprise although I'm not sure why. Zack was my world for the past ten years. Regardless of what he has done, being without him has made me feel terribly alone. But coming home to an empty house with no one to talk to about my day isn't reason enough to brush aside his deceit and fall back into his arms.

'Are you sure?' he asks. 'Only, you look a bit pale and tired.'

His comment irritates me. It might have been made from concern, but in my fragile, hungover state it sounds more like veiled criticism.

'That'll be the booze and late nights,' I say, making it sound as though last night's one-off is a regular occurrence. 'I've got my freedom back and I'm making the most of it, but that's no concern of yours now. You lost the right to have any say in what I do when you finally found the decency to tell me you'd been letting me live with false hope for years. This break-up is your doing, Zack, no one else's.'

'I deserve that,' he says.

There is sadness in his voice, but I'm not in the mood for forgiveness.

'Yes, you do. I've had time to think about all the opportunities you had to tell me the truth, but you chose not to. So many pregnancy test kits and thousands of hours of hope all gone to waste because you weren't man enough to come clean.' The volume of my voice is increasing with each spiteful word. Fortunately, there is no one else in the shop or my employment with Stems might have been shorter than the previous girl's. 'What you thought might happen if you'd been honest with me from the start has happened. Maybe I should feel sorry for you, but I don't.' He flinches, but I'm on a roll now. 'I don't think I'll ever get past the heartbreak you've caused me. I appreciate your coming to check up on me, but it doesn't change anything. You can tell that to Annabel when she calls to ask how it went.'

'Annabel?' Zack says, furrowing his brow. 'What's she got to do with anything?'

'Please don't add insult to injury, Zack. How else would you have known where to find me?'

'Hayley, at Ring o' Roses,' he replies. 'She was surprised to see me when I called in to buy a housewarming present for one of the other teachers at school. She thought we'd moved away when she got the call from your boss here asking for references.'

The enormous feeling of relief that Annabel hasn't been communicating with Zack behind my back is tempered by my lack of faith in her. I didn't want to believe that my best friend could have betrayed me after I'd confided in her, but it seemed like the only plausible solution.

'Oh, right,' I respond, struggling to find anything meaningful to say.

'It's taken two weeks for me to pluck up the courage to come and see you, and I had to fake a migraine to take the day off as I thought Saturdays would be too busy for you to talk to me.'

'Well, I'm sorry it was a wasted journey. Like I said, I'm fine. This is my life after Zack and it's going pretty well so far,' I say, hoping that I sound convincing. I'm thirty-five years old and single for the first time in a decade. The comfortable rug of a happy future with Zack and our children has been pulled from beneath my feet. I'm alone, but worse than that, I'm lonely. My life is not going particularly well. In fact it's barely 'going' at all. But, of course, I'm not going to tell him that.

Zack is examining my face, maybe searching for signs of weakness and a way back into my heart, but my mouth is fixed in a half-smile and my chin is slightly raised in defiance. I watch his shoulders slump forward in defeat before he forces them back.

'If that's what you want, Charlotte.'

'It is,' I say, thankful for the tinkle of the bell above the shop door signalling the arrival of a customer. 'How can I help?' I ask, turning to a smartly dressed woman approaching the counter.

'It's my boss's wedding anniversary and he forgot... again! Can you do something big and flashy to be delivered before half past four? That's when they need to leave to get into London for the dinner that I've just booked. Men,' she says, shaking her head in disbelief. 'They're all the same.'

Zack turns back to look at me before he leaves and my heart contracts. Not only had he recently remembered our tenth anniversary and organised what he thought was a special treat, he never forgot any of our other anniversaries, or my birthdays or Valentine's Days. Men are not all the same. I could stop him leaving and we could try to work things out, but even before the door closes behind him, I realise it's too late. The damage is done.

'Any preference for colours, or particular flowers?' I say to the woman, who is impatiently tapping a credit card on the counter.

She shrugs. 'Your choice.'

The door clicks closed behind Zack as if to underline that my choice is already made. I still have feelings for him and probably will for a long time to come, but he hasn't been honest with me. I doubt I could ever fully trust him again when everything about our time together was built on a lie.

SIX

As if this day could get any worse, the fine drizzle drifting on the breeze as I locked the door to Stems and dropped the keys in the secure box turned to a torrential downpour before I walked halfway home. Normally, I carry an umbrella with me even if the forecast doesn't mention rain, but this morning I forgot to pick it up. It shows how hung-over I must have been.

My face, already wet from the relentless rain, now has an added saltiness as I give myself permission to cry the tears that I held back earlier after Zack had left the shop. Seeing him today has reopened the wound that had started to heal. His concern appeared genuine, and it made me question whether I've made a terrible mistake.

Myrtle Cottage is a welcome sight as I turn off the main street that runs through Bray village and quicken my pace still further in my urgency to get inside. My jeans are so wet they are sticking to my legs, and my knee-length quilted coat is no match for the cloudburst I'm stuck in the middle of.

Although I left a message for my landlord to report the faulty central heating, I don't expect anyone will have been around to fix it yet, so I'm imagining myself sinking into a hot bath to warm up as I turn the key in the lock and push the door open. I start to unfasten my coat before heading straight upstairs to run myself a bath when the sound of voices coming from my kitchen stops me dead in my tracks.

It's taking me a while to adjust to living on my own. Before I go to bed each night, I double-check that I've locked and bolted the back door and put the deadlock on the front. My heart starts to thump against my ribs at the thought that someone may have broken in. I'm telling myself not to panic, but my hands which moments earlier were so cold that I could barely undo my coat now have sweaty palms.

I'm fingering my mobile phone, debating whether to call the police or make a run for it, when Annabel's voice calls out from the kitchen.

'Is that you, Charlotte? We're in here.'

The tension drains away from my body with the relief of hearing a familiar voice but is quickly replaced by questions. Why is Annabel still at Myrtle Cottage? And who is the other person? For one awful moment, I wonder if I was right with my original thought that Zack and Annabel are in cahoots. After his coming to the shop ended in failure, maybe he contacted Annabel and she suggested he should come to my home for a second attempt at reconciliation with her there to support his corner.

I fling the kitchen door open, ready to give them both a piece of my mind, and I'm pleasantly surprised to see my land-lord, Gary, and Annabel sitting at the kitchen table, each with a mug in hand. That's when I notice, despite being chilled to the bone from my walk home, that the house is much warmer than when I left it a seven o'clock this morning.

Gary pushes his chair back and gets to his feet. 'I didn't know what time you finished work, so I called around at six on the off-chance because the forecast is predicting overnight snow and I didn't want my tenant freezing to death. Your friend let me in,' he says, inclining his head in Annabel's direction.

I glance over at her with my eyebrows raised.

'I'll tell you when Gary's gone,' she says.

'Actually, I need to be getting off now or I'll miss my little boy's bedtime story and that will land me in hot water with my wife. Speaking of which, you should probably run yourself a bath to warm up, although the radiators should be up to full temperature soon.'

'You managed to fix the heating?' I ask.

'There was nothing wrong with it,' he replies. 'You must have accidentally knocked the switch in the airing cupboard from the winter to the summer setting, so you still had hot water, but the radiators were off.'

I can feel my cheeks colouring up in embarrassment.

'I'm sorry to have dragged you out for nothing,' I say, moving to one side as he carefully steps over the puddle of water created by my sodden coat dripping onto the expensive wooden flooring. 'And I'll get this mopped up straight away.'

'No worries,' he replies, wafting his hand dismissively as I follow him out into the hall. 'I wouldn't have rented the place to you if I didn't think you'd look after it.' He opens the front door to the elements. 'What a filthy night. I'm glad I was able to get you up and running with the heating.'

'Me too, thank you.' I watch him duck his head against the rain as he hurries down the path. The wind snatches the door from my grasp, and slams it shut behind him.

'What a nice chap,' Annabel says, leaning against the kitchen doorframe. 'Such a shame he's happily married.'

I shake my head at her in exasperation. 'Don't you start matchmaking. I'm nowhere close to being over Zack yet and definitely not ready for another relationship.'

'I don't know what you mean,' Annabel says, an innocent expression on her face.

'Oh, I think you do,' I reply, a small shiver running through me. Although the heating is back on, there's no way I'm going to thaw until I get out of my soaking wet clothes.

Annabel must be reading my mind. 'You need to get out of those wet clothes,' she says. 'Why don't you do as Gary suggested and I'll bring you a cup of tea up.'

'Are you sure you don't mind?' I ask.

'Of course not. And if you throw me a towel down, I'll mop up the puddle you've left on the kitchen floor,' she adds.

'You're the best,' I say, making my way upstairs to start the bath running. I turn the taps on and choose a bath foam scented with sandalwood. While the tub starts to fill, I select a large beach towel from the airing cupboard and launch it from the top of the stairs, watching as it flies through the air and lands in the hallway in a brightly coloured heap.

It's a relief to finally peel off my wet clothes. I place them in the wicker washing basket in the corner of my bedroom, slip into my towelling dressing gown and head back to the bathroom. The foam is billowing just below the rim of the tub, and both looks and smells inviting as I reach to turn the taps off before getting in. There's a fraction of a second as my freezing toes touch the water when I can't feel if the water is hot or cold, but as the remainder of my body sinks beneath the foam the warmth of the water envelops me.

Resting my head back, I savour the aroma of sandalwood with a hint of coconut and am instantly transported to a tropical beach. How I long for the feel of sun on my skin and sand between my toes. I close my eyes with images of swaying palm trees filling my mind.

SEVEN

'Here we go,' Annabel says, pushing open the bathroom door with her foot. In one hand she's carrying my mug of tea and in the other the wicker chair from my bedroom. 'I thought you might like some company,' she adds, handing me the mug and setting the chair down at the taps end of the bath.

If I'm honest, I'd have preferred a bit of me time to reflect on how I'm feeling after Zack showed up at Stems, but that seems a bit selfish after the way Annabel's been looking out for me since my split with him.

'Be my guest.' I wriggle myself into a more upright position to take a sip from my mug without spilling any. 'Just how I like it,' I say appreciatively.

'We've known each other long enough for me to know how you take your tea,' she says, tucking her legs beneath her to get comfortable on the bedroom chair.

She's right about us knowing each other a long time, long enough for me to get the sense that something isn't quite right now. I take another sip of tea before setting the mug on the side of the bath and allowing my shoulders to slip back beneath the water. Although the heating is on, there is only a towel rail in the bathroom, and it hasn't warmed the whole room yet. Guessing that there's something she wants to get off her chest, I stay silent, giving her the opportunity to steer the conversation.

'I'm sorry I stayed on here without asking,' she says. 'I should have rung to make sure you didn't mind.'

'Of course I don't mind. If you hadn't been here when Gary showed up, I'd still be without heating.' I give her a moment to explain why she hasn't gone home, but she's not forthcoming. 'Is everything okay with Finn?'

She nods. 'I rang him earlier to tell him you needed me. I just wanted a bit of time to think about my feelings for Finn after our conversation last night.'

My mind switches to overdrive trying to remember exactly what I said that could have Annabel questioning her commitment to Finn. He's been her longest relationship by far, after a decade of flings that could be counted in weeks rather than months or years. All her friends, me included, thought that in Finn she'd finally found her forever love. It would be awful if she threw away the chance of happiness because of something I said. 'I was pretty drunk last night, Annabel. I might have exaggerated my feelings for Zack.'

'In my experience, we're at our most honest when we're drunk. The filters are off, so we just tell it how it is.'

I don't disagree, so I stay silent.

'I woke up this morning with the mother of all hangovers,' she begins, a few moments later. 'We really did have a skinful, didn't we? I don't know how you made it to work. I think it was the G & Ts that finished me off. Anyway, I was lying as still as I could in bed, and it gave me time to truly examine mine and Finn's relationship. Don't get me wrong, I do love him, but I'm not sure that it's in the all-consuming way you loved Zack.'

Annabel uses the past tense regarding my feelings for my ex, but she could be a little premature. I can't just erase ten years of love in a month. I'm sure I once read in an article about relationships in a women's magazine that it takes a month for every year you were together to get over someone. If that's the case, it's one month down and nine to go, and if I'm honest that seems quite optimistic after seeing him earlier.

'He came to the shop today,' I say.

'Finn?' Annabel asks, her brow furrowed in confusion.

'No, Zack.'

'Of course, that makes much more sense. Hold on a minute though, how did he know where to find you?'

I take another sip of my tea to buy myself some time. I don't have to tell her about my suspicion now, but look where people being less than truthful has landed me.

Clearing my throat, I say, 'I'm a bit ashamed to admit that I assumed you contacted him after our heart-to-heart last night and told him where I was working.'

'Why would I do that?' Annabel says, the hurt obvious in her voice. 'If you wanted him to find you, you'd tell him yourself.'

'True. I guess I wondered if you thought I'd overreacted about the whole baby situation and were trying to save the relationship while you hoped there was still a chance.'

'It's not my place to try to change your mind. I think it's a shame that things haven't worked out, but imagine how awful it would be if you two got back together because of something I said and then it all went belly-up again? You'd blame me. I wouldn't want to risk our friendship over some bloke.'

It's weird to hear Annabel refer to Zack as 'some bloke'. He's been my boyfriend, my partner, my other half, a constant in my life for ten years. Although Zack and I never discussed getting married, I always believed it was because we were a strong enough partnership without a legally binding piece of paper and a band of gold or platinum on my finger. At least it made the split simpler. We haven't got to file for a divorce or argue over possessions. I was living in the flat Zack bought after his ex-wife left for Australia with their boys, so almost everything in it is his.

'What did he want?' Annabel asks.

'He said he was just checking that I was okay.'

'And are you? It must have been a bit of a shock, him turning up out of the blue.'

She's right, it was a shock, although, in a way, I was pleased that he'd come all the way to Maidenhead to see me. It reassured me that Zack did care deeply about me and possibly still does. It was also important for him to understand what his deception did to me. The truth is, I wish Zack had felt that he could tell me about his vasectomy. If he had trusted me enough, we could have discussed options, maybe even a reversal. But he wasn't honest about it for whatever reason, and it feels as though we're too far down the road of betrayal to come back from it. I didn't think I wanted to see him, but in retrospect it was strangely cathartic to know that he seemed as sad about the whole situation as me.

'It'll take a while for me to get over Zack and the life I thought we would always share, but I still think I've done the right thing,' I say with more conviction than I'm feeling. 'Trust is vital in a relationship. Without it, there's nothing.'

'Trust is vital in a friendship too,' Annabel says, a look of reproach in her eyes.

'I know. I'm really sorry I doubted you.'

'That's okay, just don't let it happen again,' she says, a smile returning to her face. 'Did he say why he didn't he tell you that he'd had the snip?'

'He said he was afraid of losing me.'

'And now he has.'

'We've lost each other,' I say, unable to keep the sadness from my voice.

Annabel swings her legs down and comes over to my end of

the bath to wrap her arms around my foamy neck. We hug for a minute or so until she releases us from the embrace.

'Thank you,' she says.

'What for?'

'For making me see that there's no such things as perfect when it comes to relationships, but there is something called right. Finn and I are pretty good together, aren't we?' she asks, clearly seeking reassurance.

'You're more than pretty good,' I reply. 'Like I said last night, he's the best thing that ever happened to you. You just have to believe in what the two of you have.'

'As a reward for your unwitting advice, I'll rustle us up some dinner,' she says, picking up the chair and heading towards the door.

'There's not much in,' I say. 'I haven't really fancied cooking.'

'You're not kidding. I had a look through your cupboards and fridge earlier. It was like tumbleweed, but I reckon I can throw a pasta dish together before I head home.'

It will be good to share a home-cooked meal with someone – something I haven't done since walking out on my former life. Cooking and eating solo isn't much fun, but I still think it's preferable to living a lie.

EIGHT

THURSDAY 8 MARCH

I love the sound of a busy coffee shop. The chink of cutlery, the clatter of crockery and the spluttering of the milk frother, not to mention the chatter of people who have stolen a few minutes or a couple of hours for a long overdue catch-up, which is what I'm doing here at Sally Teaspoon's when I should be at work.

I say 'should be at work', but Michaela was happy to give me this morning off as a thank you for all the evenings I've stayed late to keep the shop open. She can't believe her luck that she's finally found someone who isn't rushing home to cook dinner, get ready to go out or read a bedtime story to a little one. These are all things I would love to be doing, but I have no life outside work, so willingly stay a little longer if I'm needed.

When I asked her about the possibility of having this morning off after Tiffany messaged me out of the blue to suggest meeting up with her and Annabel, Michaela insisted that I should go. Maybe even she is starting to feel sorry for her 'Billy No-Mates' employee.

'What are you smiling at?' Annabel says, placing her mocha latte and coffee and walnut cake on the table before pulling the chair out to sit down. I've seen less of her since the night she stayed over at mine, but I haven't taken it personally. Obviously, she felt she had a bit of soul-searching to do after our confessions night. I hope she sees sense and stays with Finn, as they do make a very good couple.

'I was just thinking how nice it is to be meeting up with you and Tiff. It's been ages since we last did anything like this.'

Annabel and Tiff have been close friends since she, as the most experienced model at Faces, took Annabel under her wing on their first assignment together. They both did something similar with me, but although I'd consider Tiff a good friend, I didn't have as much time to build the kind of friendship the two of them have. Annabel and I grew much closer when Tiff retired from modelling, so she meets up with us individually, but Tiff and I only see one another when it's a threesome. We chat on the phone from time to time and I try to keep up with her life on Facebook, but it's a bit one-sided as she's not a social media fan and rarely posts anything. I think the most recent was of her winning the egg-and-spoon race when her eldest daughter, Melody, who's now in her teens, was still at primary school.

'Was your boss all right about you having the morning off?' I ask Annabel, taking a sip of my cappuccino. I should probably have waited for Tiff who is at the counter paying, but the creamy froth decorated with a chocolate palm frond is far too inviting to resist. Annabel only gave up modelling a year ago and surprised us all when she announced she'd gained an AAT Level 2 qualification in accountancy after doing an online course. It's a complete change of direction for her, but she's hoping to start her own business once she's achieved her AAT Level 4.

'Let's just say he couldn't really refuse me permission to go to an emergency dental appointment.' My shocked expression must say it all because she continues, 'You don't seriously think Scrooge would have given me a couple of hours off to meet up with my girlfriends for a coffee? We don't all have Michaela for a boss, and I would hate to have missed out on a get-together after we've been trying to do it for so long.'

I don't miss the slight edge to Annabel's voice. We both accept that it's tricky for Tiff to meet up, with the girls to look after and her husband JJ often working away, leaving her with all the fetching and carrying to do. But Annabel has always been more critical of me for not making as much time for her as I used to before Zack and I became an item. The sad thing is, she's right. I missed the simple pleasures of going for a coffee or to the cinema with the girls throughout my relationship with Zack. I'd always reply to Annabel's criticism by saying that true friends don't need to see each other all the time to stay friends, which I honestly believe, but I can't deny feeling excited when I took an extra bit of care getting ready this morning in anticipation of the three of us being back together.

I notice Tiff hasn't lost any of her model grace as she makes her way towards us, mug and plate in hand. She's insisted on paying for everything as meeting up was her idea. She sashays between the busy tables, the swish of her long copper hair following suit. An observer might assume we're old classmates from school, but she is at least ten years older than me. She was one of Faces most established models when I joined at the tender age of sixteen. Considering that she is the one with teenage daughters, she looks incredible. On second thoughts, maybe having teenagers around all the time is what is keeping her youthful.

She puts her plate down on the table alongside her mug. In the process, a couple of mini pink and white marshmallows escape from the top of her hot chocolate. 'Finally,' she says, sitting down opposite me. 'How can a simple thing like meeting up for coffee have taken so long to organise? Cheers,' she adds, raising her mug, losing another couple of marshmallows. She casts a backwards glance over her shoulder. 'I didn't leave a trail of them, did I?'

We all follow her lead in checking for a pink and white Hansel and Gretel-like trail leading to our table. There's nothing, so we continue with our toast.

'To us,' Annabel says, touching mugs first with Tiff and then me.

'To the old gang,' I add, joining in with the mug chinking.

'Less of the old,' Tiff says, before taking a sip of her hot chocolate. Judging by the expression on her face and her trim figure, I'd hazard a guess that it's not a treat she indulges in very often.

'I was just thinking how amazing you look,' Annabel remarks. 'You haven't aged a bit since the last time we all got together. I think that must have been around the time that Tamsin started school, so you were celebrating freedom from young children hanging onto your legs and asking you to play with them.'

Tiff and Annabel laugh while I take a quick sip of my cappuccino to prevent myself from reacting to a throwaway comment which would not be hurtful to anyone but me. I really need to stop overreacting whenever anyone says anything negative about being a parent, even though I would give the world to have infants bothering me twenty-four seven.

It's a wonder I agreed to come today, knowing that at some point the conversation would turn to her family. I had to give myself a stern talking-to this morning, because she has everything I want: a husband, children and a lifestyle that enables her to be a stay-at-home mum. No getting up at the crack of dawn and battling the elements to get to a freezing-cold flower shop to open up for the early bird customers, not that I'm complaining really. At least I love my job and have a great relationship with my new boss, unlike Annabel. And anyway, I suppose Tiff has to be up early to get the girls' breakfast and drop them at school. But the rest of the day is hers to do with as she pleases, and judging by the shiny hair and toned thighs I'd say some of it is spent at the hairdressers or the gym on a fairly regular basis.

'It can't be that long ago, surely,' Tiff says. 'Tamsin's thirteen and Melody's fifteen next month.'

'You're kidding,' I say. 'It doesn't seem two minutes ago since we were passing her around for a quick cuddle at her christening ceremony. I was only twenty, but I reckon that was the start of my broodiness.'

It's only a quick exchange of looks between the two of them, but I catch it and Tiff knows I have.

'I'm sorry you and Zack have split up,' she says.

I glance at Annabel, who is studying her mocha latte intensely, a slight flush travelling up her neck.

'So, obviously you two have been talking,' I say. I suppose it was inevitable, but I would have preferred to speak to Tiff when I felt ready. 'How much has she told you?'

'Just that Zack had the snip before he met you and omitted to mention it when you started talking about wanting a baby.'

'So, everything then. At least it saves me getting upset by having to repeat it all, although I did think we were talking in confidence,' I say, throwing another look in Annabel's direction.

'We were,' she says. 'It's just that I was struggling to understand how you could give up on a relationship where you were both so clearly in love just because he could never father a child with you. I figured that Tiff, as a mum herself, would be able to give me a better perspective on it...'

'And did she?'

Tiff reaches her hand across the table and squeezes mine. 'I told Annabel that I couldn't understand how any loving man would allow his girlfriend to go through the cycle of hope each month knowing full well the despair that would follow each time. Frankly, I didn't have Zack down as a cruel person, but after Annabel told me, it was the only conclusion I could draw. JJ would never have made me suffer like that.'

Annabel fills the gap in conversation that is widening because I can't trust myself to speak by saying, 'How is JJ? Still working away a lot?'

'More than ever,' Tiff says, a cloud passing across her perfect features. 'That's the trouble with being self-employed, you have to take the work when the phone rings, even if it means long periods away from home. If you don't, there'll come a day when your phone stops ringing, and the work will go to someone else. He's paranoid that younger, trendier photographers will make a move on his celebrity clients and that he'll spend the rest of his career doing weddings and christenings.'

'Would that be so bad? At least he'd still be working,' I say, forcing myself to re-join the conversation.

'For some, maybe not, but JJ is in the world of high fashion and pop music, shooting in the most fabulous locations around the world. Somehow, I don't think photographing a family wedding in Essex would satisfy his creativity.'

The image of Tiff and JJ's wedding photo flashes into my head. Tiff was on a fashion shoot in South Africa. She flew into Johannesburg a single woman and came home six weeks later married after a whirlwind romance with the photographer. The wedding photos were of the two of them standing side by side on the edge of a ravine with their backs to the camera, Tiff's veil caught by a gust of wind. The accompanying text message sent to friends back home simply said, 'We've taken the plunge.'

That was the last modelling assignment Tiff undertook. She only flew home to collect some clothes and put her flat on the market before re-joining her new husband in South Africa. I didn't get to see her because I was on a modelling assignment of my own. A little over a year later, Tiff flew home with four-month-old Melody for the christening. She wanted the service to be held in England so that her elderly grandparents could attend, but it was all a bit awkward when JJ had to cancel at the last minute because one of his high-profile clients wanted him to do a shoot in Barbados. In fact, weirdly, in all the years that Tiff and JJ have been married, I've never had the chance to meet him. Nor have I seen any photos of him, which is not as unusual as it might sound. Photographers are generally much happier behind the camera than in front of it.

'Is he away at the moment?' Annabel asks, breaking a piece of her cake off with her fingers and popping it into her mouth. 'OMG, that is divine.'

'He's in Scotland doing some new shots for a golf course website, but back next weekend for a whole week before jetting off to photograph some celebrity wedding or other. I say celebri-ty,' Tiff says, rolling her eyes, 'but most of the names he throws around these days are huge on Instagram and YouTube and I'm embarrassed to admit I've never heard of them. Still, the good thing is, they've heard of JJ, so the work keeps coming, thankfully.'

'I don't know how you cope with him being away so much,' I venture. 'I felt lonely when Zack went to Amsterdam for a couple of nights on a stag do. I didn't know what to do with myself.'

'Could you have called your two oldest friends for a night out?' Annabel asks, her voice loaded with sarcasm. 'I'm sure they'd have obliged.'

I shake my head in mild exasperation. 'To hear you talk, you'd think we never met up while I was with Zack. You seem to have conveniently forgotten all the foursomes we endured with your various boyfriends down the years.'

'Touché,' Annabel acknowledges.

'To answer your question, it's probably one of the reasons JJ and I are still together,' Tiff says. 'So many of the mums at the school gate are either already divorced, going through one or thinking about it. Making a marriage work involves a lot of compromising – something today's young couples don't seem so willing to do. I was thirty-four when JJ and I tied the knot, so I'd already lived a bit, but these days couples seem intent on pairing up when they've only known each other two minutes.'

'Says the woman who got married after knowing her groom for six whole weeks,' Annabel says. We all laugh and take a sip of our respective drinks. My stomach gives a little grumble as Annabel breaks off another piece of her cake. She clearly sees me eyeing it as she puts her hand around it protectively and says, 'Should have got your own. Tiff did offer.'

'Here,' Tiff says, pushing her plate in my direction, 'have some of mine. I don't mind sharing. And, Annabel, for your information, when you know, you know. I was certain JJ was the man I wanted to spend my life with after twenty-four hours.'

'I felt that way about Zack. I thought he was my happy ever after.' The crumbs from Tiff's sponge cake suddenly feel dry in my mouth, making it difficult to swallow.

Tiff's hand is back over mine, gently squeezing it. 'We all thought Zack was your one. If only he'd been honest with you from the start. If having kids was such a big deal for you, you would have had the choice of not getting too heavily involved or coming up with a plan B, like reversal or adoption. You invested time in him and the relationship which you might not have done if you knew. It was a shitty thing to do and unbelievably selfish.'

'Thanks, Tiff. I've had a few wobbles since he dropped in to Stems unannounced, but deep down I know that I'll never be able to completely trust him again. He left me no choice, just like you said.'

'Then let's just chalk him up to experience. You're still young, only a year older than I was when I married JJ, and considering what you've just been through, you look amazing. I think this calls for project "find Charlotte a new boyfriend". Don't you agree, Annabel?'

Annabel doesn't answer and appears to be concentrating on something.

'Earth to Annabel,' Tiff says, good-naturedly.

'Hold on a minute. Did you say you were thirty-four when you got married, so thirty-five when you had Melody, who is soon to be fifteen? You always claimed to be eight years older than me, but the numbers don't add up cos I'm thirty-seven.'

'Oops, rumbled,' Tiff says, at least having the good grace to look a little sheepish. 'Everyone lies about their age, don't they? It's no biggie.'

'I don't,' Annabel replies, looking at me and adding, 'do you, Charlotte?'

'I've not felt the need to since I first started modelling and was trying to get into clubs with you two. I can't believe you're fifty!' I exclaim, taking in Tiff's immaculate appearance once more.

'Nearly fifty. JJ and I both have our big five-oh birthdays this year, starting with mine in June.'

'You need to throw a party,' Annabel immediately says.

'Actually, that's a great idea. I'll invite some single male friends so that we can get to work on finding you a new boyfriend, Charlotte.'

I groan, but a little part of me is grateful that my best friends want to help me get back into dating without resorting to the online variety. I'm not ready yet, but maybe by June I will be, I think, finishing up the remainder of my cappuccino.

'You'll need to ditch the moustache first, though,' Annabel says, taking a mirror out of her handbag to let me see my frothy white top lip.

'Thanks for having my back.' I draw my hand across my mouth to remove it.

'Well, I couldn't let you go back to work like that,' she replies.

'That's not what I meant. You two have reaffirmed that I did the right thing and there will be life after Zack, eventually,' I say, although in my heart that still feels a long way off.

'Of course there will,' Annabel encourages. 'Sorry to be a party pooper, but I'm going to have to go,' she adds, draining her mug and getting to her feet. 'I wouldn't put it past old misery guts to ring the dentist to check up on me. Let's not leave it so long until the next time!' The last sentence is thrown over her shoulder as she heads towards the door.

'June! My fiftieth,' Tiff calls out. 'I'll be in touch with details.'

Every head in Sally Teaspoon's has turned to stare at my gorgeous auburn-haired friend. I know what they're thinking. How can she possibly be almost fifty?

I, on the other hand, am thinking how sad it is that someone else I'm close to has been lying for years, even if it's only a little white lie.

NINE

MOTHERING SUNDAY 11 MARCH

Today was always going to be extra tough for me, so it's a blessing that I've slept in until almost midday. I finally got off to sleep just before dawn, which surprised me considering how tired I was after such a full-on day at work yesterday. Even with the lie-in, I haven't awoken feeling particularly refreshed, so it's a good job I haven't got anywhere to go or anything to do because I'm pretty sure I'll need a snooze at some point this afternoon. Normally, this thought would make me smile and provoke an inner voice saying, *you're only thirty-five not eighty-five*, but it's doubtful that I'll be able to find anything funny today.

The downside of sleeping in is that I've missed the time I promised to ring my mum, so she won't be too happy with me. Roxanne, my older sister, has arranged to pick Mum and Dad up at noon and take them for Mother's Day lunch at a posh restaurant in Poole where they all live, along with her husband, their three children and her mother-in-law. A happy family gathering, although most likely Mum will spoil it at some point with her acerbic tongue. It's funny, I always think of life as a journey, where along the way we are supposed to learn lessons to make us better people. If our lives depend on how quickly we master the lessons, my mum might be the first person to make it to a hundred and fifty. Even as I have the thought, I try to banish it from my mind. It was mean, and I don't usually do mean. It must be because I'm tired.

Yesterday, Stems was every bit as manically busy and heart-breaking as I'd imagined it would be. Michaela and I worked on bouquet after bouquet of glorious flowers, each accompanying card saying 'To the Best Mum in the World', or words to that effect. From huge hand-tied arrangements to a few simple stems of roses, from pot plants to a bunch of tulips, each was a loving and thoughtful gift to the person who gave them life.

We started making up our creations at 6 a.m. and finally shut up shop at 8 p.m., three hours later than usual on a Satur-day, and neither of us had taken a break other than to pop to the loo or make a coffee while the other held the fort. We were both utterly exhausted by the time she flipped the sign on the door to closed.

'Thank you so much for today, Charlotte,' Michaela said, as we collapsed onto the wooden chairs in the small kitchen area at the back of the shop. 'I absolutely couldn't have done it without you. I've got a couple of cans of gin in a tin in the fridge. Do you fancy cracking them open while we get our breath back?'

I wanted to say no and slink off home to wallow in self-pity, but it felt ungrateful, particularly as she'd recently given me the morning off to meet up with Annabel and Tiff.

Two cans of G & T turned into four, then six, before we finally locked up and went our separate ways, but not before I'd learnt that Michaela was divorced with two young teenagers and an elderly mum to look after at home. It's funny how you think you know someone, working alongside them every day, but you only know what they want you to. I'm glad I stayed behind for a chat. I liked my boss before, but I like her even more now. And I can add admiration to my feelings about her after the way she has bounced back to open a successful business, following her cheating husband walking out and leaving her with two under school-age kids. I wonder if he's stayed with the woman he left his wife for or whether he gave up on that relationship too.

Just as I'm having these thoughts, my phone pings with a text. I reach for it, expecting the message to be from Roxanne telling me how upset Mum was that I didn't call at the allotted time, but am pleasantly surprised to see that it's from Michaela. She must be telepathic.

Hi Charlotte – thanks again for yesterday and for letting me sound off. The kids woke me up this morning with breakfast in bed, and my mum has made her speciality lemon drizzle cake for us to have after lunch. They're not a bad bunch really. You must have thought I sounded really ungrateful – I've got so much more than many people do. See you Tuesday. Michaela x

I swallow the lump that has formed in my throat. I will not give in to tears today no matter how far I'm pushed.

I dash off a quick reply to Michaela before throwing back the covers and positively jumping out of bed. I'll have some coffee and toast and then go for a walk while all the mums are being treated to lunch. In fairness, Roxanne did suggest me going down to Poole to meet up with them, but I couldn't face the questions about why I'd let Zack slip through my fingers. Mum always had a soft spot for him and was noticeably nicer to me when he was around. I'll have to face her disappointment at some point, but today's not the day.

Okay, so not all the mums were having lunch with their families. I eventually gave up on my walk around the nature reserve after half an hour of constantly having to move over to the long grass to let large family groups pass. Buggies, prams, scooters and bikes were all out in abundance. It felt like a veritable parade of happy mums, proud mums and mums-to-be, and was all too much for me. I've returned home and am now halfway through a pack of dark chocolate Hobnobs which I'm dunking into my tea in defiance as I know Zack wouldn't have approved.

I can't settle to read my book, so I put the television on instead, searching for a Netflix series that I haven't yet watched. There aren't many left that appeal to me. Since I split with Zack, I've become a Netflix junkie for two reasons: it gives me something to do in the evening, but also something to talk about with people who I have nothing in common with otherwise. My new hairdresser, a recommendation from Annabel, is a prime example. Her main two topics of conversation are her kids and what she is going to be cooking for her family when she gets in from work. I can't contribute to either of those topics and listening to her speak about a home life I can only dream of makes me sad. Chatting about my latest watch on Netflix is a great alternative.

I've just settled on a period drama that I'd been thinking of trying when my phone pings. This time it is Roxanne.

Just checking that you are planning on ringing Mum at some point today. She was pretty upset that you hadn't called when I picked her up earlier. Lunch was great – you should have come. We've just dropped her and Dad back home.

No sign-off. No row of kisses. My sister and I get on all right, but we're too different to be close like some siblings are.

I type my reply.

*Thanks for letting me know she's back from lunch and that
you had a good time. I'll call her now xxxx*

I add the row of kisses as an afterthought, one which
Roxanne will probably misinterpret and assume that I'm being
facetious. Whatever, I think, taking a deep breath before
tapping Mum's number on my phone and muting the television.
I don't want to give her the ammunition of knowing I've been
indoors watching TV when I could have gone to visit. Maybe I
could tell a little white lie and say that my car is in for a service.
Or maybe not. I shouldn't have to make excuses about my
choices.

She answers on the fifth ring, probably deliberately as she
wouldn't want me to think she'd been waiting for my call, and
then doesn't say anything, waiting for me to speak first.

'Hi, Mum,' I offer brightly. 'I hope you've had a nice day so
far?'

'So far?' she asks, without acknowledging that it's me calling. 'There's nothing else planned as far as I know.'

I try again. 'Did you get the card and the biscuits? I thought
you'd like the cat ones, and you could use the tin afterwards to
store Milo's treats.'

Milo is Mum's ginger cat. He is the gentlest, most docile cat
a person could own and yet she still manages to complain about
him if he accidently scratches her while he's perching on her lap
during a stroking session. She really doesn't deserve him, nor my
dad for that matter. Mum is the centre of my dad's world. In his
eyes she can do no wrong, which is lovely for her, but not so
great from my point of view. I don't know if he's as disappointed
with my life choices as Mum is because he simply goes along
with her decisions. Maybe it's to avoid confrontation because he
is definitely the more easy-going of the two.

She ignores my suggestion, instead saying, 'I wish you

wouldn't waste your money sending me flowers, they'll be dead in a week.'

I resist the urge to say, 'only because you don't top up their water' and change the subject. 'How was your lunch with Rox?'

Her tone changes. 'They're such a lovely family. I can't believe how quickly Verity is growing.'

Verity is my sister's youngest child and much longed-for daughter. She and David had their first two children, Rory and Alfie, in quick succession, only fourteen months apart. They originally agreed that they would only have two, but Roxanne was desperate for a daughter, so they decided to have another go. Eight years after Alfie was born, they were blessed with Verity. The entire family, my mum included, has been besotted with her since she made her appearance on Boxing Day just over four years ago. To be fair, she looks like an angel with her curly blond hair and blue eyes framed by impossibly long eyelashes, and on the occasions I've seen her, she behaves like one too. I wonder if her hair will get darker as she grows older, as mine did. When I was modelling, I always kept it very blonde as it seemed to help me to get work, but Zack persuaded me to go back to my natural colour, a mid to dark brown. Maybe I should go back to being a blonde, they're supposed to have more fun, and I could definitely do with some in my life. Or I could dye it a coppery red, similar to Tiff's. I'm just wondering whether Tiff's is still natural or if it comes out of a bottle when I realise Mum has stopped talking. I'd tuned out while she was gushing about my sister's perfect family and now I have no idea what she just said.

'Sorry, Mum, I lost you for a minute there. The mobile signal isn't that good here. What were you saying?'

'Maybe you should have stayed with Zack. The signal there was always fine. I was asking if you'd heard from him. Is there any chance he might take you back?'

I bite down hard on my lip to stop me saying something I

might regret. If it wasn't Mothering Sunday, I might not be so considerate.

'It was mutual, Mum,' I lie, crossing my fingers as I used to as a child when I was being economical with the truth. 'In the end, we realised we wanted different things.' It's true, at least from my perspective, but I'm not prepared to divulge what the different things are because I suspect Mum would find a way of blaming me.

'Well, you'll be lucky to find yourself another Zack,' she persists. 'And you're not getting any younger.'

'Thanks for pointing that out,' I say, finally reacting to the constant prodding. She's made me feel like a bull trapped in a ring and at the mercy of the toreador. I need to end the call before I see red and charge at her full force. 'I'll let you go and arrange your flowers. I made sure there were no lilies that might harm Milo. Remember to top the water up midweek and change it next weekend if you want them to last a bit longer.' My finger is hovering over the end call button.

'There's no need to speak to me like I'm a child, Charlotte,' she's saying as I hang up.

Two minutes later, my phone starts to ring. I take a deep breath. Maybe it was a bit rude terminating the call like that.

'Hi, Mum, we must have got cut off,' I start.

'Sorry, it's me,' I hear Annabel say. 'I can ring back later if you're waiting for a call from your mum.'

'I just had a call with her, one that ended rather abruptly, I'm afraid.'

'Up to her usual tricks then?'

'Yep. I honestly don't know what I ever did to make her dislike me so much,' I say, taking a few gulps of air to try to normalise my heartbeat which always seems to sky-rocket when I've been talking to my mother, even for a few minutes.

'You were on a loser the minute you broke the mould of

getting a dead-end job in your hometown, meeting a nice young man and delivering grandchildren.'

'I was all for delivering the grandchildren, it was her beloved Zack that scuppered that one.'

'Have you told her that?'

I sigh. 'There's no point. She would somehow twist it to be my fault. It's easier just to say we wanted different things.'

'So, not a great call with your mum, but how are you holding up otherwise? Do you need me to come round? I can be there in ten minutes.'

'It's nice of you to offer, but I won't be very good company. Me and the biscuit tin are going to hang out and watch a bit of Netflix. I'm fine... really I am,' I add, although I suspect Annabel knows that I'm not being entirely truthful, given that this is my first Mother's Day without any real hope of becoming a mum myself by the time the next one comes around.

'If you're sure?'

'Positive,' I reply.

'Okay.' She pauses. 'There was something I wanted to ask you. You know the whole split with Zack unsettled me a bit.'

My heart sinks.

'You haven't done anything stupid, have you?'

'Define stupid. If you mean, have I walked out on Finn, then the answer is no.'

I exhale heavily.

'But we did have a long chat about us and our future, during which I may have mentioned that a week apart might give us a better idea of how we feel.'

'Oh, is that all? Of course you can come and stay here for a week to see how much you miss Finn. That's no problem,' I say, the relief evident in my voice.

'Well, almost, except that instead of my coming to you, how would you fancy a week away with me on holiday, all paid for by Finn?'

'Are you serious?' I'd contemplated taking a holiday, spending some of the money I'd been squirrelling away to contribute to a deposit on a house if Zack and I needed a bigger place to accommodate our family. I won't be needing it for that now, and a mortgage will be out of reach on my salary. Anyway, despite the appeal of long lazy days on a beach somewhere, I can't imagine holidaying on my own, particularly dining alone. And it's probably sensible to have savings to fall back on while I navigate the next phase of my life.

'Absolutely. Finn's all for it. He'd much rather the two of us go somewhere than for me to be let loose on my own. Are you up for it?'

'I'll have to check that it's all right with Michaela, but apart from that, point me in the direction of the sun cream.'

'Brilliant. I knew you wouldn't let me down. I'll have a look for some last-minute offers flying out around the middle of next month and I'll book it once you've got the okay from Michaela.'

'I don't know what to say, except my weekend just took a massive turn for the better. I might not even finish the packet of Hobnobs now that I need to be bikini ready. You really are the best friend in the world. Thank you,' I gush.

'You deserve to have something nice happen to you. We'll have a ball. Let me know ASAP what Michaela says. Oh, and finish the pack of biscuits, there's nothing of you.'

She ends the call, leaving me staring at my handset, barely able to believe my good fortune. It's been a rough weekend, or more accurately, a rough couple of months, but maybe this will be the start of a new chapter in my life.

I turn the sound on the TV back on, put my feet up on the pouffe and reach for a biscuit. I've been dreading today for weeks and, despite a less than perfect morning, it's turned out to be the best day of the year so far by a country mile. I bite down into the biscuit, savouring its buttery saltiness, grinning from ear to ear.

TEN

THURSDAY 19 APRIL

The sound of the waves breaking rhythmically against the shore must have lulled me to sleep and for the moment before I'm fully awake, I think I'm in the middle of a fabulous dream. As consciousness takes hold, I remember that this is not a dream but the most surreal reality.

My eyes start to open, and I reach instinctively for my sunglasses to protect them against the bright diamond sparkle of the sun on the rippling waves further from the shore.

'Not a bad view, is it?' Annabel says, clearly having noticed my movement.

'Utterly fantastic.' I wriggle into a more upright position on my sun lounger to take in more of it.

At one end of the beach is a small jetty where holiday-makers are strapping themselves into life jackets before taking to the water on windsurfers or pedalos, while at the other end a couple on horseback are following their guide as he leads them to a place away from sunbathers where it will be safe for them to have a canter.

I turn to Annabel. 'You know, when you mentioned a week's holiday, I thought you meant Portugal or Spain. I had no idea you had paradise in mind. I don't know how I'll ever be able to repay you for your thoughtfulness, and Finn for footing the bill. I have to keep pinching myself to make sure this is all actually real.'

'I can see that from the bruise on your arm,' Annabel says.

I miss the humour in her voice and look down to my arm before I realise she's teasing me.

'We might not have had the torrential downpours in Spain or Portugal,' she continues, wrinkling her nose slightly, 'but this is now classified as winter in Mauritius, so I guess it's only to be expected.'

It was a bit of a shock on our first morning, waking up not to the gloriously blue skies of the previous day when we'd arrived at our resort after a twelve-hour plane journey, but to the leaden grey colour more associated with the country we'd left behind. By the time we were finishing breakfast, the first drops of rain were falling and we'd only just reached our room before it had turned into a full-on downpour. At least the rain is warm, and when we've not been so lucky on a couple of occasions and got drenched, we've dried out really quickly in the heat of the sun as soon as the storm has passed.

Somehow, you never imagine rain in places like Mauritius, but I guess that's what keeps it so lush and green. Annabel had looked at Dubai, which was slightly cheaper, but she'd remembered that Zack and I had holidayed there a couple of times. She opted for Mauritius as the safer bet as she was worried that I might have spent the entire week crying into my beer, or in my case cocktails.

The mere thought of cocktails has me scanning the beach between the neatly lined-up thatched parasols, seeking out our waiter, Hemant.

'Already on their way,' Annabel says. 'I ordered when I nipped to the loo while you were asleep. I also popped back to our room to get the money and gave it to Abdul for our sarongs.'

'Wow, you're really on it today,' I say, glancing up at the struts of our parasol where the brightly coloured fabric of the sarongs we acquired yesterday are fluttering in the gentle breeze.

'Glad you came?' Annabel asks.

'Is that even a real question?' I respond. 'Look around you. It makes me feel happy to be alive. I came here feeling part of a sad group of women who yearn to be a mother and can't. I thought my life was as extinct as the dodo.'

'And all the beach weddings and the honeymoon couples haven't upset you?'

'Far from it. Seeing the vast range of ages has given me hope that there might be someone else out there for me.'

I don't think a day has passed so far without a wedding taking place. The old me would never have considered tying the knot so publicly, with a bunch of holidaymakers spectating from the comfort of their sunbeds. I've sneaked the odd glance or two, interested to see the bride and groom's outfits, but some people openly stare. That said, the atmosphere has been so joyful and celebratory that I could possibly be persuaded to change my mind. All I need to do now is find a groom, something my mum thinks will be highly unlikely given our conversation on Mother's Day. Sitting on this idyllic beach, that conversation seems a lifetime ago and yet it's only been a month... a month in which I've not spoken to her. Maybe part of the reason I've longed for motherhood is so that I could develop the kind of bond that I wish wasn't so sadly lacking between me and Mum.

'Ladies,' Hemant says, delivering our piña coladas with a flourish. 'Enjoy the rest of your afternoon.'

'This is the best piña colada I've ever tasted,' Annabel says, taking a sip.

'Made with locally produced rum!' we both chorus, laughing before Hemant can repeat the line he has delivered every time we mention how good the cocktails are.

He does a strange little half-bow. 'I think maybe I've said this before, so you already know the rum is local.'

'Local and excellent,' I say, anxious that we may have upset him.

'Like me.' He smiles as he backs away a couple of paces before turning to hurry off and take another order.

'Phew! I was worried he was going to take that the wrong way,' I say.

'Not Hemant. He has a good personality and the looks to match,' she says, raising her eyebrows as she takes another long sip of her drink.

'I hope you're not matchmaking.'

She shrugs. 'A little fling wouldn't do you any harm. You must be missing sex.'

I put on my best shocked face, and say, 'I can't believe you just said that!' before dissolving into laughter, in part to cover my embarrassment. Annabel has hit the nail on the head. I miss the physical side of my relationship with Zack terribly.

'It's good to see you laughing again,' Annabel says. 'You deserve another shot at happiness after the past few months.'

'I'll cheers to that,' I say, chinking my glass against hers before taking a huge sip of my cocktail through the paper straw.

'I wanted you to be in a happy place, Charlotte, because I have something to tell you.'

I lower my drink. The flippancy of a minute ago has gone. There's a serious note to Annabel's voice.

She continues, 'Please don't be cross with me, but I haven't been completely honest about my reason for coming here. It's true, I did need some thinking time away from Finn, but not because we're breaking up. He... he asked me to marry him,' she says, almost apologetically.

Her tone makes me feel like a very bad person. She shouldn't feel guilty sharing such amazing news with one of her best friends.

'Oh wow! Congratulations,' I say, raising my glass, not quite ready for the full-on hug that would be more appropriate. 'I must admit I didn't see that coming. When did he propose?'

'It wasn't long after the night I spent at yours, which probably prompted him to do it because he said that he'd hated waking up without me by his side. He must have been planning it for a while as he popped the question with a beautiful emerald and diamond ring. He knows how much I love the colour green,' she says, a tremor in her voice.

'What did you say?' I ask, glancing down at Annabel's ring finger where the emerald and diamond ring is noticeable by its absence. I've made the effort to keep my voice light and joyful because I truly am happy for my friend, despite the churning feeling in my stomach.

She looks sheepish. 'I said it was a big commitment and that I needed a time-out to think about it. It was Finn who suggested a week away.'

'So, we're five days into that week, are you any closer to reaching a decision?'

'You probably think I'm crazy, but no. I need to be sure that I'd being saying yes for the right reasons. Finn's kind, loving and generous to a fault, as you now know,' she says, indicating our stunning surroundings. 'But he's not even thirty until his next birthday. Is marriage and all the trimmings what he really wants or what he thinks he should want?'

'That's his decision,' I reply. 'We're talking about yours. Everyone always says that age is just a number, and he honestly never strikes me as being a lot younger than you. You're good together. I've said it before, but it's worth repeating. You've kissed a lot of frogs, maybe you've finally found your prince.' A thought occurs to me. 'Does Tiff know?'

'Yes,' Annabel says, an embarrassed look on her face.

'Oh, right,' I say, the penny suddenly dropping. 'So that was what the impromptu coffee date was all about. Tiff wanted to gauge whether I'd be able to handle your good news because my cosy little life had just imploded.'

'Something like that,' Annabel mumbles.

'And obviously, she didn't think the timing was right, otherwise we wouldn't be here together now,' I say, a hint of 'spoilt brat' in my voice.

'That's not exactly true. Finn had already suggested the week away because of my hesitation before we met up. There's no way Tiff can just up sticks and have a week away from the girls, although between you and me, I think she would benefit from a week of being Tiff, rather than just a mum and a wife. The ideal scenario would have been for the three of us to come so you two could have persuaded me that I'd be an idiot to throw away a chance of settling down with a poor fool who is clearly crazy about me. But in Tiff's absence, the ball is in your court, Charlotte. My destiny is in your hands,' Annabel says dramatically, winking at the same time.

'Ever the drama queen,' I remark, grateful that my petulance appears to have gone unnoticed. My friends were just being thoughtful, nothing more and nothing less. 'Tiff must have given you her opinion though?'

'Of course. She said I should seize the opportunity to be more grown-up, as she put it, but then Tiff is happily married to her love at first sight. She was never going to say anything else. But things haven't been so straightforward for you.' She reaches across with her free hand and places it on mine. 'In a way, your advice will be more valuable because sometimes love at first sight doesn't work out. Your split with Zack was a sobering reminder of that.'

I wait for the heart-wrenching pain that normally accompanies the belief that Zack and I were a forever couple. It doesn't come, at least not with the ferocity I've grown to expect.

'You've got two more days to really weigh up your feelings for Finn. Forget how he feels about you and concentrate on how you feel about him. Do you love him enough? It might not be the fireworks that Tiff and I experienced, but sometimes all that's left of the explosive display is ash. Love changes in all relationships,' I say, thinking again of my own experience with Zack. At first, I was totally in love with him, but it changed to something much deeper as time went on. I loved him with every fibre of my being, but in the end that wasn't enough because he hadn't been truthful with me. 'It's whether you think your love will stay as strong as it already is or possibly grow even stronger. Either of those, and you and Finn will have a good chance of making it work. And for what it's worth,' I add, 'you and Tiff were right about not telling me last month. I wasn't ready and wouldn't have been able to say any of what I just have, whether it turns out to be useful or not.'

Annabel turns away for a moment, looking towards the distant horizon.

'Thanks, Charlotte,' she says, turning back to face me. 'I may have underestimated how much I needed your approval. Who knew the baby of our group would turn out to be the wisest?'

Am I though? Only time will tell if the decision I've made and the one I'm urging Annabel to take will prove to be wise.

ELEVEN

FRIDAY 20 APRIL

'I'm so sorry, Charlotte,' Annabel says. 'I don't think I can face dinner. It's either something I ate at lunch or the boat journey back from the island. Either way, I feel as though I'm about to throw up.'

We booked the island visit as a treat for our last full day in Mauritius. Each morning, we watched the boat leave the jetty filled with enthusiastic holidaymakers, staff, and the where-withal to make a barbecue lunch on the beach. The only thing stopping us was Annabel's predisposition to motion sickness, but we decided to risk it as the boat journey was only half an hour on normally calm seas.

It was like a millpond on the outward leg first thing this morning. We wandered around the island. It didn't take us long to circumnavigate, so thirty minutes later, we settled on our sun loungers, the legs of which were half in and half out of the sea, while the hotel staff prepared salads to serve with the freshly caught barbecued fish. It all tasted delicious and even more so because of the idyllic location. It felt otherworldly in the best possible sense of the word.

The return journey was slightly earlier than we'd been

anticipating, and the reason soon became apparent. A storm was brewing and despite their best efforts to get us back to the resort before it hit, we got caught in the heavy rolling swell. Annabel was looking greener by the second. The moment we got back to our room, she lay flat on her back on her bed, refusing even a sip of water. We were both expecting her nausea to pass quickly, but she's still struggling three hours on.

'No worries. It won't hurt me to skip a meal. I feel like I've put on a stone since we've been here,' I say, patting my stomach.

'No, you go. I know how much you've been looking forward to another meal in the beach restaurant and we were so lucky to get a table. I'm sure I'll be fine by the morning.'

The Attitude Hotel, like many all-inclusive resorts, has a main buffet-style restaurant and several other themed à la carte restaurants that require a reservation. Despite booking our restaurant choices directly after checking in, the beach restaurant was only available on the second night of our stay. We both loved it so much, we'd asked to be put on the cancellations list and sure enough, there was a message yesterday saying that a table for two had become available for tonight. Much as I really want to go, I can't leave Annabel on her own.

'I wouldn't dream of it,' I say. 'I can order room service.'

'To be honest, I think that trying to get some rest with the smell of food in the room would make me worse,' Annabel replies. 'It's not as though all the staff don't know you. I'm just sorry I've ruined the plans for our last night here.'

Reluctantly, I agree to go on my own and head into the shower. When I come out of the bathroom thirty minutes later, after running the dryer over my freshly washed hair and applying a 'no make-up' make-up look, I find Annabel sleeping, so creep out of the room as quietly as I can.

Even though I'm no stranger to the beach restaurant as we've been having our buffet lunch there most days, I still feel awkward standing next to the desk waiting to be escorted to my table.

'Good evening, Miss Charlotte,' Vikram, the restaurant manager, says, approaching me with two menus in his hand. 'Would you like to sit or have a drink at the bar while you wait for your friend?'

'I'm dining alone tonight,' I reply. 'My friend isn't feeling too well.'

'I hope she will feel better soon. Please follow me.' He leads me to the only vacant table, laying the napkin across my lap once I've sat down and handing me the menu. 'What would you like to drink?' he asks.

I'm about to say I'd like a Diet Coke but change my mind. It's been a wonderful week at a fabulous resort and although I'd rather be celebrating my new mood of optimism with Annabel, it still deserves recognition.

'I'll have a glass of Prosecco, please,' I say, 'and a bottle of water.'

The daytime temperatures have been in the low thirties, and it doesn't drop much in the evenings. Add to that the high humidity with it being rainy season and I've drunk more water in a week than I would normally in a month at home, although most of it seems to leak from my skin. I surreptitiously pat at my forehead, nose and cheeks with my napkin and haven't even had time to open the menu before my drinks order arrives courtesy of Hemant. I can't believe how long the days are for the staff. Hemant will have started at 10 a.m. serving drinks on the beach and will be serving drinks in the beach bar, including drinks for diners in the beach restaurant during service, until midnight. Annabel and I discovered this on our previous visit to the beach restaurant when he'd virtually closed the bar around us just after midnight, apologising profusely but explaining that he was back on duty in ten hours.

'No Miss Annabel tonight?' he asks, placing my Prosecco on

the table and flipping up the rubber stopper of the water bottle before pouring me a glass.

'I was just saying to Vikram that she's not feeling too well.' I raise my water glass and taking a long drink from it.

Hemant waits for me to place it back on the table, then refills it before heading off to deliver the remaining drinks on his tray.

I sip my Prosecco, the bubbles tickling my nose, and glance down at the menu. There are so many delicious things to choose from, I hardly know where to start. I can see Vikram heading in my direction and I'm nowhere near ready to order.

'Could you just give me a few more moments?' I say as he reaches my table.

'Of course, Miss Charlotte, take your time. But I have a favour to ask of you. As you know, we are fully booked tonight. There is a gentleman, also a lone diner, who really wanted to eat here tonight but couldn't get booked in. He came by the restaurant to see whether anyone hadn't turned up for their table. He noticed you dining alone and wondered whether you might consider sharing your table with him. Please feel free to say no if it makes you feel uncomfortable.'

It's not unusual to approach people at bar tables and ask if they'd mind if you joined them, but in a restaurant? I'm about to say no when I catch sight of the man waiting by the entrance desk. He raises his hands in a silent prayer, the corners of his mouth turning down slightly.

I hesitate for only a moment before saying, 'That's fine. It will be nice to have company on my last night.'

Vikram turns and indicates with his hand, and I watch as the man mouths thank you and starts to make his way across the sandy floor of the restaurant. From a distance, he looked handsome, but the closer he gets, I realise that is a bit of an understatement. He has dark wavy hair, a little on the long side, giving him a slightly bohemian appearance, and a strong clean-shaven jaw.

'Are you sure you don't mind?' he asks, meeting my gaze with eyes that are a similar shade of green to my own.

Annoyingly, I know I've coloured up, but I'm hoping he hasn't noticed because I'm already sporting a pinkish tinge to my tan. I underestimated the intensity of the sun on the island earlier.

'No, please,' I mutter, indicating the chair opposite me. 'We only managed to get this table because someone else cancelled, so the least I can do is share my good fortune, particularly as we've eaten in here before.'

'We?' he asks, glancing around. 'Are you dining with the Invisible Man? I'm not about to sit on his knee, am I?' He looks suspiciously at the upholstered chair that Vikram has pulled back.

He has an easy manner. Maybe I'm going to enjoy my final evening in Mauritius more than I anticipated.

'Sorry, I should have explained better. My girlfriend was supposed to be eating with me, but she isn't feeling well.'

His eyebrows raise almost imperceptibly, but it makes me realise what I've said.

'Not girlfriend in the relationship sense,' I rush on, feeling flustered. 'She's my friend and she's female.'

'No need to explain, I'm very open-minded,' he says, a hint of amusement in his voice. 'I'm sorry to hear she's not well, of course, but it's a stroke of luck for me.' He sits down and takes the menu that Vikram is offering.

'Can I get you a drink, sir?'

'I'll have a glass of the house Chablis, please.'

I drop my eyes to study my menu, trying to hide my embarrassment and collect my thoughts. It seems that my ten-year relationship with Zack has removed my ability to talk to an attractive member of the opposite sex without getting tongue-tied. I can feel his eyes on me. He clears his throat and I risk glancing up.

'Have we met before?' he asks. 'Only you look vaguely familiar.'

That has to be the worst chat-up line ever.

'I don't think so,' I reply. I'm sure I would have remembered.

'I'm Justin, by the way.'

'Oh, right. I'm Charlotte. I guess if we're going to spend the night together, we should at least know each other's name.'

The look he gives me is one of surprise followed by amusement. Oh God, I can't believe I just said that. Do I stumble around trying to explain myself, or pretend I haven't realised what I implied?

'Am I making you nervous, Charlotte? Because, honestly, that's not my intention.'

'No, not at all,' I manage, although, in truth, he is. It's a long time since I had dinner with a stranger, and a very good-looking one at that. 'I guess I wasn't expecting to engage in conversation tonight, so it's caught me off guard. Are you holidaying alone?' I ask, trying to move the focus away from me.

'Not holidaying at all,' he replies, as Hemant arrives with his glass of white wine. 'Are you ready to order?'

I nod. I've decided to have the baked fish and stir-fried vegetables that the diners on the next table to ours are having. It looks delicious.

'Good, I'm starving,' he says, addressing me before turning to Hemant. 'Would you ask the waiter to come and take our order, please?'

Hemant bows his head and retreats. He's probably wondering who on earth my dinner companion is. He's not the only one.

'So, if you're not on holiday, do you live here?' I ask.

'I wish. But no, I'm over here working at the moment.'

'Oh really? What do you do?'

He seems to be giving his answer a fair amount of consideration before he replies, 'I make my clients look good, which is sometimes easier said than done.'

I'm intrigued. He hasn't answered my question, but maybe he'll be more forthcoming as our evening goes on, particularly if he continues downing his wine. Either that, or he's in some dodgy business he is sworn to secrecy about.

'Are you ready to order, sir?' Vikram asks, pad in hand.

'Ladies first,' Justin says.

'Can I have the deep-fried Camembert with the masala wine sauce, followed by the baked fish please?'

'Certainly, Miss Charlotte, and for you, sir?'

'I'll have the same as Miss Charlotte,' Justin says, a mischievous smile on his face.

'Very good, sir. And would you both like another drink?' Vikram asks, indicating our empty glasses.

I'm quite surprised that my drink is already finished. It must be the nerves.

'Oh, go on then, you've persuaded me,' I say, flashing Vikram my best smile.

Justin nods in agreement and waits for Vikram to leave before saying, 'So, how about you?' At my puzzled expression, he adds, 'What work do you do? Are you a model or something? You're very beautiful and you have amazing bone structure.'

For a moment, I toy with the idea of telling him that I used to be a model but decide against it. What would be the point? It might prompt questions about why I gave it up and I'm not ready to discuss my relationship and subsequent break-up with a total stranger.

'Wow!' I exclaim. 'That's almost as bad a chat-up line as "have we met before?".' The Prosecco has clearly relaxed and emboldened me.

'It wasn't a chat-up line,' he protests. 'I genuinely thought you looked familiar, and you are good-looking enough to be a model.' I can feel the colour creeping up my cheeks again. 'I guess I should learn to filter my thoughts before speaking, though.'

For the first time since he joined me at the table, he doesn't seem quite so self-assured. Maybe he puts on an act of being super confident but underneath it all he's shy. I decide to give him the benefit of the doubt.

'Actually, I work in a florist. It doesn't pay that well and it's long hours, but I really love creating beautiful flower arrangements for special occasions or handing over a bunch of tulips to children who've bought them with their pocket money,' I reply, feeling the most relaxed I have since Justin joined me because I'm now on safe territory.

Flowers have always been a passion of mine. As a small child, I had my own patch of garden where I grew candytuft and cornflowers from seeds. I can remember checking my little flower bed every morning before school, waiting for the first signs of green to push through the soil and the feeling of elation when they appeared. There wasn't a moment of hesitation when my parents suggested getting a Saturday job to help make ends meet at home. I went straight to the flower shop on the corner of our street, asked for a job and started work that afternoon. At first, it was mostly serving customers with readymade bunches of flowers and quite a lot of sweeping up, but I can still recall the thrill of making up my first hand-tied bouquet and the look of delight on the customer's face. I would probably have made a career of it, maybe even have had my own shop, if I hadn't been spotted by a modelling agent.

My life took a totally different path, but I have no regrets, and at least I had something to go back to when I gave up modelling. Everyone assumed that Zack wanted me to give up my career, but the truth was I didn't want to spend time away from him and modelling was nowhere near as glamorous as people outside the industry assumed. My first swimsuit shoot on deserted white sand beaches in the Caribbean meant a week of 5 a.m. starts so that the make-up artist had time to make me look like I wasn't wearing any make-up before the photographer lost the early-morning light. It was all smoke and mirrors, nothing was as it seemed. I soon realised it wasn't what I wanted to do for the rest of my life, but I'd been lured away from school at sixteen without any qualifications. Then Zack came into my life.

I stuck the modelling out for a few more years, each trip away becoming increasingly difficult. I hated the goodbyes and the jet lag often made me grumpy. I simply wasn't enjoying it anymore and I was starting to feel broody as my thirties beckoned. When the Ring o' Roses florist shop opened a five-minute walk from Zack's flat, I took it as a sign. I went in, asked for a job and a week later told the model agency I was quitting. I was sad to leave the shop after six happy years, but Zack forced my hand.

'Flowers can always raise a smile,' I say, 'whatever the occasion.'

'With the possible exception of funerals,' Justin says.

It was a glib remark and I'm about to say that flowers bring a huge amount of comfort on a difficult day, but I can see Hemant and Vikram approaching with our drinks and starters, so I stay quiet.

'Sorry, that was uncalled for.' Justin sounds contrite. 'You clearly enjoy your job, which is more than can be said for most people.'

I can't help wondering if he's including himself in that statement, but I'll have to wait to find out as conversation is suspended while we get started on our food. The first cut of the knife into the wedges of breaded cheese releases the melted centre, allowing it to ooze out into the deep red of the wine sauce.

I close my eyes to savour the divine taste and when I open

them, Justin is watching me with those intense green eyes, an amused expression on his face. There is a stirring of something deep inside that I hadn't expected to feel so soon after my split with Zack. In fact, there have been times over the past three months when I wondered if I would ever feel it again. I swallow my food and take another forkful so I don't have to speak. There's no doubt my dinner companion is a very handsome man, but it's more than that. He is charming and funny and interesting. What a shame our paths didn't cross earlier in the holiday.

TWELVE

'I'm absolutely stuffed.' Justin leans back in his chair and pats his non-existent stomach. 'But how good was that dessert?'

Annabel and I devoured a 'bombe surprise' between us when we'd had dinner at the beach restaurant earlier in the week. Although I've spent the evening with Justin, it didn't seem appropriate to suggest sharing our pudding, so I gave up on finishing mine, even though in my humble opinion it's the food of the gods.

We've decamped to the beach bar after Justin waved away my protestations that I should get back and check on Annabel, saying she'd most likely be sleeping off whatever her ailment was. To be fair, I didn't raise much of an argument. I'm enjoying his company. As the evening has worn on, we've talked about a variety of things, from music and favourite movies to holidays and childhood pets, but neither of us has broached the subject of our personal lives and there's been no further mention of Justin's job. It's as though we've known each other for years rather than a couple of hours.

The bar is an old fishing boat complete with carefully angled sails to provide some shade during the day. The tables and chairs are constructed from empty oil cans all painted in bright colours. There is a definite feeling of being at sea, although I'm pretty sure the movement I'm experiencing is a result of the brandy I ordered on top of half a dozen glasses of Prosecco, not some clever technology.

Hemant appears to have taken on the role of protective older brother. He knows exactly how much I've had to drink this evening and clearly thinks it's enough. When he brought my brandy a few minutes ago, he seemed to bang the glass down on the table in a disapproving manner. He made his point though, as I now have a black coffee in front of me which I'm hoping will help me to sober up.

'I don't think your pal's too happy with me for plying you with drinks all night.' Justin indicates Hemant with a slight nod of his head and takes a sip of his double espresso. 'Blimey, that's strong. Do you think it's to mask the taste of the poison?'

I suppress a giggle and take a sip of my own coffee, grimacing at the taste. It's so strong, I'm surprised that the crystallised sugar stirring stick didn't stand up in it on its own. 'It's quite sweet really,' I reply. 'Not the coffee, obviously. He's been looking after my friend and me all week.'

Justin raises his eyebrows and I realise how my words could have given him the wrong impression. I've managed to get through most of the evening without making a fool of myself, but now I'm back to the clumsiness of our early exchanges. Maybe the brandy was a drink too far. I take another sip of my hideous coffee to hide my embarrassment.

'Of course he has. If your friend is even half as attractive as you, he'll have been falling over himself to serve you both. We men are a shallow lot. We'll do anything for a pretty face,' he says, lowering his cup onto the saucer.

'It's probably more about earning himself a decent tip at the end of our holiday, which, in fairness, he deserves,' I reply, my words slightly slurred.

'Maybe we should call it a night?' Justin suggests. 'I don't think I can stomach any more of that coffee.'

I agree with him on the coffee, but I'm sad our time together is almost over. It's been an unexpectedly pleasant evening. I make a move to stand but lose my balance and sink back down onto the cushioned seat.

'I think I'd better walk you to your room.' Justin gets up from his chair and offers me his arm for support.

'Are you sure you don't mind?' I say, taking hold of his arm to pull myself up onto my feet. 'We're right at the other end of the resort, near the reception.'

'All the more reason to escort you back,' he replies. 'I wouldn't want you falling into a bush in your inebriated state and being set upon by wild dogs. I'd never forgive myself.'

'Are there wild dogs in Mauritius?' I link my arm through Justin's and wave goodnight to Hemant, who is already heading towards our recently vacated table to remove the coffee cups.

'I have no idea, but it's best not to risk it,' he says, steering me towards a leafy archway and the path beyond.

It's the first time in months that I've been in such close contact with a member of the opposite sex. The shudder of pleasure it sends through me catches me off guard. Annabel's words from yesterday force their way into my head. '*A little fling wouldn't do you any harm.*' I can feel Justin's firm biceps through the linen fabric of his jacket sleeve and find myself imagining what the rest of his body is like.

'I don't suppose you'd be up for making me a decent cup of coffee?' I hear myself suggest. 'I probably should try to sober up a bit...'

It's less snoring, more a gentle vibration as Justin breathes in and out through his nose in a regular pattern. In the dim light cast through the open bathroom door, I can see the outline of his toned shoulders and torso. In a way, I'm sad that this is the last night of our holiday as I would have liked to get to know Justin better.

He was so kind when we got back to his room, making me a coffee, and opening the sliding doors to his balcony to let the warm night air in when I shivered at the cool air-conditioning. As he put his linen jacket around my shoulders, I noticed his cologne for the first time. It was CK One, a unisex fragrance I enjoyed wearing when I was first with Zack. Smelling it brought back vivid memories of the heady days at the start of our relationship when we couldn't get enough of each other. Something inside me just clicked then. I devoted ten years of my life to Zack, and I didn't want to spend the rest of my life dwelling on what might have been. I needed to start living again and I felt a powerful physical attraction to Justin.

I don't really remember who kissed who first, but I do remember him saying, 'You really are very beautiful.' It was as though the starting pistol had been fired at the beginning of a track and field race. Within minutes, we were pulling each other's clothes off and exploring one another with our hands and our tongues. Everything was moving very quickly, but I do remember him pausing before entering me and saying, 'Are you sure you want this?' My response was to wrap my legs around him and pull him towards me. In truth, it was all over far too quickly, but it satisfied a growing need. His final kiss was gentle before he turned over and fell asleep.

Much as I don't want to disturb him, I'm desperate for a wee and I should probably be getting back to check on Annabel. Carefully, I wriggle towards the edge of the bed and drop my legs to the floor. I feel quite exposed and cast my eyes around for my dress and underwear. I pick them up on my way to the bathroom and squeeze through the door so as not to throw too much light into the room and possibly wake Justin.

The bathroom light is harsh and bright, and I blink rapidly

until my eyes adjust. My reflection in the mirror is best described as dishevelled. Silently closing the door behind me so that I won't feel self-conscious, I pad across the cool tiles under-foot and sink down onto the loo.

It's when I'm lathering the bar of soap to wash my hands that I see it. My blood runs cold. On the shelf above the taps is a wide gold band with a row of diamonds running along it. I grip the washbasin with both hands to steady myself. I was already feeling a little shocked at my own promiscuity; jumping into bed on a first date has never been my style, and to describe the chance encounter with Justin as a date is a bit of a stretch in anybody's book. But having sex with a married man has always been a complete no-no for me. My shock quickly turns to revul-sion, even though I had no way of knowing that he was married.

My first instinct is to wake Justin and demand to know why he didn't tell me. How dare he think it's all right to treat two women with such disrespect? Then I play the events of the evening over in my mind. Had I come on to him so much that he simply couldn't resist? Had he been so drunk by the time we got back to his room that his morals deserted him?

The question I'm asking myself is what would confronting him achieve? I'm going home tomorrow, so I'll never see him again. I feel ashamed by my own behaviour and disgusted by his. It's a lose/lose situation. If he showed no remorse, I'd feel dreadful that I'd allowed myself to be attracted to him, but if he felt guilty and expressed regret, I'd feel even worse about what we'd done.

I just want to get out of his room and back to mine to take a shower. But something tells me that no amount of foaming body gel will cleanse how dirty I now feel.

THIRTEEN

FRIDAY 8 JUNE

I'm in the middle of tying a beautiful arrangement of white calla lilies, pink oriental lilies, and white and pink roses when my mobile starts to ring. I can see it's Annabel calling, but I can't answer it until I've secured the twine around the stems or I'll spoil the display that I've been working on for the past twenty minutes.

Seeing her number reminds me that she also rang yesterday, and I forgot to return her call. I've barely seen her since we got back from Mauritius, apart from a very clumsy attempt on her part to set me up with a friend of Finn's at the dinner party to celebrate their engagement. I guess after my fling in Mauritius, she thinks I'm completely over Zack and ready to start dating again, and she was just trying to get the ball rolling.

It was supposed to be a 'couples' dinner, with Tiff and JJ and two friends of Finn's with their partners. An eligible bachelor was rustled up for me, so that I wouldn't feel awkward as the only single person. To say we had absolutely nothing in common is an understatement, and there wasn't even the tiniest spark of attraction on my part. It could have been mutual as he excused himself before dessert saying he had an early start. It was his loss, as the passion fruit pavlova was divine.

The whole evening hadn't quite gone to plan. Tiff and JJ had to cancel at the last minute as their younger daughter, Tamsin, had caught chickenpox from one of her school friends. In children, it's itchy and unpleasant, but adult chickenpox is 'horrendous' according to Tiff and she should know as she and Melody had caught it at a mother and baby group. Like me, most of the dinner party guests had it in infancy, but Annabel hadn't and Tiff was erring on the side of caution. Another of the couples arrived an hour late as their babysitter's car had broken down and you could have cut the atmosphere with a knife between the last couple, who'd clearly had an argument before arriving and were barely speaking. All in all, it wasn't the joyful occasion it should have been, although Annabel did a good job of covering her disappointment, aided by the best part of a bottle of gin.

We'd planned to meet for a catch up over lunch last week, but Michaela surprised everybody by booking a last-minute half-term holiday in a villa in Portugal for her mum and her kids. I'm chuffed that she felt she could trust me to hold the fort. It's lovely that she has faith not only in my ability to make up the flower arrangements, but also to leave me in sole charge. It's meant that I've been rushed off my feet though, hence forgetting to return Annabel's call yesterday.

I finish tying the twine, snip the ends and then wrap the whole arrangement in the shop's branded tissue paper with an outer layer of cellophane and hold it in place with several rounds of Sellotape. Then I take another piece of cellophane and press it into the cardboard holder, fill it with a small amount of water, place the arrangement into it and gather up the sides of the cellophane to tie with a grosgrain branded ribbon. I'm sure Mr Harrington will be delighted when he picks it up on his way home from the station tonight.

There's no one in the shop, so I decide to flip the sign on the door to closed and take my lunch break early. I haven't fancied breakfast for the past couple of weeks so I'm always starving by half past eleven.

With the kettle coming to the boil, I unwrap my sandwich and take a bite of cheese and pickle, before glancing down at my mobile. There's the missed call notification from Annabel, but she's also sent a text.

Hi stranger, I hope you're not avoiding me since I tried to set you up with Phil? Sorry, Finn's recommendation... not your type at all!! Anyway, Tiff messaged to ask if Finn and I are going to her 50th birthday bash next weekend. She said she hadn't heard back from you either, so asked me to check. Call me when you get this xx

Replying to Tiff's invitation is something else I've forgotten because I've been so busy, although that's not much of an excuse as I could have done it last Sunday on my day off. Instead, I went back to sleep until midday after getting up for the loo around 7 a.m., and then spent the afternoon on the sofa watching catch-up TV after a whistle-stop trip to the local supermarket. A soak in a foamy bath followed and I was fast asleep in bed before 10 p.m. Age seems to have caught up with me since I got home from Mauritius, or maybe it's jet lag. I've been constantly tired.

I have another bite of my sandwich, pour the boiling water onto the coffee granules and dial Annabel's number. She answers on the second ring.

'Charlotte, at last. I was starting to think you'd run off back to Mauritius to be with your waiter.'

As expected, Annabel hasn't let this topic of conversation drop. When I arrived back at our room on that final night in

Mauritius, she was lying on her side with her back to me and appeared to be sleeping. I showered as quietly as I could and crept into bed. Nothing much was said the next morning over breakfast, but when we arrived at the beach and a different waiter arrived to take our drinks order, Annabel immediately jumped to the wrong conclusion.

The minute the waiter was out of earshot, she turned to me and said, 'Wow! What did you do to the poor guy?'

Obviously she hadn't been asleep as I'd assumed when I got back to our room in the early hours. For a moment, I considered correcting Annabel's assumption that it was Hemant who I'd been with the previous night, but I quickly realised that there was no point. She knew nothing about my dinner with Justin and I wasn't in the mood for a lecture about hopping into bed with a stranger. I decided that by calling in sick, Hemant might have done me a favour. I chose my words carefully so that I wasn't actually lying.

'Perhaps he thinks last night was an error of judgement and he'd rather forget about it,' I said. 'He would know he'd have to face me if he came into work today, so he stayed away to protect us both from feeling embarrassed.'

Annabel pulled a disbelieving face before saying, 'There's nothing to be embarrassed about. You're both adults, and he clearly fancied the pants off you. So long as it was consensual from both of you, it's completely normal. It's 2018 not 1918.' When I didn't answer, she added, 'It was consensual, wasn't it? He didn't force you, did he? Is that why you don't want to talk about it?'

'Nobody was forced into anything,' I assured her. 'There might have been a fair amount of alcohol involved, but not so much that we didn't know what we were doing.'

That had been true for me of course, but not for Justin. He knew he was breaking his wedding vows even if he was the worse for drink. And given that he's married, Justin might not be his real name. Not that it matters, as I'll never have to lay eyes on him again. I felt nervous throughout breakfast in case I ran into him. I've no idea how I would have reacted, or how he would have for that matter after I snuck out of his room in the middle of the night. Fortunately, there was no sign of him, but my twitchiness must have been obvious.

'And?' she asked.

'And what? I'm not going to give you a blow-by-blow account.'

'But it must have been good, or you would have been back before 4 a.m.,' she persisted.

'Let's just say it satisfied a need,' I replied, wanting to close the subject down without arousing suspicion. 'I'm sorry I woke you. I was trying to be really quiet.'

'You didn't. I woke up hungry and saw your bed was empty. I pretended to be asleep when I heard the key in the lock in case you didn't want to talk about it. I knew I'd get the truth from you eventually.' She prodded me in the ribs with her finger. 'You always were a terrible liar.'

I'm not that bad a liar as I've managed to keep the truth from her, although it's not something to be proud of. I've allowed her to think that my night of passion was with a waiter in the hope that she would eventually get bored of talking about it, but it hasn't happened yet.

'Sorry, Annabel,' I say, ignoring the comment about Hemant. 'I was going to call you last night, but I fell asleep in front of the TV, and it was too late by the time I woke up. It's just so full-on at work with Michaela away. I'll need another holiday to recover once she's back.'

'Maybe you could go back to Mauritius?' she says, as though to underline her previous comment.

'Ha ha, you're so funny,' I respond.

'I know, that's part of my attraction. Your boss is back tomorrow, isn't she?'

'Yes, but not until the evening, so I've got another manic Saturday on my own. She's covering my shift on Monday though.'

'It's the least she can do,' Annabel says, sounding mildly indignant on my behalf. 'You could maybe go shopping for something to wear to Tiff's party. I could meet you in my lunch hour if you like?'

The thought of a quick dash around the Maidenhead shops isn't that appealing. I'd rather shop online and try things on at home, even if returning things is a nuisance.

'I'll take a rain check on that. The house hasn't seen a duster since we got back and one of the provisos of my low rent was that I kept the garden looking tidy. I think Gary thought I would be a keen gardener because I work in a florist shop, but the two are chalk and cheese. It's like a jungle out there at the moment.'

'But you are going to Tiff's party? Like I said in my text, she was asking.'

The thought of making small talk with a load of people, most of whom I won't know, is daunting, but it's a milestone birthday for her so I'll have to make an effort.

'Of course,' I reply. 'As long as you and Tiff promise not to try to set me up with a date.' Before Annabel can follow up, I hear the rattle of the shop door handle. 'Look, I'm going to have to go. There's someone at the shop door and I haven't finished my brunch yet.'

'Ooooh, brunch is it,' she says in a mocking voice. 'What happened to good old breakfast?'

'I haven't been fancying anything first thing just lately.'

'You're not pregnant, are you?' she asks, and then gulps. 'Sorry, that's insensitive. I'll give you a call on Sunday and we can discuss outfits for the party.'

Annabel ends the call, and the rattling of the door handle becomes a determined knocking, but I can't move. Her words, spoken in jest, have struck a chord. I've been super tired and feeling too queasy to eat breakfast. Come to think of it, I'm well overdue for my period. My mouth is suddenly as dry as the Sahara.

What if I am pregnant? What will I do?

FOURTEEN

SATURDAY 9 JUNE

Five o'clock couldn't come quickly enough for me today. I was literally watching the second hand move around the big white clock face whenever I was alone in the shop and it seemed to be moving at a snail's pace. The moment the minute hand hits twelve with the hour hand on the five, I flip the sign on the door to closed. Ten minutes later, I've locked up, dropped the keys in the secure box and am striding out in the direction of Bray.

After my call to Annabel yesterday, I spent the day in a bit of a daze. On my way home, I called in to the late-night chemist and bought a pregnancy test, but when I got home, I couldn't bring myself to take it. I had to go into work today, and if I'd done the test and it was positive, I'm not sure I could have held it together. Without saying why, I messaged Annabel late last night and asked her to come over for pizza in front of Saturday night television. Fortunately, she and Finn had no plans other than a boxing match on pay per view which he wanted to watch and Annabel wasn't so keen on. I suggested she brought an overnight bag just in case.

Since I got home from work, I've been pacing around the kitchen table, where the box containing the pregnancy test is lying. My emotions are all over the place. I've been desperate for a baby for so long, but that was when I was in a settled relationship. My situation now is completely different.

I almost jump out of my skin when the doorbell rings. I can see Annabel's outline through the frosted glazed panels as I head down the hallway and, unsurprisingly, she appears to be holding a bottle of wine that I won't be touching if things go as I suspect they might.

'Well, this is unexpected,' Annabel says the moment I start to open the door. 'I've brought supplies.' She brandishes the bottle of red in one hand and a box of Maltesers in the other, then pauses. 'Are you okay? You look like you've seen a ghost.'

I absolutely didn't mean to cry and have no idea why I am, but I'm bawling my eyes out before she's even across the doorstep.

'What the hell?' She ushers me inside, closing the door and putting the wine and chocolates on the Victorian hall stand before flinging her arms around me. 'Is it Zack? Has he been to the shop again?'

I cling to her for a moment. What happens in the next few minutes has the potential to change my life forever.

'Thank you for coming,' I mumble through my tears. 'I couldn't do this alone.'

'Do what?' she asks, gently taking hold of my shoulders and pushing me out to arm's length so that she can see my face.

I lead the way into the kitchen and move around to the other side of the table. Her eyes register the blue and white box.

'Oh, my God. Are you actually pregnant with the waiter's baby?'

Once again, I don't correct her assumption. 'I haven't done the test yet,' I say, resting my hands on the table to stop them shaking. 'I wasn't brave enough to do it on my own. That's why I asked you to come over.'

Annabel takes a deep breath and holds it a moment before

exhaling. 'Well, let's get on with it. There's no point getting stressed and upset until we know what we're dealing with.'

She has no idea how much her use of the word 'we' means to me. I've felt so alone since I first considered the possibility that I might be pregnant.

'Come on.' She takes hold of my hand in one of hers and picks up the pregnancy test with the other. 'There's no time like the present.'

Annabel holds both my hands very tightly between hers while we wait for the message to appear in the little window. Neither of us speaks; it seems pointless until we know the outcome of the test.

When the word pregnant appears, it's almost as though it's taunting me. I've visualised it so often, willing it to happen throughout the last five of the ten years I was with Zack. For a few seconds, I can't be sure if it's real or imagined.

'Well, at least we know now,' Annabel says, her eyes moving away from the pregnancy test to connect with mine. 'How do you feel about it?'

I can't answer her immediately. I'm beyond shocked to have fallen pregnant during a night of drunken passion. I'm struggling to believe that what I've longed for and dreamt about for the past five years has happened so easily and naturally. To my mind, there is only one problem. The father of the child I'm now carrying is not Zack but instead someone I barely know, who also happens to be married to someone else.

When I still haven't replied a few minutes later, Annabel says, 'Come on, let's go downstairs and consider all the options. I don't know about you, but I need a drink.'

She grabs the bottle of red from the hall and settles me on the sofa while she fetches a couple of wine glasses and the corkscrew from the kitchen. I watch as the deep red liquid flows into Annabel's glass, a tiny splash landing on her pale pink jeans, but I stop her from pouring anything into mine. She raises her eyebrows in an unspoken question before bringing her glass to her lips and draining it.

'Does that mean you are intending to keep it then?' she asks, refilling her glass.

Annabel's use of the word *it* when referring to the tiny person growing inside me makes me flinch.

'It means I may already have inadvertently done some damage to the baby,' I reply emphasising the word. 'I'd rather not do anymore until I've had time to think things through.'

'Fair enough,' she agrees, downing her second glass of wine in as many minutes. For whatever reason, all I can think about is how few glasses make up a bottle when you're on home measures. 'Are you going to think things through on your own?'

'You know how much I value your opinion,' I say, 'but I'd really appreciate if we could keep this between the two of us for now.'

'That's not what I meant,' she says.

That's when I realise that I'm going to have to tell Annabel the truth about what happened on the last night of our holiday.

FIFTEEN

The wine bottle is almost empty, even though I haven't touched a drop.

'So, let me get this straight,' Annabel says. 'You had dinner with some random guy, got pissed and went back to his room for a quickie without using any protection?'

I nod. Put like that, it makes me sound incredibly irresponsible.

'Quite apart from the fact that he could have been some knife-wielding psycho,' she says, struggling to keep the incredulity from her voice, 'why on earth didn't you insist he wore a condom?'

'I wasn't thinking straight. I've been with Zack for so long and obviously we never used them. It never entered my head that I might get pregnant.'

'It's not just about getting pregnant,' she says, shaking her head. 'But that's the situation you find yourself in. The question remains, regardless of who the father is, are you going to keep it?'

Without realising, I place my hand on my belly in a protective gesture which doesn't go unnoticed.

'I'll take that as a yes then,' she says, the tone of her voice becoming gentler.

I haven't had much time to get used to the idea, but from the moment I saw the two-syllable word, I think I knew I couldn't give up the chance to become a mother after wanting it for so long. I've cried so many tears when each month my period has arrived to taunt me and I've raged at all the women who opted for terminations of unwanted pregnancies when I longed so desperately to be a mother. In all conscience, there's no way I can take that path. There's no doubt that I should have been more careful, but now there is another life to consider. I don't believe I have the right to snuff it out before it has begun.

'It's very early days, Annabel. Anything could happen in the next few months. But I can't kill my unborn child,' I say, making eye contact with her for the first time in several minutes. 'It isn't his or her fault that they were conceived outside a loving relationship, and it won't mean I'll love them any less.'

'What about the father? Justin, did you say his name is? Are you going to try to find out who he is and tell him?'

I knew Annabel would ask me this from the moment she found out that the baby's father was not Hemant, but I haven't yet told her that Justin is married. He won't want anything to do with me and, to be honest, the feeling is mutual.

'I wouldn't know where to begin,' I admit, trying to find reasons to dissuade Annabel from looking without having to tell her that I slept with a married man. 'If I knew his last name, maybe the hotel would be able to help, but I don't, and besides, it's probably against data protection to give out other guests' information.'

'We could try. We could say that something of his is unexpectedly in our possession, which isn't a million miles from the truth,' she says, giving me a wry smile. 'We know at least one of the dates he was staying at the resort, and you know his room number, so that would be something for them to work from.'

When I don't say anything, she continues, 'Look, he probably won't want anything to do with the baby, but as its father, don't you think he has a right to know?'

'There's no "probably" about it,' I say, rubbing my fingers on my forehead.

'You can't know that for sure. He may surprise you and turn out to be the man of your dreams. Let's face it, the two of you clearly clicked and you said he was a bit of a looker. Maybe this is the universe at work,' she says, an enthusiasm to her voice that I'm about to crush. But she's on a roll. 'Perhaps you've been thrown together for a reason, and you'll live happily ever after. You could even get married on the beach in Mauritius to celebrate the fact that your paths first crossed there. Maybe I could even persuade Finn to have a joint wedding. That would be amazing, wouldn't it? What?' she asks, finally realising that I'm not joining in.

'It's never going to happen,' I say, shaking my head.

'Unlikely, I agree, but you don't know for sure.'

'Yes, I do. I had to use the bathroom after we'd... well, you know.' I pause to take a deep breath. 'Part of the reason I didn't correct you when you assumed that I'd been with Hemant was because I was so disgusted with myself.'

'I'm not following,' Annabel says.

'There was a gold ring on the shelf in the bathroom. Justin's married. I slept with a married man.'

'But you didn't...' she starts to say before I interrupt.

'No, I didn't know, but it changes things. He has a life and maybe even a family.'

'Well, he should have thought about them before leaving his wedding ring off and then seducing someone who was a bit the worse for drink.' Annabel bristles, all thoughts of a romantic double wedding clearly now abandoned.

'I wanted it just as much as him.'

'That might be true, but you weren't cheating on anyone. How can you not be angry with him?'

'When I saw the ring, I felt disgusted with myself and disrespected by Justin. And I was furious with him for cheating on his wife. But when I got back to our room, I lay in bed replaying the evening in my head and decided that it wasn't really his fault.'

Annabel tries to interrupt, but I hold my hand up to stop her speaking.

'The fact of the matter is, I wanted to have sex with him. I enjoyed spending the evening with him. He wasn't flirting with me, but he made me feel attractive and desirable. To be honest, it felt good to just let myself go without the pressure of trying to conceive. I know,' I say, reacting to Annabel's expression, 'how ironic is that? The point I'm trying to make is that I don't think he went to dinner with the intention of inviting someone back to his room, although why he wasn't wearing his wedding ring is something of a mystery. Maybe he takes it off to shower and forgot to put it back on. I'll never know the answer to that. But what we did should never have happened and he's probably regretted it from the moment he woke up the next day. The last thing he needs is a permanent reminder of his infidelity.'

Annabel puts her wine glass down and pulls me into a fierce hug. 'I'm so angry with him for treating my friend this way.'

'I know, but don't waste your energy. Holding on to anger is like drinking poison and expecting the other person to die. Nothing will be gained by either of us being mad at a total stranger.'

'I suppose you're right. I should just be grateful that I'm not his wife. She's the one we should feel most sorry for, oblivious to the fact that she's married to a lying, cheating arsehole.'

'You still sound angry.'

'I'll get past it,' she says. 'And don't worry, Charlotte, whatever your decision, you won't be facing it alone. Tiff and I will be there for you and I expect Finn will see it as a practice run for us having kids of our own.'

She glances down at the emerald and diamond ring sparkling in the lamplight and it brings a lump to my throat. I always thought Zack and I would be married with a couple of kids before Annabel settled down. I'm so pleased she accepted Finn's proposal after we returned from Mauritius. But hearing her mention having children with Finn when she has always been so adamant that she didn't want any underlines that life really can throw some curveballs.

'Thank you,' I say, returning her hug with a vengeance. 'I'm so lucky to have such great friends. But like I said earlier, can we keep this between the two of us for now?'

'Mum's the word,' she says, holding her index finger up in front of her lips.

'Quite literally,' I reply, joining in with her joke, even though I can't really see the funny side.

SIXTEEN

SATURDAY 16 JUNE

I apply my coral lip gloss, shot through with tiny specks of gold, and smack my lips together before taking a step back from the full-length mirror propped up against the wall. Taking in the whole effect, I must admit that I don't look too bad. I've managed to cover the dark circles under my eyes with concealer and by adding blusher I don't look quite so pale and tired as I did when I arrived home from Stems a little over an hour ago.

I haven't slept well since last Friday when the possibility that I could be pregnant first surfaced and I'm still feeling nauseous in the mornings. Neither has contributed to me looking my best. Thankfully, I'm blessed with well-behaved hair and lots of it, which will draw attention away from my face. It falls loosely around my shoulders in big bouncy curls as I release it from the elastic band that held it back while I was doing my face.

The coral floral dress shows off perfectly what is left of my Mauritian tan, which I topped up a bit while I was tidying the garden on Monday – the only day this week that we've had a bit of sun. I didn't go crazy, just some gentle weeding and mowing the small patch of lawn, interspersed with relaxing on the sun lounger sipping orange squash while I did a bit of online shopping. Obviously, I'd have preferred a cocktail or two, but, having given my baby a boozy start, it will be mocktails for me not only at the party but for the rest of the year.

When Annabel left on Sunday morning, I was non-committal about whether I'd be going to Tiff's fiftieth birthday party. I was physically exhausted from looking after the shop on my own for a week and emotionally drained following the positive pregnancy test and talking through the various scenarios until the early hours of the morning.

Although Annabel has said she and Finn will be there to help in whatever way they can, I don't have an actual plan of how I'm going to manage bringing up a baby on my own. One thing we both agreed was that I couldn't go back to live with my parents. For some, it would be the obvious solution, but not for me. My mother can convey her disappointment in me and my life choices by raising one eyebrow. There is no way I would give her the satisfaction of admitting that my pregnancy was a mistake. As far as she is concerned, my pregnancy has resulted from a sperm donation which to some degree is true. From a distance, the pretence will be easy to keep up, but it'd be impossible if I was under their roof and existing on their charity.

My main reluctance about going to Tiff's birthday bash is because I haven't told her yet that I'm pregnant. I'm not lying to her, but I'm not being completely honest either, which doesn't sit well with me, particularly after the whole episode with Zack. I was vague in my text message to Tiff, saying that I hoped to see her at the party, but I should have known she wouldn't be fobbed off with a 'maybe'. She turned up at Stems in person on Thursday, asking if she'd upset me somehow and if that was why I didn't want to go to her party. I explained to her that I'd been feeling shattered since getting back from Mauritius, which wasn't a lie, but I wasn't ready to share the truth yet. I could hardly stay away after she'd taken the trouble to come to the shop.

Fortunately, I ordered a couple of dresses in my online spree on Monday as the one I really liked the look of in the pictures was hideous in real life. The pattern was garish, the shade of purple too bright and the fabric felt as though it would go up in flames if anyone lit a cigarette near me. The coral one is perfect, though. It has a crossover bodice with a slightly plunging but not too revealing neckline and several rows of shirring elastic, creating the high waist from which a generous amount of fabric falls. It should see me through the summer months and disguise the fact that my waistline is expanding.

I rest my hands on my currently smooth stomach, an action I've repeated many times this past week. It's hard to believe there is a tiny human growing inside me, its cells multiplying in the time it took me to do my make-up and hair for the party. It's not the way I would have planned it, but I'm thankful for the miracle which will finally make me complete. Some women are ambivalent about being a mum, others actively don't want it, but I've always yearned for motherhood and after the initial shock, I'm willing the next seven months to speed by.

The sound of the door knocker prevents me from indulging in the daydream that has occupied my mind for most of the past week. Annabel and Finn are here to give me a lift to the party. There'll be plenty of time for wondering whether my child will be a boy or a girl in the months ahead.

'Coming!' I call, grabbing my bag and the huge hand-tied bouquet that Michaela refused to take any money for. It's not very original, but better than taking a bottle of bubbly, which might draw attention to me not drinking if I refused a glass.

'Wowser!' Finn says as I open the front door. 'You look amazing. Positively radiant.'

I throw a concerned glance towards Annabel in the front passenger seat of Finn's car. She gives a slight shake of her head in answer to my unspoken question.

'Thanks, Finn,' I say, pulling the door closed behind me. 'You don't look so bad yourself.'

SEVENTEEN

It's the first time I've been to Tiff's house since she and JJ moved from their flat in Fulham the summer before their older daughter, Melody, was due to start school. Winkfield Row is a small village not far from Windsor and the purpose of the move was smaller class sizes, cleaner air and more outdoor space. Even from the outside, as we pull up in the gravel driveway which already accommodates half a dozen cars, I'm guessing they've probably ticked the box on all three.

Finn manoeuvres expertly into a space between Tiff's Audi and a four-seater Smart car before coming around to open the doors for Annabel and me. He certainly behaves in a very mature way for someone who is yet to reach thirty, but there isn't an age limit on manners.

As we approach the front door of the double-fronted Victorian house, it opens and a young woman brandishing a tray of drinks greets us. 'Champagne, Buck's Fizz or orange juice?' she asks, a warm smile lighting up her pretty features. 'I suppose it depends on who is the designated driver.'

In the end, that was the reason we came up with for me not drinking. I suggested driving Finn and Annabel home at the end of the night in return for them giving me a lift. I could have picked them up and dropped them home in my Mini, but it would have been a tight squeeze with the flowers and the helium balloon. Going in Finn's car was the perfect solution.

Annabel has already helped herself to a glass of champagne and hands me an orange juice, thoughtfully served in a champagne flute to make the non-drinkers feel an equal part of the celebration.

'Mum said you'd be on the champagne, Auntie Annabel,' says the young woman with the drinks tray.

'Oh, my goodness, is that really you, Melody? Last time I saw you, you had your hair in pigtails, and you were thrashing around a net thing on the end of a stick,' Annabel says.

Melody laughs, a tinkling joyful sound. 'Ha, I remember that. You came to a lacrosse game with Mum when I was in Year 8. I think the two of you lasted on the side-lines for about five minutes before retreating to the warmth of the car.'

'You've got a good memory,' Annabel says. 'Did you win the match?'

'I've no idea, so it's obviously not that good,' Melody replies.

Annabel takes another flute of champagne and hands it to Finn.

'This is my fiancée, Finn.' She waggles her finger to show off her emerald and diamond engagement ring. 'And I'm sure you remember Charlotte?'

'I'm not sure we've met before, have we?' Melody says.

'Not since you were far too young to play lacrosse,' I reply. It's sad to think there is a whole side to Tiff's life that I've hardly been part of, and that it's mostly because Zack and I were always so wrapped up in each other.

'But you're the one who works in a florist,' she says, gesturing towards the bouquet I'm holding. 'They're gorgeous, and they match your dress. Mum's going to love them.' She turns and leads the way into a beautiful entrance hall, which is bigger than the whole of the downstairs of Myrtle Cottage. 'Let's go and find her. She was out in the garden last time I saw her.'

Despite the size of the house, it's still bursting at the seams with people. As we follow Melody into the lounge and then through folding glass doors which span the whole width of the room out on to the raised decking, I experienced a warm glow of pride at each compliment for the flowers I spent the best part of an hour arranging.

'Mum, look who's here,' Melody says, placing her hand on Tiff's shoulder.

'You came,' she says, pushing the flowers aside and enveloping me in a fierce hug.

'How could I not?' I reply, returning the embrace with equal vigour.

'You look amazing,' Annabel tells Tiff, making it into a group hug. 'The blue of your dress matches your eyes. If we weren't here to celebrate your half century, no one would ever believe you're fifty!'

'Thanks for the reminder.' Tiff takes the helium balloon that has been bobbing along above Finn's head as we made our way through the crush of people. 'I've a good mind to let it go.'

'You will when you read what it says on the back,' Finn remarks, grinning.

Tiff hands Annabel her drink to hold while she pulls on the string until the balloon is in her grasp. 'It's all downhill from here,' she reads. 'You won't find it quite so funny when you get to my age.'

'Old age is a privilege and preferable to the alternative,' Annabel says.

'Are you calling me old now?' Tiff remarks.

'I wouldn't dare. Although you are only two years younger than my fiancé's mum,' Annabel laughs.

'Oooh, my fiancé,' Tiff mimics. 'It does have a nice ring to it, to match that rather beautiful engagement ring. Did you choose it yourself, Finn, or had my friend here been dropping hints despite insisting that it came as a total surprise?'

'My sister Ella helped me,' he says, without a trace of embarrassment. 'I told her that green was Annabel's favourite colour and also mentioned that we started dating in May. Ella said that an emerald would be perfect as it was the birthstone for May so would be like a permanent reminder of the birth of our relationship.'

'Oh, that is so sweet,' Tiff remarks. 'Maybe your first baby will be born in May too, although make it in the first three weeks, otherwise it will be a Gemini and we all know how tricky they can be,' she adds, tapping the side of her nose knowingly.

There's a ripple of laughter as we acknowledge Tiff's self-deprecation, but all this talk of birth is making me uncomfortable. 'I'll take the flowers through to your kitchen and stand them in the sink,' I say.

'Probably better in the utility room, the caterers have the nibbles laid out on every available work surface in the kitchen. Melody will show you.'

'No worries, I'm sure I'll find it,' I reply. 'Melody's busy with the meet-and-greet. I'll be back in a minute.'

Even in a house this size, the kitchen is easy to find, not least because of the delicious aromas emanating from it. Tiff was quite right: every surface is crowded with trays of finger food. Mini beef wellingtons, baked new potatoes, French-bread-sized Welsh rarebit – the choices seem to go on and on. As does the endless stream of waiting staff returning to the kitchen with empty trays and heading off again with full ones. My stomach rumbles, and I realise I haven't eaten since my brunch sandwich just before midday. I know 'eating for two' is a myth, but I'll have to pay more attention to what and when I eat over the coming months.

I put my glass of orange juice down to take a potato from a passing tray and pop it into my mouth while looking around for the utility room. The potato is filled with a pat of herb butter which dribbles from the corner of my mouth as I savour the delicious taste for a moment. I hate to think how much a bash like this must cost, but then fifty is a big birthday and JJ does have an extensive celebrity client list, according to Annabel.

I'm right with my first guess on what lies behind the door in the corner. I walk into a utility room which is already housing a dozen or more bunches of flowers, although, casting my professional eye over them, none is quite as opulent as the one I've brought. The Belfast sink is full, so I decide to leave my flowers in their water-filled cellophane and stand them on the draining board instead. Maybe I should have thought of something more lasting and original, but hindsight is a wonderful thing.

Instead of going through the hall and lounge to get back into the garden, I exit onto the decking through the glass kitchen doors. As I step outside, a drinks waiter is blocking my path back to Tiff as he chats to some of the guests. I reach for a new glass of what I presume is orange juice and then decide to check.

'Sorry to interrupt,' I say. 'I'm just checking this is orange and not Buck's Fizz.'

The glass is already halfway to my lips but seems to slip through my fingers as the waiter turns. In the split second before the champagne flute shatters on the decking, splintering into a thousand shards, I see the shock I'm feeling register in Justin's eyes. What are the chances that two months after a night of passion six thousand miles away, our paths would cross at a party at my friend's house?

At the sound of smashing glass, all conversation around us pauses and the partygoers' eyes are on us. Mine, however, are focused on the gold band Justin is wearing on the third finger of his left hand. He follows my gaze, then looks back into my eyes as a voice says, 'I knew it was a bad idea having you as a waiter.'

It's Tiff, making her way towards us with Annabel and Finn in tow.

I feel dreadful. Whatever deception Justin practised on me, I wouldn't want him to get fired.

'Please don't fire him,' I say. 'It was entirely my fault.'

Tiff and Annabel are giving me weird looks and then Tiff bursts out laughing.

'Of course,' she says, barely able to contain her amusement. 'I forgot that you two have never met. Charlotte is one of my best friends from my modelling days,' Tiff tells the waiter before addressing me. 'And this is my husband JJ, who, as you can see, could learn a thing or two from the professionals.'

A waitress is scrambling around my feet, clearing up the mess I've made. People have restarted their conversations. Tiff is still talking, something about her husband and daughters taking on the roles of waiting staff because she always waits on them hand and foot, but her voice seems to be coming from the end of a long tunnel. I want the ground to open and swallow me up. I can't believe this is happening.

'Are you okay, Charlotte?' Tiff says. 'You've gone very pale. It was only a glass, after all. Caterers expect breakages at big parties.'

'Erm... yes. Fine. Just a bit shocked, I guess.'

That is quite possibly the biggest understatement I will ever make in my entire life. Not only have I just come face to face with the father of my unborn child, who I assumed I would never lay eyes on again, but he turns out to be married to one of the few people in the world I can truly call a friend.

'I was just saying to Finn that you three make me sick with your Mauritian suntans. I've had to resort to fake tan thanks to the rubbish weather here.'

I need to pull myself together or Annabel, who has been

looking at me with an odd expression on her face, might put two and two together.

'At least it's fine for your party,' I say, taking another glass of orange from Justin's tray, now being held by a real member of the catering team. 'I'll try not to drop this one.' I take a huge sip to quench the dryness in my mouth. 'So, you've been in Mauritius too?'

I'm not sure what passes across Justin's eyes. It could be relief that I'm not going to blow the whistle on him – at least, not at his wife's fiftieth birthday party. Or it could be gratitude.

'Yes. I spent six weeks out there taking photos for one of the hotel chain's online brochures,' he replies, managing to keep any anxiety he might be feeling from his voice. Maybe he's not as appalled as I am by the situation we find ourselves in, but then he doesn't know about the baby. 'One of my biggest clients recommended me after she redesigned the interiors for two of the hotels.'

'If we'd known you were going to be there, we could have arranged to meet up,' Annabel says. 'It must get quite lonely being away from home for such long periods.'

Do I detect a hint of suspicion in her voice?

'Not really. As you know from your modelling days, it takes a team of people to get the shots, not just the photographer. Speaking of which, as I'm now relieved of my waiting duties,' he says, smiling at Tiff, 'I'll go and get my camera so that we'll have a decent record of the occasion, rather than just snaps from people's phones.'

As Justin disappears into the crowd, Tiff remarks, 'He's so sniffy about phone cameras. I quite like the natural look, but he's all about getting the angles and the lighting right. I suppose it's just as well that his clients feel the same way, as that's what's paying for all this. Come on, girls, let me introduce you to some more people. Maybe even find you an eligible bachelor, Charlotte.'

'Tiff,' Annabel warns. 'I told you that didn't go so well when Finn and I tried it. I think Charlotte will sort it for herself when she feels ready.'

Tiff shrugs and I shoot Annabel a grateful look. What I really want to do is go home, crawl into bed and go to sleep for a hundred years so that I don't have to think about the consequences of what I've done. The whole situation was a lot easier to handle when my baby's father was a one-night stand I'd never see again. Granted, I may not see much of Justin, or JJ as his wife calls him, but I will be seeing Tiff. And I now have the mother of all secrets to keep from her, because there is no way I can ever tell her the truth.

EIGHTEEN

Tiff

The funny thing about throwing a party is that other people often enjoy it more than the host. I'm not saying that I'm not having a good time but looking around our beautiful garden at the various animated groups laughing and chinking glasses or posing for JJ's camera when they notice him pointing its lens in their direction, everyone else seems to be having a wonderful one. Though I'm not so sure about Charlotte. Since the incident with the smashed glass, she's been a bit quiet and withdrawn and she's just excused herself to go to the loo again for what must be the fifth or sixth time.

'Is Charlotte okay?' I mouth to Annabel when I catch her eye.

She comes to sit next to me on the bench Charlotte has recently left. 'She mentioned something about feeling a bit fragile on the way over. Why?'

'She seems to have spent half the evening in the toilet.'

'Really? I know she was a bit stressed looking after the

flower shop on her own while her boss was away. Maybe it's left her with an upset stomach. It was quite a big responsibility when she's only been there a few months.'

'True, but she's so good at what she does. I've always thought it's a shame that she didn't start her own business. That arrangement she brought for me is by far the most beautiful of all the flowers I've had today.'

'I don't know about Charlotte, but you could start your own florist shop with the amount of flowers you've had. I had no idea you knew so many people. I'd struggle to make a list of fifty, but there must be over a hundred here.'

'That's what happens when you put JJ in charge of the invitations. He went through my address book and invited people I've had no contact with for decades,' I say, laughing.

'I thought it was a bit strange that you'd invite Courtney and Karen when neither of them kept in touch with you after you quit modelling,' Annabel muses. 'Who'd have thought they'd become an item. I had no idea they were gay, did you?'

'No clue,' I admit. I probably wouldn't have invited half these people, especially those who I wasn't particularly close to.

'It's funny how everyone expects all male models to be gay and yet we're surprised when female models are.'

'Not all male models are gay,' I say with a speed I immediately regret.

'Something you want to tell me?' Annabel asks, raising her eyebrows.

I can feel my face colouring slightly under my fake tan.

'I was joking,' she says eventually, touching my arm reassuringly. 'It's all water under the bridge since you met JJ. Do either of you realise how lucky you are to still be so in love. The way he's been looking at you all evening is enough to melt the coldest of hearts.'

Annabel's right. We are lucky. So many couples that we

know have grown apart and are only sticking things out until their children are older. Maybe JJ's constant work trips play a part in keeping everything fresh and new. My heart still flutters when he kisses me on his return from even a few days away.

'He's been extra loving and attentive in the run-up to my birthday. I guess he's aware of what a big milestone turning fifty is, especially as it's his turn in September. Either that or he's having an affair,' I say, and we both laugh.

'So, we've accounted for two people from your extensive guest list, but what about the rest?' Annabel dramatically flings her arm out to indicate the crowd on the lawn and almost sends a tray of drinks flying.

'Careful,' I say. 'We don't want a repeat of what happened earlier. Well, a few of them are JJ's friends, but mostly it's local parents. That's what comes of having kids. You get to know a lot of mums and dads at the school gates over the years. But you'll find that out for yourself once you and Finn start reproducing.'

'Reproducing?' Annabel laughs. 'There's the slight matter of a wedding to organise first.'

I'm glad Annabel has mentioned it because I find it difficult talking about the wedding and her potential future children when Charlotte's around, for fear of upsetting her. 'Have you got a date in mind yet?' I ask.

'Not really, but don't worry, we'll give you and JJ plenty of advance warning.'

'It's not me. I'm always available, but JJ gets booked up quite a way in advance, as do wedding venues,' I say, pointedly.

'I know. From the few tentative enquiries I've made so far, all the best venues are already booked up for the rest of this year and some for next year too.'

'We should probably change the subject,' I say, nodding my head in Charlotte's direction as she makes her way back towards us. 'She already seems a bit edgy after the glass. It was only a glass for heaven's sake and not even one of our decent crystal ones. I don't want to make things worse by talking about weddings.'

'She might be more over Zack than you think,' Annabel says, giving me a knowing look.

Before I have chance to ask her what she means, Charlotte has re-joined us and over her shoulder I can see JJ descending on us with Courtney and Karen.

'Look who I've found,' JJ says.

I've already had chance for a chat with the two of them, but there are lots of squeals as they hug and air-kiss with Annabel and Charlotte.

'Oh my God!' Courtney says. 'I barely recognise you, Charlotte, with that mane of dark hair. You were always spiky and blonde on the jobs we did together.'

A look flicks across JJ's face as though he's suddenly realised which of my friends from our modelling days Charlotte is. Courtney's right; she really is almost unrecognisable from her headshots back in the day, apart from the high cheekbones and beautiful green eyes.

'My boyfriend preferred me au naturel,' Charlotte says. 'But as we're not together anymore, maybe I'll go back to blonde.'

There's a defiance in her voice and I think back to Annabel's comment a few minutes earlier. I can't help wondering if the girls are keeping something from me. Has Charlotte met someone new?

'I thought you might like a group shot of the five of you together for old times' sake,' JJ says, waving his camera.

'Great idea, but only if we're allowed to pose,' I say, putting my hand on my dropped hip and puckering my lips into a pout. I'm a bit disappointed when JJ doesn't plant a kiss on them, but instead sets about arranging the five of us for his perfect photograph. It's an opportunity he wouldn't normally pass on, but I guess he's gone into work mode now he has a camera in his hand. There'll be plenty of time for kisses later tonight when everyone has gone home, a thought that arouses the usual feelings of desire and reminds me how lucky I am to have found my 'one'.

NINETEEN

MONDAY 18 JUNE

Charlotte

I'm not fully awake, but something has disturbed me. My bedroom is in darkness so it must be very early as dawn breaks around 5 a.m. at this time of year. I lie very still listening out for any sounds from downstairs, conscious of my heart thumping against my ribs. There's no sound, but I turn to reach for my phone on the bedside table making as little noise as possible in case I need to make a 999 call. Before my hand can close around it, a searing pain shoots through my lower abdomen, causing me to cry out in pain. Instinctively, I bring my knees into my chest as I always do when I have bad period pains and then reality strikes. These can't be period pains; I'm pregnant. Panic builds in my chest and as I reach my hand up gently to push my hair back off my face, my forehead feels cold and clammy. I take a couple of shallow breaths, not wanting to inhale too deeply for fear of experiencing another excruciating stab of pain which I'm now sure is what woke me up.

Carefully, I reach out for my phone again, my first thought being to ring Annabel. I don't really want to disturb her so early, but I have no one else to call. Then I remember that she and Finn have a rule of no electronic gadgets in their bedroom and that includes their mobile phones. No one will be at my doctor's surgery for hours so I can't call them and I'm not sure that the pains I'm experiencing warrant an ambulance crew being called out. Keeping my knees tucked up towards my chest in the foetal position, I go back over the preceding thirty-two hours in my head, searching for an alternative cause of the pains other than the unthinkable.

I was sorely tempted to leave the party early, but, of course, I was driving Annabel and Finn home. Having made the decision to stick it out, I spent the remainder of Tiff's party dodging JJ without making it look too obvious. I had to have a few photographs taken and join in with the silly poses and facial expressions even though it was the last thing I felt like doing, especially with JJ behind the camera, seemingly so at ease. A couple of times when it all got a bit much, I snuck off to the loo. I knew Annabel would think it was to do with my pregnancy so would cover for me if I was missed, but she had no idea of the real reason for me absenting myself from the party. I'd just sat there in Tiff and JJ's immaculate bathroom wondering how he could act so normally in front of his wife when we were both keeping something momentous from her.

We said our goodbyes shortly after midnight. There was a very awkward moment on the front steps when JJ leaned in to give me a hug and whispered, 'Do we need to talk?'

I made the hug as brief as possible without it looking as though I'd been scalded by a kettle and made a big play of saying, 'It was lovely to finally meet you. I've heard so much about you from Tiff. I wonder if it will be another fifteen years before our paths cross again?' I hoped he'd understand I had no desire to have a conversation about what had happened between us.

'Oh, I hope not,' Tiff said. 'I want the five of us to have

regular dinner dates now that our girls are old enough to not need babysitters.'

'Childminders, Mum,' Melody said, rolling her eyes. 'And we haven't legally needed them since I turned fourteen.'

'You'll always be my babies,' Tiff replied, putting an arm around each of her girls and pulling them into a hug which JJ joined in with by reaching his arms around the three of them.

My heart plummeted. I needed time to think about what to do after finding out that Justin and JJ are the same person. One thing was certain. I could never reveal the true identity of my baby's father because it would tear this family apart. I couldn't do that to Tiff and the girls.

Finn is a very affable drunk and chatted away, telling dreadful jokes all the way back to their place. It was just as well, as it kept Annabel preoccupied enough to not notice how quiet I was. When we got back, the two of us helped Finn negotiate the stairs to their first-floor apartment and I left Annabel to put him to bed, saying that I was shattered. I wasn't lying; I was physically and emotionally drained. It was a massive relief to slip between the cool cotton sheets in Annabel's spare bedroom. Although a part of me would have preferred to be in my own home, the thought that Annabel was just across the hall was somehow comforting. I allowed myself a few tears before starting to think about how to handle the huge problem I'd created. And it wasn't just one problem either.

By the time I finally fell asleep just before dawn, I'd concluded that there was no way I could tell Annabel that the man I slept with in Mauritius is married to her best friend. If she knew, she would want to tell Tiff and that would certainly be the end of Tiff and my friendship, possibly the end of her marriage to JJ, and even, looking at the worst-case scenario, the end of my and Annabel's friendship too. As a single person with a baby on the way and very few friends, I can ill afford to lose the one person I will need to rely heavily on.

But the dishonesty wouldn't end there. Tiff is bound to ask questions about the baby's father when I tell her I'm pregnant. Once she's got past the fact that I'm not in a steady relationship but still want to go ahead with the pregnancy, I know she'll be supportive and happy for me because she knows just how much I've wanted a baby. I've no idea how I'll be able to look her in the eye though if she starts talking about baby names and asking what I'd like as a gift. Worse still, she's bound to mention my pregnancy to JJ.

The decision not to contact my baby's father was made because I knew he was a married man, and I didn't want to affect his family life. None of that has changed just because I happen to know his wife and family. JJ doesn't know I'm pregnant and I've every intention of keeping it that way for as long as possible. If he tries to contact me when he eventually hears it from Tiff, I'll simply say that he's not the only lover I've had since my break-up with Zack and that the dates don't stack up. More lies, but ones that need to be told to protect people I care about.

I slept fitfully but stayed in my room because I needed to gear myself up for any probing questions from Annabel. I was worried that she may have had further thoughts on the amazing coincidence of JJ being in Mauritius at the same time as us. I'd never considered what JJ might be an abbreviation of, but what if Annabel knew? If only I hadn't mentioned Justin's name...

No wonder I was anxious when I eventually showed my face a little after midday, my grumbling stomach having finally got the better of me. Even so, I declined the full English that Finn was making, apparently none the worse for wear after his skinful at the party.

I made my excuses about needing to clean and tidy the house and escaped soon after 2 p.m., refusing a lift in preference for a long walk to try to calm my racing mind. It didn't help, and the housework didn't get done as I opted for a relaxing bath instead. The water hadn't felt overly hot, but maybe it was and that is what my body is protesting about. I don't think I've eaten anything too spicy that might have caused a flare-up in my gut. In fact, thinking about it, I haven't really had much to eat at all over the past two days.

'I'm sorry, baby,' I whisper, my hands cradling my stomach. 'I promise to try to do better if you just hang on in there.'

My body responds with another sharp, cramp-like pain. A tear trickles from the corner of my eye, creating a trail as it runs down the side of my nose. I lick the salty liquid from my top lip, but it is quickly replaced with more as the tears I've been holding back flow freely. I know the circumstances aren't ideal, but it doesn't diminish the love I already feel for the tiny being growing inside me.

Please don't let this be what I think it is, I silently plead to an empty room. *I've waited so long, and I want this so much. I'll never ask for another thing in my life. Don't take this chance of motherhood away from me.*

I must somehow manage to fall asleep because it's light when another stab of pain has me crying out again. I feel around, searching for my phone which had slipped from my grasp as I slept. It's 7.15. I select Annabel's number and call, willing her to pick up. It rings six times before going to voicemail and I hear Annabel's cheerful voice inviting me to leave a message.

'Annabel,' I manage to say through my tears. 'It's me, Charlotte. Please come, I think I'm losing the baby.'

TWENTY

A frantic hammering on my front door and someone calling my name wakes me and I instantly realise it must be Annabel. The thought of dragging myself out of bed to go downstairs and let her in is almost overwhelming, but I don't really have a choice. With a huge effort, I push the bedcovers back and manoeuvre myself into an upright position and am about to attempt standing when I hear Annabel's voice more clearly.

'Thank you so much. I'm sure she'll be fine. Sorry to drag you out,' she says, before the door closes, and I hear her footsteps racing up the stairs. 'What happened?' she asks, rushing over to me and flinging her arms around me.

It takes a few minutes before I'm able to explain to her in faltering sentences what happened during the night. While I talk, she has one arm around my shoulders and with the other hand she's gently stroking my hair back off my forehead. She promised to help throughout my pregnancy and be a shoulder to cry on, but there's no way I could have known how literally and how soon I would need that help.

When I eventually finish speaking, she says, 'Right, well, let's get you settled back in bed, and I'll make a call to the GP surgery. They might want you to go in to see a doctor. Do you think you could manage that?' My horrified expression must answer her question, as she adds, 'Or maybe I can request a home visit.'

'Do you think they might come out?' I ask.

'Well, it's worth a try.' She lifts my legs back into bed and pulls the covers over me. 'I'll call them while I'm waiting for the kettle to boil. You look like you need a cup of tea.'

'Would you be able to call Michaela too,' I ask, handing her my mobile. 'I was supposed to open the shop an hour ago, so we've already missed all the early morning trade.'

'I'm sure she'll understand when I tell her you're ill,' she replies.

'You won't tell her the reason...' I start to say.

'Stop worrying, I've got this. You just relax.'

I am so lucky to have a friend like Annabel, who is always calm and collected in a crisis.

It's several minutes before I hear her footsteps on the staircase. She places the panacea of all illness, a hot sweet cup of tea, on my bedside table. Then she props a pillow behind my head and sits next to me on the bed, holding my hand.

'I ran into a bit of resistance from the receptionist,' she says, 'but in the end I persuaded her to arrange a call-back from the duty doctor. No promises, but there's a possibility of a subsequent home visit if they deem it necessary.'

I've known Annabel a long time and there is no mistaking the sadness in her voice. It makes me feel guilty as the pains in my belly have stopped and I'm wondering if it was all a false alarm. I wriggle into an upright position and take hold of the mug Annabel is handing me.

'Be careful,' she says, 'it'll be hot.'

I blow across the top of the pale brown liquid before taking a sip. I don't normally drink tea with sugar and the unaccustomed sweetness catches me by surprise. I lower the mug.

'I'm sorry I dragged you over here. I was in a panic, but I think it may have been a false alarm. I bet you're dreading the next seven months if I'm going to be this needy.'

The look in her eyes is akin to the one my dad had when he had to break the news to a seven-year-old me that Rusty, our cat, had been knocked over and killed on the road outside our house.

'Really,' I add, attempting to reassure her, 'I feel a lot better now. It was probably my IBS reacting to all the orange juice I had at Tiff's.'

Gently, Annabel removes the mug from my hand. 'There's... there's quite a lot of blood,' she says.

It's as though she's slapped me.

'I'm so sorry, Charlotte. I know how much you wanted this baby.'

I push the bed covers down and there is a bright red stain spreading across the bottom sheet either side of my thighs. 'There wasn't any blood before. I don't understand. The pain has stopped now. I thought my baby was...' I can't finish my sentence. My body starts to shake and then the tears come; huge wracking sobs for the tiny human that I've already grown to love so much.

'Let it all out,' Annabel says, her arms around me, rocking me back and forth.

I'm still sobbing uncontrollably a few minutes later when Annabel's phone starts ringing.

Untangling herself from our embrace, she glances at the phone screen. 'It's the GP surgery. Can you speak to them?'

I shake my head as she accepts the call.

'Hello. Yes, that's me. Erm, as you can imagine she's quite distressed, so she's asked me to speak on her behalf.'

There's a pause while the person on the other end of the call is obviously speaking.

'I think it's quite likely,' Annabel says, her voice calm.

Another smaller pause.

'Yes. Quite a lot.' Annabel listens and then says, 'That would be amazing if you could. I'm not sure she's up to coming into the surgery.' She's looking at me and nodding. 'Not a problem. I can stay with her all day. Thanks so much.' She ends the call. 'The doctor is going to call round when open surgery is finished. Probably around midday.'

'What's the point?' I say, my voice sounding dull and flat. 'My baby's gone. It's punishment for getting drunk and having unprotected sex with a married man. I'm not fit to be a mother.'

Annabel ignores that, saying instead, 'Dr Aktar needs to do a few checks to make sure you're okay.'

Something inside me snaps. 'I'm not okay,' I shout at my best friend. 'I'll never be okay again.'

'I'm sorry, Charlotte,' she says, trying to put her arms around me, but I push her away. 'Look, it was a poor choice of words. What I meant is they need to make sure everything has... come away cleanly and that you're not still bleeding.'

The anger from seconds earlier evaporates. I have no right to blame Annabel for anything when all she's trying to do is help. 'It's me who should be apologising,' I say, my shoulders slumping forward in acceptance.

She reaches for my hands and squeezes them tightly between hers. 'Don't be silly. You've had a terrible shock and you needed to lash out. And that's what friends are for, in good times and in bad.'

'Thank you,' I mumble.

She reaches for my mug of tea. 'This feels a bit cold now. How about I make you a fresh one and maybe some toast to go with it?'

All the while I was pregnant, even before I knew it, I'd felt too sick to eat early in the morning. As if to underline the fact that my pregnancy is over, I suddenly feel ravenous and yet I know that if Annabel makes me toast, my throat will be too tight to swallow it.

'Just tea please,' I say, adding in my head that I no longer have to make sure I'm eating well for my baby and me.

It's almost midday when the doorbell rings.

'That'll be the doctor,' Annabel says. 'I'll go and let her in.'

She runs down the stairs, opens the front door and I hear muffled voices. I can't catch what they're saying, but that's probably intentional.

Moments later, Annabel reappears in the doorway of my bedroom with a woman at her side who is probably around my age, if not slightly younger. She looks tiny standing next to my lofty ex-fashion model friend.

'Good morning, Charlotte. I'm Dr Aktar,' she says, stepping into the room. 'Will it be all right if we open the shutters so that I can have a look at you?'

I nod my agreement and Annabel does the honours before going back to stand by the door.

'Are you in any pain now?' Dr Aktar asks, looking down at me.

I shake my head. My throat feels too tight to speak. She has come to confirm what we all know has happened. The past few hours have dragged by. Despite Annabel's attempts to comfort and console me I just feel so empty. Right at this moment, I'm finding it difficult believe that I will ever feel happy again.

'Well, that's good. Are you happy for me to feel your tummy? I'll be very gentle,' she says, her voice soft and reassuring.

'There was never a bump,' I manage to say. 'I was only a few weeks pregnant. I didn't even know it until last weekend.'

She gently pulls the covers back and I notice her looking at the bloodstain on the sheet which is starting to take on a brownish tinge as it dries.

'Are you still bleeding?' she asks.

'I don't know. I haven't dared move since I saw...' My voice tails off.

'Okay. Can you pull your waistband down for me?' she asks, slipping her hands into surgical gloves.

I oblige and she applies gentle pressure to the area directly above the pubic bone, asking whether I feel any pain as she does so. I say I don't. I don't add that all I feel is numb.

'Well, it's good that you're no longer in physical pain,' she says. 'Breakthrough bleeding is far more common in the first few weeks of pregnancy than people imagine.' For a moment, I experience a tiny glimmer of hope, which is almost immediately extinguished when she continues, 'But with the amount of blood you've lost, I'm afraid it is much more likely that you have miscarried.'

The pressure in the centre of my chest is almost unbearable. It's as though someone is crushing my heart. Even though it's what I was fearing the doctor would say, hearing the actual word is possibly the biggest blow of all.

'Aren't you going to do an internal examination to be sure?' Annabel asks as the doctor places her surgical gloves in a disposal bag.

'We will in a couple of days when everything has had a chance to settle down. But so long as Charlotte is comfortable and has someone with her for the first twenty-four hours, it's better to wait, just in case.'

I want to scream, 'just in case what?' It feels cruel to give me any kind of lingering hope when she is clearly sure that I've had a miscarriage.

'I'll stay as long as she needs me to,' Annabel says. 'Will it be okay for her to have a bath?'

'A shower would be preferable until we've done a thorough check, but it's a good idea to have a little clean up if she feels up to it.'

The two of them are talking about me as they would about a small child with a fever.

'I'm right here in the room, you know,' I shriek. 'Talk *to* me, not *about* me!'

'I'm sorry,' Dr Aktar says kindly, turning her attention back to me. 'Sometimes patients find it hard to absorb information, particularly when they've gone through something as emotional as this. If you need to talk to someone about how you're feeling, we have specialist helplines run by women who've had a similar experience.'

I nod, embarrassed by my outburst and mutter, 'Thank you.'

'We'll email your appointment details over and what you need to do before coming in, but if you've got any concerns in the meantime, you've got the surgery number,' she says.

'Thank you for making a home visit, Dr Aktar,' Annabel says. 'I'll just be a minute while I show the doctor out,' she adds, addressing me. 'Okay?'

I watch the two of them leave my bedroom and hear their hushed voices as they go downstairs. Dr Aktar has been in my home for less than ten minutes and is taking with her my future hopes and dreams. I want to cry, but the tears won't come. The pregnancy was an accident. At first, I thought it was the universe answering my plea. It wasn't how I'd hoped, but I was going to be a mother and I was determined to give my baby all the love it could ever need. But perhaps love alone is not enough. Maybe I wouldn't have been able to cope on my own. Maybe fate stepped in because this child – JJ's child – was never meant to be. The truth of who the baby's father was, if it had ever come out, had the potential to tear lives and families apart. Much as I don't want to believe it, perhaps this personal tragedy for me is the best thing for everyone else.

PART TWO

TWENTY-ONE

THURSDAY 31 JANUARY 2019

The irony isn't lost on me. It's exactly a year to the day since Zack and I celebrated the tenth anniversary of the day we met and now someone new is about to enter my life. I didn't plan it this way; in fact, I should have met George ten days ago, but he had other ideas. I can't be mad at him though, particularly as I thought this day might never come.

It doesn't seem possible when I think back to the day in June when my world appeared to have come crashing down. At the time, I blamed myself, as I'm sure all women in that situation do. Had I damaged the tiny little being growing inside of me because of the alcohol that I'd consumed at the time of conception and continued to indulge in until I knew I was pregnant? I hadn't touched a drop of alcohol from the moment my eyes rested on the first positive pregnancy test, but I couldn't stop myself from wondering if it was already too late.

In the days following Dr Aktar's home visit, I tried to come to terms with my loss, telling myself that perhaps the baby could never have been viable and that I should be thankful that I wasn't further along. It was unimaginable to think about the women who carried their babies to full term only for them to be stillborn. I don't think I would have been strong enough to survive that, even with Annabel's help.

She was brilliant, staying with me for the whole three days until I felt able to follow the instructions on the email before my appointment with the GP. When I first read that I needed to take a pregnancy test before the doctor's internal examination, I burst into floods of tears again. How utterly cruel. There had been so much blood, surely there was very little doubt that I'd had a miscarriage.

Annabel rang the surgery on my behalf to ask if it was absolutely necessary for me to do a pregnancy test, explaining that I'd been trying for a baby for five years without success and had been witness to dozens of negative results. She argued that it might have serious consequences for my mental health which I was just about holding together. Even Annabel, with her undoubted powers of persuasion, was unable to change their position. They wouldn't do a full internal examination unless I provided them with a negative pregnancy test result and if one wasn't performed and there was an issue that went undiagnosed, it could affect my chances of a successful future pregnancy.

In the end, having talked it over at great length, I agreed to pee on the stick if Annabel was the one to check the result.

I will never forget the look on her face as she emerged from the bathroom holding the white plastic test in her hand. It was a combination of confusion, disbelief and guarded joy. 'You're not going to believe this,' she said, 'it's saying you're still pregnant.'

The two hours until my 9.30 a.m. appointment felt like an eternity. I hadn't dared to hope that the test could be accurate as I wasn't sure if I would be able to deal with the crushing disappointment if it wasn't. I had to do a repeat test at the surgery, peeing into a container which Dr Aktar then tested. 'Well,' she said, her warm smile reaching her eyes as she spoke, 'I'm pleased to confirm that you are still pregnant.'

It's a physical impossibility, but it felt as though my heart stopped while I tried to absorb what she was saying. I had a million questions for her, mostly about whether I now had to be particularly careful throughout the rest of my pregnancy, but she assured me that having survived the bleed, my baby was a 'tough little cookie'. Nevertheless, she said that they would keep a close eye on me with blood tests and scans to monitor everything and make sure my baby was developing as it should. I didn't care how many blood tests or scans I would have to endure, I was simply overjoyed that I'd been given what felt like a second chance. She did also warn me that the baby could potentially come early. But clearly nobody told George, which is why I'm at the hospital ten days later than my due date.

I rest my hands on my distended belly, sensing that another painful contraction is on the way. 'Come on, little guy,' I whisper. 'I'm desperate to give you a cuddle.'

I have wondered whether he will bear any resemblance to JJ and if he does, whether anyone will remark on it. I guess with babies it's harder to see familial similarities, despite the number of people who insist that a baby is just like one or other of the parents.

I decided on the name George the moment I discovered I was having a boy at the twenty-week scan. George was my grandfather's name and is my dad's middle name and I need my parents to accept their new grandson. It's also the name of the young prince, William and Kate's firstborn, and to me, my baby will be a prince. I just wish he'd hurry up and arrive.

The contractions are more frequent now but still ten minutes apart. Annabel has popped to the loo so she can be at my side uninterrupted throughout the birth, just as she has been over the past seven months. She has undoubtedly been my rock, but, to be fair, I've had support from elsewhere too.

Michaela has been particularly understanding. As a mum herself, she was able to fill in some practical gaps in Annabel's knowledge, despite the number of books she's read on parenting. While I'll be eternally grateful for Annabel's commitment, I could have done without some of the information she relayed. I spent the latter part of my pregnancy breathing into my hand first before serving people in Stems as some expectant mums experience bad breath. Not to mention the little snippet about the uterus expanding to over five hundred times its normal size... how is that even possible? Books are all well and good, but there is no substitute for first-hand experience when it comes to children. Michaela's also been great in allowing me time off for the additional antenatal appointments I've had to attend, not to mention gifting me some of the baby clothes she hadn't been able to part with. She's also made it clear that my job will be held open for whenever I feel like returning to work after the baby is born.

Tiff, although initially shocked, was thrilled to hear my news. I didn't single her out not to tell, but I made the decision that I would keep my pregnancy to myself and Annabel until the baby would have been viable as a premature birth or until I started to really show, whichever came first. As it was, it was the end of September by the time I told her. At twenty-two weeks, when I was unable to wriggle out of attending JJ's birthday bash despite it being the last thing on the planet I wanted to do, I looked pretty much as normal, just a little thicker around the waist. By twenty-five weeks, a pronounced baby bump appeared almost overnight, so I invited Tiff and Annabel over to Myrtle Cottage for a 'girls' night in'. She was obviously a little hurt that I hadn't shared my news with them both at the same time, but Annabel did a great job of explaining my reasons, saying she was only in the loop because she'd been the one to check the pregnancy test.

Of course, Tiff immediately asked who the father was, so I had my answer prepared. I told the same story to everyone, including my parents, who haven't been as judgmental as I thought they would be. I simply said that I'd used a sperm donor, which everyone who knew how much I wanted a baby accepted. It isn't quite the truth, but it's not a total lie either. There was never the opportunity for a relationship between me and JJ from the moment that I discovered he was married, let alone the fact that his wife was one of my closest friends.

I've often wondered why he wasn't wearing his wedding band on the night we got together in Mauritius. Was it deliberate or did he always take it off when showering and had simply forgotten to put it back on? For Tiff's sake, I sincerely hope it was the latter. I hate the idea that I might not be the first indiscretion in his marriage. It's one of the things I've really struggled with when deciding to keep Tiff in the dark about what we did. What if he's done it before? What if he has a fling every time he goes away? Tiff is my friend; doesn't she deserve to know? I've wrestled with the question so many times over the past few months when I was unable to sleep because of the heartburn my pregnancy was causing me. I always came to the same conclusion: if he was a serial adulterer, he would eventually be caught out. I didn't want to be the one to blow her world apart.

The door from the corridor opens, allowing the sounds of a busy hospital into my quiet space for a few moments.

'Did I miss anything?' Annabel asks.

'No, but another one is about to start,' I say, bracing myself for the excruciating pain.

She's at the bedside in an instant, offering the breathing advice that we practised at the NCT classes. When we arrived together at the first one, people assumed that we were in a gay relationship. How the world has changed, become more accepting. It's not many years ago that the assumption would have been that we were sisters.

'You're doing great,' she says as I breathe through the pain.

Funnily enough, I've never worried too much about the

labour. I accepted it was going to be painful, but it doesn't last forever, and judging by the number of women who have a second baby within two years, it is soon forgotten.

Gentle contractions started yesterday at work, much to the concern of the regulars at Stems, some of whom have given me little gifts for the baby. Mrs Cartwright, who knitted a hat and mittens in a soft yarn in a lovely shade of blue, calls in every Thursday for a bunch of flowers to take on her visit to her nonagenarian mum. 'I'm surprised to see you here, dear,' she said. 'I thought you'd have had that baby by now.' When I told her I was in labour, she couldn't get out of the shop fast enough, probably not wanting to get roped into an emergency delivery. When Michaela and I had first discussed how close to the birth I would be working, I'd considered finishing at Christmas. But the thought of being stuck at home alone with no one to talk to didn't hold much appeal and the money, albeit not a huge amount as I was working shorter hours, would be useful.

The mild contractions continued throughout the afternoon, but by the time I arrived back at Myrtle Cottage, they had become stronger and more frequent. At midnight, I messaged Annabel to pick me and my overnight bag up and drive us to the hospital.

Nothing much happened during the night, but from about six this morning the contractions have restarted with a vengeance. Although when I was last checked, I was still only seven centimetres dilated. The nurse said she would be back to check on me at eight, but it's now after nine. I'm wondering if maybe I've been missed in the changeover of their shift.

Annabel has popped out again, this time to get a sandwich from the cafeteria. She must be starving as it's now past midday and George is still refusing to put in an appearance. The nursing staff, while not overly concerned, have now attached electrodes to his head so that they can monitor him, which they maintain is completely normal in a lengthier delivery to make sure the baby isn't in distress. I have faith that they know more about delivering babies than I do.

I've been asked several times if I want anything other than gas and air to relieve the pain and even though I've refused to this point, I'm starting to consider it as the gas and air is making me feel sick. My worry is that if George's arrival is imminent, a painkilling drug administered to me might make him a bit drowsy and less likely to feed well, something discussed at one of my NCT sessions.

I'm weighing up my options when the midwife, who has told me to call her Scottie, and a nurse come into the room. To say they look worried is probably an overstatement, but they are certainly not as calm as on their previous visits.

'How are you holding up, Charlotte?' Scottie asks.

'I'm getting a bit tired if I'm honest,' I reply.

'Yes, it's been a while, and the monitor's showing signs of distress in baby. Has anyone spoken to you about a C-section if this continues for much longer?'

Some of the women at my NCT class were having elective caesarean sections, but I've been adamant that I want a natural birth with as little intervention as possible. But if George is getting distressed, that casts a new light on everything. The last thing I want is to put my baby at risk.

'Not really. Do you think it will become necessary?'

'Well, let's take a look and see how things are progressing. If you're not any more dilated than you were earlier, I think you should perhaps consider it,' Scottie says, lifting the sheet that is covering my lower half. 'There are more risks both for you and baby if we leave it too long... Actually, Charlotte, I don't think it will be necessary after all. Is your friend still here?'

'She's just gone to get something to eat. Neither of us have had anything since last night.'

'Well, I'd message her to get back ASAP, or she could miss the finale,' Scottie says with a wink.

All these months I've spent talking to my tummy will soon be over. I can hardly believe I'll be meeting my baby. Before I can grab my phone to message Annabel, another contraction grips me.

'I feel like I want to push, Scottie,' I say, panting a little.

'You're not quite ready, but nearly there. What's your friend's name? Nurse will message her for you,' she says.

'Annabel,' I say through gritted teeth while trying to control my breathing.

I hear the ping of the message arriving on Annabel's phone as the door from the corridor opens.

'I've always had terrible timing,' she says. 'Is he coming?'

'I think we'll be able to start pushing with the next contraction,' Scottie replies. 'Are you ready, Charlotte?'

It's hard to stay focused even though Annabel and I have practised for this moment so many times over the past few weeks. I'm already exhausted and the hardest bit is yet to come.

'Come on, Charlotte, you've got this,' Annabel encourages me. 'Not long now and you'll be cuddling baby George.'

'I can feel the next one coming,' I say. 'I want to push.'

'Wait until I tell you,' Scottie instructs. 'And remember what I said about using all your energy for the push rather than crying out.'

I can't help wondering if Scottie has ever had a baby herself. I'm pretty sure I won't be able to keep completely quiet during the final stages, although I haven't done too badly so far.

The vice-like grip takes hold again. It's like nothing I've experienced previously. It's ten times worse than even my most agonising period pains. I'm hanging on to Annabel's arm for dear life. If this doesn't put her off having babies of her own, I don't know what will.

'All right, now push,' Scottie says. 'Keep pushing for the

whole contraction. Well done,' she says when I finally fall back onto my pillows, breathing heavily, spent with the effort.

I hardly have time to catch my breath before I feel the tightening start again.

'You're doing great,' Annabel says, trying to mop the sweat from my forehead with a towel.

'Don't touch me!' I snap, pushing her hand away. 'There's another one coming.'

'I think we'll have him with this one,' Scottie remarks, 'but wait until I tell you to bear down.' Moments later, she's saying, 'Here he is. Just one more little push for his shoulders and you'll be able to hold him before you know it.'

'Is he okay?' I ask. 'Shouldn't he have cried?'

'You've been watching too many hospital dramas. Not all babies cry straight away. You just concentrate on that final push and then I can get him cleaned up and weighed.'

Even through my pain, I'm sure I detect a degree of urgency in her voice.

'Now?' I ask.

'Yes, keep pushing. Here he is, got you, little fella,' she says almost to herself.

I'm desperate to see my baby. He still hasn't made a sound. I need to know he's all right.

'Can I hold him?'

'Just give me one minute to clean him up a bit and clear his nose and mouth.'

'Can you see him, Annabel? Is he okay?'

'He's not red and wrinkly like I was expecting,' Annabel replies. 'And he's so big. I'm not sure those size 1 Babygros I've bought him are going to fit.'

From the other side of the delivery room, there is a noise similar to a suction unit at the dentist's, followed by the sound I've been so desperate to hear. George announces his presence and relief floods through me.

'Your friend is right, he's a big chap – 9 lbs 5 ounces to be precise and quite a pair of lungs on him,' Scottie says, the worry I thought I detected in her voice moments earlier now gone. 'Here you go, Charlotte.' She places my son in the crook of my arm. 'He's all yours.'

I'm sure she says that to all the women who have just given birth, but in my case it's true. There is no loving partner or husband to share my moment of overwhelming joy, tinged with relief that George has arrived safely. Of course, there will be friends and family, but for the most part it will be just the two of us, and that's fine by me.

TWENTY-TWO

It probably sounds obvious to say that I know my life has changed forever the instant Scottie hands me my newborn son, but it's the truth. I have dreamt about this exact moment and the way it would make me feel for almost six years, but nothing could have prepared me for the pure unadulterated surge of love I experience as I cradle George against my bare breast. He has stopped crying and is lying still in the crook of my arm, gazing up at me with blue eyes that won't be able to see me clearly for the first few weeks of his life. But I can see him, and I drink in every perfect tiny detail.

His eyes are a deepish shade of blue, the small amount of hair he has is dark and, as Annabel pointed out, his skin is smooth and creamy in colour, with not a wrinkle in sight. I bend my index finger to gently stroke his cheek and marvel at the softness of his skin. His mouth is puckered as though he is trying to form a kiss and I move my hand to touch it with the tip of my little finger. George immediately begins to suck on it with a strength that surprises me.

'Looks like someone is hungry,' Scottie says. 'Do you remember being shown how to introduce baby to the breast?'

For a moment I panic. What did they tell us to do? I look up to make eye contact with Annabel who is sitting on the chair next to my bed, gazing adoringly at George. There's no doubt she is going to be a wonderful aunt. She transfers her gaze to me and smiles reassuringly. The instructions for breastfeeding come flooding back.

I nod, cupping my right breast and slightly flattening the nipple before presenting it to George's Cupid's bow mouth as an alternative to my finger. He immediately latches on, his little tongue curling. The unfamiliar sensation feels a little uncomfortable to begin with, but watching his downy head moving backwards and forwards in tiny jerking movements as he settles into his rhythm soon distracts me from any discomfort. All I can think about is how my baby is still totally reliant on me for his survival, just as he has been for the previous nine months. I'd wondered if the magical bond we've developed would break the moment he was born, but if anything, it is even stronger.

'Well done, George,' Scottie says, before turning her attention to me. 'It looks like you've got a good feeder there. It's often the case with bigger babies, and they're able to take more milk at each feed, which should hopefully give you longer gaps between them. You may find he starts going through the night without waking up for a night-time feed earlier too.' While Scottie is talking, she is busy taking care of me. 'The downside of bigger babies is that sometimes we get a tear during the birth, but don't you worry, Charlotte, a couple of stitches will soon sort that out. You won't feel a thing after the numbing injection and these days they are self-dissolving.'

George feeds for fifteen minutes or so before his eyes start to close. The effort of suckling has clearly exhausting him. The nurse takes him away from me and lays him in the cot at my bedside and Annabel goes to ring Finn and Tiff with the news of George's arrival.

While she's gone, the junior doctor 'tidies me up', as he puts it. Scottie has been right about most things during the whole birth process, but she's rather underestimated the stitches being painless. At least it doesn't take long and I'm just lying back on my pillows to rest when George regurgitates everything he consumed in his first feed. I immediately buzz for the nurse, who comes very swiftly with Annabel hot on her heels, an anxious expression on her face. The nurse isn't overly concerned when she sees what the problem is. While she's cleaning George up, she explains that sometimes a baby who has become distressed during labour, particularly one who is post full term as he was, excretes a substance called meconium in the womb.

'We found traces of it in the amniotic fluid when George was born. You may have heard some suction noises?' she asks in her singsong Welsh accent. 'That was us clearing his mouth and nasal cavity in case he'd swallowed some of the meconium that had built up in his gut during gestation. Don't worry,' she reassures me, clearly reacting to the fear in my eyes. 'It was just a precaution. We're fairly confident that everything is fine because he was a good colour at birth and he's not experiencing breathing difficulties. There you go, little man.' She lays George back in his cot. 'All nice and clean again. Give him an hour or so and then try him on the breast again.' She places the soiled clothes and the cloth she's used to clean him up in a bin to be collected for laundering. 'We'll move you both onto a ward at some point this evening.'

Annabel, who kept out of the way while the nurse sorted my baby out, goes over to his cot and says, 'We could have done without the excitement, George.' She turns her attention to me. 'Are you okay?'

'Yes. Just shattered, but I suppose I'd better get used to it because I'm sure there'll be plenty of sleepless nights to come despite what Scottie said about bigger babies. I hope I'm up to the challenge.'

'There's no doubt that it's going to be tough on your own, but I have every faith in you. And just look at that little face.' She turns back to the cot. 'He's worth every sleepless night and more.'

'You sound as though you're getting broody.'

Annabel shrugs. 'I just don't want to leave it too late and then regret it. Seeing your face when you held him for the first time really resonated with me.'

'It's magical,' I say, unable to keep the wonderment of it all from my voice. 'I still can't believe I'm a mum. Whatever it takes, I'm determined to give my boy the best of everything.'

Annabel stays with me until it's time for George's next feed, then heads off home, saying she'll be back to collect us tomorrow. He feeds well again, but, unfortunately, just as with the previous feed, he is sick shortly afterwards. This time, the nurse shows a little more concern.

'I'm sorry, Charlotte, but the best thing for George will be to pump his little stomach. It will get rid of any residual meconium which could be irritating his gut. It's not that uncommon and we'll have him back with you in a few hours,' she says, wheeling him out of my room.

I hate being apart from my baby, having only just met him for the first time, but obviously I want the best for him. While we're apart, I'm shown how to express some breast milk for him to be given from a bottle during the hours he's under observation and just after 8 p.m., I'm moved onto a ward with three other new mums, all of whom have their babies at their bedside, which upsets me. Why does my baby have to be the one to have swallowed meconium?

George is brought back to me around midnight and although I'd been concerned that he might not want to feed from me after being bottle-fed, I needn't have worried as he latches straight on again. Once he's finished feeding, he promptly falls asleep, his tiny hands clasped together touching his rosebud mouth.

George sleeps soundly for several hours. This I know because I barely close my eyes, due in part to being watchful after his rocky start but also for the sheer wonder that I nurtured this tiny human and would now have the job of continuing to do so for at least the next eighteen years.

When he stirs at 4 a.m., I gently lift him from the cot at my bedside to feed again before changing his nappy in the half-light so as not to disturb the other mothers and babies on my ward.

I don't notice anything untoward until the next time I lay him down to change his nappy at around 9 a.m. George's belly seems distended, and his face, each tiny feature of which I committed to memory the moment I laid eyes on him, seems to be rounder than I remember. Not wanting to seem like an over-anxious first-time mum, I change his nappy, despite it not being soiled, before returning him to his cot.

Around 11 a.m., Doctor Radley comes to check my stitches to make sure I'm in good shape to go home and asks if I've passed urine or been to the loo. I tell her that I've had a wee, unlike my baby son, who seems to be holding it all in. She makes no attempt to disguise the look of concern that flashes across her face as she turns to George's cot and rolls him onto his back.

'I think I'll have a colleague give George a quick examination,' she says, unlocking the wheels on the cot and pushing it towards the door. 'No cause for concern. We'll be back before you know it.'

If her remark is meant to reassure me, it doesn't. My baby has been taken away from me for the second time in his first twenty-four hours and this time with no explanation.

I've been trying to take deep calming breaths, but it isn't

working, so by the time Mr Carter appears on the ward around thirty minutes later, I've worked myself up into quite a state.

'What's going on?' I demand. 'Where's my baby?'

TWENTY-THREE
FRIDAY 1 FEBRUARY

In my experience, it's not ideal for a sentence to start with, 'Try not to worry, but...' as it usually means there's plenty of cause for concern. Those words have just been uttered by Mr Carter, a consultant paediatrician at Hatherwood Maternity Hospital, followed by 'George has a medical problem which requires more specialist care than we are equipped to deal with here.' Far from not worrying, my anxiety level has gone through the roof.

It's about twenty-four hours since George's birth and around this time I was expecting to be preparing for discharge from hospital with my baby to begin the endless round of feeding, nappy-changing and sleeping which I thought would be pretty much his life and mine over the coming months. I say his life and mine, but I knew the sleep bit for me was less likely as newborns are notorious for their ability to demand attention at all times of the day or night. Right at this moment, I would happily swap sleep to have my baby son at my side.

'What's wrong with him?' I stammer.

'As I believe you were told yesterday, it's not uncommon for babies to swallow meconium in the latter stages of delivery, particularly if they've become distressed. It's usually fairly straightforward and is dealt with by clearing baby's airways and sometimes, as in George's case, pumping the stomach.'

My hands are clammy. Mr Carter's use of the word 'usually' sounds ominous and has me instantly panicking.

'Occasionally,' he continues in a measured tone, 'the baby swallows meconium in the amniotic fluid in the final few moments prior to birth and that can result in more serious problems.'

'What kind of problems?' I hear myself ask in a voice that sounds as though it doesn't belong to me.

'Well, it can cause a lack of oxygen to the brain and that oxygen starvation can be responsible for a variety of different issues, including epilepsy, brain damage and difficulty breathing. Very rarely, it can affect kidney function, which I'm afraid is the case with George.'

I can feel the fine hairs on my arms stand to attention as Mr Carter's words register and my blood turns to ice. I want to speak, but my throat is too tight.

'His kidneys weren't functioning at all, which is why he looked swollen and has almost doubled his birth weight. He needs to be moved to a specialist unit in a different hospital, which is what we are preparing him for right now.'

'Where's my baby? I want to see my baby,' I say, finally finding my voice, which is high-pitched and hysterical.

I'm aware that the other mothers on the ward are staring at me, but I don't care.

'I know this must be very distressing, Charlotte, but the best way to help George is if we all stay calm,' Mr Carter says. 'Is your husband here or is he on his way to fetch you and George home?'

I've never felt so alone in my life. I always knew that bringing up a baby as a single parent was going to be tough, but

I only ever imagined a healthy baby. I'm not prepared for this. In fact, I don't think anyone ever could be.

'My friend is due any minute,' I manage to say. 'George is going to be all right, isn't he? Please don't let him die,' I beg, tears pricking the backs of my eyes and threatening to overwhelm me.

Mr Carter lays a reassuring hand on my shoulder. 'George is a seriously ill little boy. We've administered drugs to start his kidneys functioning, but the specialist team will assess if any permanent damage has been done. When they've reviewed his case, they'll set up a meeting to go through the options. Okay?'

I nod mutely. Mr Carter is probably in his late fifties and will have seen other cases like George's. He is sounding positive and suggesting there will be treatment options, so I must trust his expert judgement.

'We'll be moving him shortly. If you want to travel in the ambulance with him, as I presume you do, you'll need to be ready to go in fifteen minutes. Can you do that?' he asks, just as the door to the ward is pushed open.

A smiling Annabel is carrying George's baby carrier in preparation for his journey home. Tied to the handle is a helium balloon with the words 'Welcome to the World Baby George' on it. The sight tips me over the edge and the floodgates open, despite my best intentions from moments earlier. The smile freezes on her lips.

'What's wrong?' she says, her eyes darting around. 'Where's George?'

TWENTY-FOUR
THURSDAY 7 FEBRUARY

'Come in and take a seat,' Mr Kottaridis says, looking up from an open file on the desk in front of him and indicating the two rust-coloured leather chairs positioned opposite, where Annabel and I sit as directed.

I like the fact that the top of his desk is very tidy, apart from the open file, a small pile of similar files on the front left-hand corner and a coffee cup. There is a saying about tidiness and tidy minds which escapes me at the moment, but I need someone organised to explain to me exactly what is happening with George and what will be best for his future.

The past week, my baby's first on the planet, has been one long round of tests and meetings after the dash from Berkshire to Guy's Hospital in London in an ambulance with its blue light flashing. Many times, I've pulled to the side of the road to allow an emergency vehicle to pass in its rush to get to its destination and said a silent prayer for the occupants. I wonder if anyone did that for me and George as we raced against time to get my baby boy the help he urgently needed.

'Can I get you and your partner a coffee?' Mr Kottaridis asks.

He obviously noticed me glance at his cup, so is perceptive as well as tidy.

'Oh, no, thank you, we've just had one in the cafeteria. And Annabel is my friend not my partner,' I correct him.

'My apologies,' he says. 'I assumed I was talking to both parents. Is the baby's father joining us?'

I shuffle in my seat. 'Erm, no. I'm a single parent.'

'Right. So, making another assumption here, the baby's father is unaware of George's tricky start in life?'

'That's right,' I confirm.

'We'll come back to that later,' he says, 'but for now I just want to explain clearly where we're at with George and what treatment is going to give him the best chance at a long and reasonably healthy life.'

I'm trying to stay relaxed, but I can feel my shoulders tense because I'm gripping the arms of the chair so tightly. Annabel reaches across and gently squeezes my hand, leaving hers resting lightly on mine for comfort. Although she's had to go to work during the day, she's come to the hospital to sit with me and George in the ICU every night. Today she has taken the day off to be with me. I don't know how I'll ever be able to repay her.

'As you know, George had a bit of a traumatic entry into the world and a first forty-eight hours where it was all a bit touch-and-go. The good news is that his problem was spotted early, and the right steps were taken to encourage his kidneys to start working to remove waste from his body,' Mr Kottaridis says. There is the briefest of pauses, during which he takes a deep breath before continuing. 'The not-so-good news is that although they are both now working and he has been able to pass waste, George's kidneys have been damaged due to oxygen starvation. They have less than forty per cent function.'

I can feel Annabel's eyes on me as though she's expecting me to react or perhaps ask a question. When I don't, she says,

'So, to be clear, George's kidneys are now working but not as effectively as they should be?'

'Actually, they are doing a rather good job. You've got a little fighter there.' The consultant smiles at me.

For a moment, I experience a surge of pride, but it's short-lived.

'The problem George has is that with less than twenty per cent function in each kidney they won't last as long as they should.' Clearly reacting to my puzzled expression, Mr Kottaridis continues patiently but without sounding condescending in any way. 'Put simply, if a person has a life expectancy of eighty years, in normal circumstances and without abusing them, their kidneys should last their lifetime, albeit with a reduced function as they start to wear out with age. However, in someone like George where they've had to work really hard from the outset, the kidneys will wear out at a faster rate. And, of course, they had reduced function to start with.'

I'm gripping the arms of the chair even harder and Annabel still has her hand on mine. I start to tremble. 'So, you're saying that George's kidneys will wear out at some point in his thirties?' I manage to ask, having done some frantic calculations in my head.

'Not exactly,' he says, his deep brown eyes connecting with mine. 'I'm afraid the prognosis isn't as optimistic as that because of the amount of extra work his kidneys are already having to do. I know this is difficult for you to hear, but I must be honest with you for you to make the right decisions about your son's future. I would be very surprised if George made it to his twenties without intervention.'

The gasp is mine.

Annabel utters a profanity and then apologises for it before saying, 'By intervention, do you mean dialysis again?'

George was on dialysis for a short time until the drugs kicked in and he was able to rid his body of waste himself.

Although neither of us have spoken about it in the long hours we've spent together at Guy's Hospital since he was admitted, I'm pretty sure that both Annabel and I were praying that he wouldn't ever need to go back on it. The sight of my baby hooked up to a machine that was in effect keeping him alive was heartbreaking. The sound of whirring and clicking while the machine took on the job that George's body was unable to perform has already featured in nightmares on the rare occasions where I've managed to sleep deeply enough to have dreams. The thought of him relying on a dialysis machine to survive for most of his life chills me to the bone.

'Dialysis is certainly one option,' Mr Kottaridis says, his tone measured. 'It's not ideal and would mean frequent hospital visits. By frequent, I'm talking about two or three times a week from the moment his kidneys can no longer cope. It would have a major impact on his physical quality of life, particularly as a teenager. It could also result in mental health issues.'

Up to this point, I've not allowed myself to consider the awful thought that it might have been better if my baby had miscarried. It would have been utterly devastating for me, but what kind of life have I sentenced my son to?

'Is it my fault?' I whisper. 'Is it because I was drinking in the early stages before I knew I was pregnant?' It's a question that has plagued me since the nightmare dash from Berkshire to London in the back of the ambulance with my critically ill son. How will I be able to live with myself if I've caused his condition?

'Blaming yourself isn't going to achieve anything.' Mr Kottaridis shakes his head. 'There is no research to suggest that Meconium Aspiration Syndrome, which is what George suffered, has anything to do with drinking in early pregnancy, so please put that thought out of your mind. In fact, it's more common in babies who have gone beyond full term. You made him a little too comfortable in the womb, so he was reluctant to leave you. What he needs now is someone strong and focused, not someone weighed down by guilt. Can you be strong for George?' he asks kindly.

Annabel squeezes my hand again. 'You said dialysis was one option,' she says.

'Yes. There are a couple of others. Drug therapy is advancing in all areas of medicine and there is a possibility that before George's kidneys become less effective there could be a drug to maintain the level of function that he has. But that is an unknown and, of course, could have long-term side-effects that wouldn't be apparent for years. The final option, and we will need to decide on a plan as doing nothing isn't an option, is a transplant from a suitable donor. But, as with all organ transplants, it carries the greatest amount of risk and there are no guarantees.'

'By suitable donor, do you mean me?' I ask, finally glimpsing a hint of light at the end of a very dark tunnel.

'Possibly,' Mr Kottaridis says, cautiously. 'Unfortunately, it's not quite as straightforward as that, but one or other of the parents is usually the best match, or occasionally a sibling. Which is why I asked about George's father. If you did want to pursue the transplant option, we would start by doing blood tests to see which of you, if either, is the best match for George.'

The thought of having to approach JJ and tell him that he has a baby son who might need his help fills me with dread.

'But you could start by testing me,' I say, 'and if I'm a suitable match, the father wouldn't need to be contacted.'

'Ideally, we'd prefer to test you both. There are very fine margins and tiny percentages could make a huge difference to the outcome of surgery. We could certainly start by running the tests on you in the hope that you will be a perfect match if transplant is the route you think you want to go down.'

I want the best for George, of course I do, but if I'm a perfect match is there really any need to involve JJ?

'What would you do if you had a baby in this situation?'
I ask.

He considers for a moment. 'I'm a surgeon,' he says, 'so I know there are risks involved. I've had patients for whom surgery has gone well, but the organ has been rejected by the recipient. But if I had a child in George's position, I would want to give him the best quality of life I could. It would be unethical for me to try to persuade you one way or the other. Ultimately, it has to be the decision of the parents,' he concludes, placing heavy emphasis on the plural.

Clearly, Mr Kottaridis is of the opinion that George's father has a right to know what is happening with his son and should be involved in the decision-making. It is equally clear that I have some soul-searching to do. A lot of lives could potentially be destroyed if it comes to light that JJ is George's father, but my priority is my son. I will do anything to give him the best shot at life.

TWENTY-FIVE

MONDAY 18 FEBRUARY

I know there are going to be plenty of times in the coming months and years when the feelings of isolation because I'm bringing George up as a single parent might start to overwhelm me, but to be honest, I wasn't expecting it to happen so soon and for it to affect me so badly.

I was already feeling sorry for myself at the prospect of a second consecutive Valentine's Day without a partner sending me a card declaring their undying love, but I'd steeled myself to get through the day in the knowledge that I would be seeing Annabel on the Friday evening after work. Finn had other ideas.

Annabel sounded so guilty when she rang me on Friday morning to say that Finn was whisking her away for a weekend spa break. Apparently, he'd had it booked for weeks. It was a special Valentine's present as it would be their first one as an engaged couple, so he wanted to make an occasion of it. She must have sensed my disappointment even though I'd tried to keep it from my voice because she offered to cancel and go at a later date. I'm not that selfish. I assured her that George and I would be absolutely fine and arranged for her to come around to Myrtle Cottage tonight instead.

I tried to keep myself as busy as possible over the weekend. Despite the freezing temperatures, I wrapped George up and took him for long walks. I even contemplated inviting my mum for a visit but changed my mind about calling her as my finger hovered over her number on my mobile. The only person I could stand having around me was Annabel because she was the only one who knew the true reason I was feeling so stressed. The tests to see if I would be a suitable kidney donor for George started the day after the meeting with Dr Kottaridis, with the results due a week to ten days later.

'There's no point in putting off finding out if you're a match, even though I would prefer not to operate in the first year of George's life,' he said before Annabel and I left his office. 'If you are a strong match, we can take our time planning and preparing to give us the best chance of a good outcome. If you're not, we can have further discussions about involving the father. If he's unwilling to be tested, we would then put George on the organ donor register immediately as it would be a shame to miss a potential donor because we dragged our feet.'

I spent all day Friday on tenterhooks. I was anxious for the call from Mr Kottaridis but at the same time nervous in case the news was not what I wanted to hear, and I would have no Annabel to lessen the blow.

The call eventually comes at 2.30 this afternoon. Mr Kottaridis is kind and gentle as he delivers the devastating news that I'm not a close enough match to help my baby. He organises an appointment for the following day to discuss the next steps before ending the call.

For what feels like hours but is probably only minutes, I sit staring at my phone, unable to accept the news I've just received. I've been so certain that I would be a close enough match to give my son the lifeline he desperately needs and more than willing to undergo the surgery with all the accompanying risks for George to have his best chance of a long and active life. But I've failed him... again. I still feel responsible for George's condition, which I've convinced myself is a result of drinking during the early weeks of my pregnancy despite the experts telling me otherwise. And now this. There is nothing I can do to help my baby boy. I'm not a suitable donor.

Every last ounce of hope seems to have been rung out of me, but I can't just give up. My mind starts racing. As George's mother, I should have been the closest match, but it's not always the case, sometimes it's the father. I've tried to keep JJ out of things to protect Tiff and their girls, but that's no longer an option. Tiff is one of my best friends; I would do almost anything for her. But George is my family.

I head upstairs and although George is sleeping, it doesn't stop me from lifting him out of his cot and holding onto him as though my life depended on him. The irony isn't lost on me now I know that he can't depend on me for his. Silent tears stream down my cheeks as I gently rock back and forth with my beautiful boy in my arms. Eventually, he wakes and gazes up at me with eyes the colour of the deepest ocean. I'll do whatever it takes to help him.

When I open the door to Annabel just after 7 p.m., I don't need to say anything. One look at my tear-streaked face tells her everything she needs to know. She pulls me into a hug and I dissolve into floods of tears again. Although she only holds me for a few minutes, just the touch of another adult, one who understands how devastated I'm feeling, has a calming effect. There is a tiny bit of me, though, that can't help wishing it was Zack with his arms around me and that we were facing George's uncertain future as a family.

'It's not the end for George,' Annabel eventually says, taking hold of my shoulders and looking into my eyes. 'We don't give up at the first hurdle, okay?'

I nod.

'What we need now is a plan to try to trace George's father.'

I feel the blood drain from my face. Not only have I been keeping a massive secret from Tiff, I've also withheld the truth from the very person who has given me her unreserved support. There have been so many opportunities for me to tell Annabel, but I chose to ignore them. I could have told her the night after Tiff's birthday party when I first discovered I'd inadvertently slept with our friend's husband and was carrying his child. Or maybe during one of the many nights she stayed by my side at Guy's Hospital acting as my anchor in a very stormy sea. Or perhaps when we knew that George's best chance of a near normal life was a kidney transplant from a close relative. We'd had a disagreement then about setting the wheels in motion to try to track George's father down in case I proved to be an unsuitable donor. I persuaded Annabel to wait until I'd had the results of my tests, because if I was a good match, nothing else about the situation would have changed. But following the phone call from Mr Kottaridis earlier today everything has changed and I'm going to have to hope that Annabel accepts my reasons for not being honest with her.

Annabel has made us both a cup of strong sweet tea, which she places on the walnut coffee table before sitting down opposite me.

'So,' she says in her best organisational tone of voice, 'now we know that you aren't a suitable donor for George, we have to find his father.'

I go to speak, but Annabel stops me.

'I know you weren't keen to involve him, but the situation has moved on and George needs his help. I think we should go with my original idea and email the resort, giving the date of the last night of our holiday there and Justin's room number. If we emphasise the urgency of getting in contact with him, they might be prepared to relax their data protection policy. It's a long shot, but we have to try.'

'No,' I say.

'What do you mean, no?' she asks with a hint of irritation in her voice. 'It's our best hope of finding him and George's best chance of a suitable donor.'

'I mean, no we don't need to contact the hotel,' I sigh. 'I know how to find George's dad.'

'You know how to find George's dad.' She repeats my statement as though to get it clear in her head that she hasn't misheard me. 'Well, if you know, why on earth didn't you tell me?'

'Because I was trying to protect everyone from the awful truth.' I clasp my hands to my mouth, still reluctant to speak the words that could change our relationship forever.

'Which is?' she prompts. She doesn't sound angry, more confused.

I close my eyes momentarily and take a deep breath. So much is riding on the way that Annabel reacts to what I'm about to reveal. I couldn't have got this far without her by my side. If she walks away from our friendship, I don't know how I'll survive, but I've run out of options; I have to tell her the truth.

'Justin is JJ,' I say, pausing briefly to allow the information to sink in. 'JJ is George's father.'

Nothing much shocks Annabel, but this is truly the exception. All the colour drains from her cheeks while she tries to process what I've just admitted. 'Oh. My. God. I honestly don't know what to say. I can't believe that JJ would cheat on Tiff.'

'I'm so sorry, Annabel. I wanted to tell you as soon as I found out, but I didn't know how to.'

'How did you not know you were sleeping with Tiff's husband?' she asks incredulously.

'I'd never met him,' I reply. 'I've never even seen photos of him apart from the wedding one where they both had their backs to the camera.'

Annabel nods slowly as though processing what I'm telling her before saying, 'So the glass dropping incident at Tiff's party was because you recognised that Justin and JJ were one and the same?'

It's my turn to nod.

'So why didn't you just tell me then?' she asks, her confusion replaced by hurt that I would keep something so huge from her.

It's the question I've asked myself on many occasions but have only recently realised what the answer is. 'I... I didn't want to force you to make a choice between me and Tiff, especially as she is the one who has been wronged,' I say, trying to swallow back the tears that are threatening to flow again. 'I was terrified that you would choose her, and I would be left with no one.'

Annabel gets up from her chair and moves to sit next to me on the sofa. Putting her arm around me, she says, 'I would never have taken sides. I'm still not. You're both my friends and always will be. It's one hell of a mess and there's no doubt it's going to take some sorting out, but, to my mind, the person to blame here is not you, it's JJ. I'm appalled that he could have so little respect for both you and Tiff. I'm furious with him.' She pauses. 'I'm assuming that he doesn't know that George is his baby?'

'No,' I admit, beyond relieved that Annabel still intends to be my friend despite what I've just told her. The trouble is, armed with this new information and a newly acquired animosity towards JJ, what will she do next?

'Well, it's about time he did. We'll have to find a way of getting the two of you together without Tiff around so that you can tell him about George. It'll give him some time to plan how he's going to break his wife's heart.'

I flinch.

'Sorry,' she says. 'That was uncalled for. I'm just so bloody mad with him. But that's not helping me to think clearly. What excuse could we invent to have him meet up with you?' She drums her fingers on the coffee table.

I can't think of a single thing that would have JJ agreeing to a private meeting with me.

'That's it!' Annabel exclaims as though a light bulb has turned on in her head. 'Didn't you mention that Tiff suggested doing a photoshoot with George as a baby gift because you were reluctant to accept anything else? The reasons for which are now glaringly obvious.'

'Yes,' I reply. I haven't seen Tiff since George's birth, mostly because of his prolonged stay in hospital, but I messaged her with a photo of him the day we were allowed to come home. She messaged back within minutes commenting on how handsome he is and suggesting a photo session with JJ as their gift to me. I thanked her but declined the offer. There was no way I could be in close proximity to JJ, particularly with George there too.

'So, you message her and say you've had second thoughts and you think it's a lovely idea.'

'I'm not sure,' I say. I know I'm going to have to tell him about his son because he might be a perfect match for George, but I'm not sure that tricking him into doing a photo session is the best way of going about it. 'What if Tiff insists on coming with him?'

'She probably will, but you're bound to get a few moments with JJ alone. If it's not enough time to tell him the truth, make sure you get his phone number.'

'I don't know if I can be in the same space as Tiff, JJ and George,' I start to say.

'You have to.' Annabel takes hold of my hands and squeezes them gently in hers. 'Remember, this is not about you, it's about giving George a fighting chance.'

I know Annabel's right, but the mere thought of telling JJ is daunting and this will just be the tip of the iceberg.

TWENTY-SIX

MONDAY 4 MARCH

Looking at George energetically kicking his legs as he sits in his baby rocker under the bay window in the sitting room of Myrtle Cottage, no one would ever guess that there was anything wrong with him. He's a happy, smiley baby who goes four hours between feeds and sleeps for six hours straight at night-time. It's exactly as Scottie, the midwife, had suggested it might be because of George's size, even with the medical issues he's experienced.

For the first few days after I was allowed to bring him home from hospital, I was terribly nervous at every nappy change. I'd been told to look out for any changes that might suggest his little kidneys were stressed and to contact the hospital if I was at all concerned. I'm not a nurse and there were sometimes slight changes but having Annabel with me for three days to offer a second opinion while George and I settled into a routine was invaluable. There's no doubt that things are getting easier, but I won't start to relax until there's a clearly defined treatment path. And even then, it will be many months, possibly years, before George gets his transplant. I can't allow myself to think too far ahead because it overwhelms me.

It's two weeks since I learned that I'm not a good enough match to donate one of my kidneys to George. Mr Kottaridis explained to me at the hospital appointment the following day that it's to do with the split of chromosomes. I didn't fully understand, but the bottom line is that I don't have enough. The probability is that JJ does, although it's not a given. I told Mr Kottaridis that I would be contacting George's father as a matter of urgency with a view to him testing for compatibility.

I wanted to get the appointment with Mr Kottaridis out of the way before I contacted Tiff to set Annabel's plan in motion. It allowed me to carefully think things through and I arrived at the conclusion that JJ won't necessarily have to tell Tiff about our night of passion if he chooses not to. If he does turn out to be a match for our baby, he could have the operation as a non-related donor. It will be his decision whether to tell the whole truth or keep it from his wife. First things first though, I need to tell him that he's George's father and explain why his son needs his help.

When I rang Tiff to say I had changed my mind about JJ doing a photo session with George, she was genuinely enthusiastic, which made me feel terribly guilty.

'It's not something generally does,' she'd reiterated, 'but, as I originally said, you can consider it our baby gift to you as you've refused everything else I've suggested.'

So, here I am waiting for Tiff and her husband to arrive at my house, which would be unthinkable if George didn't need JJ's help. As expected, Tiff was eager to meet George and there was no plausible excuse I could think of for her not to come. They're already thirty minutes late and I'm hoping they won't be too much longer as George will start getting sleepy and then irritable if I try to keep him awake.

Even as I have the thought, there is a knock at my door.

I take a deep breath and head out into the hall. From the

outline through the glazed panels, I can tell it's JJ on the doorstep. Composing myself, I open the door.

'Hello, JJ, thanks so much for agreeing to do this,' I say in an overly loud voice so that Tiff can hear. She's waiting in their car on the yellow line outside my house so her husband can unload his gear.

'Very much under duress,' he mutters in response as he steps into the hallway with a couple of stands and lights. 'Where would you like me to set up?' he asks in a much louder voice, also for Tiff's benefit.

I direct him into the lounge, where he leaves the gear before heading back to the car for his camera bag and tripod.

'See you in a minute,' Tiff says, waving as she pulls away from the kerb to go and park her car by the village hall, giving me a vital few minutes alone with her husband.

I follow JJ into my living room, where he has already started busying himself with stands. It seems he's anxious to get on with the shoot and get out as quickly as possible, which is completely understandable. Being in my home with his wife and my baby is already awkward, so my plan is to get his phone number and call him when Tiff is not around.

'We need to talk, Justin,' I say.

'Don't call me that,' he hisses. 'I'm JJ. Tiff's husband. As far as she's concerned, I never laid eyes on you before the night of her fiftieth birthday party. Judging by what you said as you were leaving, I thought that's what you wanted too.'

He sounds tense, but I would be in his situation. He probably tried to find an excuse not to come here today, but Tiff clearly wasn't going to take no for an answer after she'd offered it.

'I need your number because I won't have time to explain everything before Tiff gets back,' I say as calmly as I can, conscious that it will take Tiff less than five minutes to park.

'Look, Charlotte, I don't know what your game is. I love my

wife and what happened between us was just a set of circumstances,' he says, in an almost apologetic tone of voice. He continues fiddling with the photographic equipment, presumably to avoid having to make eye contact with me. It's all so different from that night in Mauritius. 'I'm sorry if that upsets you, really I am, but that's the truth of the matter.'

Time is ticking and I may not get another opportunity to speak to JJ on his own. 'Give me your number, JJ, or I'll tell Tiff what happened in Mauritius.'

He stops what he's doing and turns to face me. 'You're not serious?'

'Put your number in my phone,' I say, holding my mobile out.

He locks eyes with me momentarily before snatching the phone off me and tapping the screen.

'When's the best time to call when you won't be overheard?' I ask.

'Why are you doing this?' he counters.

'We've got ten seconds before Tiff walks in the front door,' I say, having seen her go past the bay window.

'Tonight, at nine,' he hisses, thrusting my phone back at me moments before Tiff comes into the room.

'Where is he?' Tiff says, making a beeline for George. 'Oh my God, Charlotte, he's even more handsome than his WhatsApp pictures. How lucky were you with your sperm donor?'

I turn away from Tiff so that she can't see my cheeks colouring up.

'Mind you, you've got pretty decent genes yourself. Can I pick him up?' she adds.

She's already unclipping the buckle of his harness as she speaks, so it would be pointless to come up with a reason for her not to lift him out and give him a cuddle. It gives me a strange feeling seeing my friend holding her husband's son. It's obviously a feeling not shared by George, who squeals with delight as Tiff tickles his ribs.

'Is he a good baby?' she asks, blowing a raspberry into his chubby little hand.

'The best,' I reply, locking eyes with JJ behind her back. 'I wouldn't change him for the world.'

Tiff

It feels so good to finally be cuddling Charlotte's baby. I've been desperate to visit since they arrived home from the hospital, but I didn't want to rush her, particularly as George had an extended stay in hospital due to the infection Annabel told me he had picked up. It must have been a worrying time for Charlotte as a first-time mum, especially as she has no partner to share her concerns with, although Annabel has been an amazing support for her. I'm a little ashamed to admit feeling pangs of jealousy because the two of them have been so close since Charlotte became pregnant. I've felt a bit left out, if I'm honest, but now that George is here, I expect Charlotte will be more likely to call me if she needs practical advice. I have experience in the baby department that Annabel doesn't. Granted, it's from a few years ago, but that wasn't by choice. I would have loved another baby, especially a son, but it wasn't meant to be.

I pull George closer into my chest. At five weeks old, some babies are floppy and seem unaware of what's going on around them, but not George. He's a solid little chap. Charlotte's obviously doing a great job in the breastfeeding department. And he's scrupulously clean, with no hint of a smell of vomit. I close my eyes for a moment and inhale deeply, savouring the sweet aroma of baby shampoo and powder. When I open them again, JJ has stopped what he's doing and is watching me.

'Are you okay?' he asks.

'Of course,' I say, smiling at him. 'I'm just enjoying my first cuddle with George and hoping it will be the first of many.' I direct my attention to Charlotte.

She returns my smile but seems a little tense. Surely she has confidence in me that I'm not about to drop her baby, but to allay her fears, I sit down on the small sofa that she's pushed back against the wall to give JJ more space to set up and lay George along my thighs, his head supported by my knees.

'You look so comfortable handling him,' Charlotte says. 'You seem to know all the things he likes instinctively.'

'Only because I should imagine most babies like similar things,' I say, gazing down at George. He takes hold of my finger with a surprisingly firm grip and returns my gaze with his deep blue eyes. Melody's were the same shade of blue but turned to a dark green at some point during her first year, which is quite common if one parent has green eyes. Charlotte's are green, so I guess it will depend on what colour his father's eyes are as to whether they will stay blue or not.

'Right, I'm all set. Let's make a start, shall we?'

JJ's voice seems unnecessarily sharp. I know he's doing this as a favour for me, but it's not as though he had anything else on today.

'Good idea,' Charlotte says, coming over to me.

I lift her son off my lap, carefully supporting his head, and hand him back to his mum.

'George is all smiles now,' she continues, 'but he'll start getting grumpy when he's ready for his sleep.'

'Where would you like him, JJ?' I ask, getting to my feet, keen to be as involved as possible.

George couldn't have been any better behaved for his photo session and although JJ sounded a bit sharp at one point, he was great with him. Between us, Charlotte and I used every trick in the book to get the best shots of her baby son. I clicked my fingers and squeaked toys above JJ's head for the perfect eyeline, while Charlotte pulled funny faces and clapped her hands to keep George alert and smiley while JJ was snapping away with his camera.

He also took some shots of Charlotte holding George, which I'd suggested to him on the drive over. I don't know what Charlotte's plan to support her and George is, but I've still got plenty of contacts in the world of modelling if she's willing to consider some mother and baby work to earn a bit of extra money. I'm pretty sure the work would come rolling in for them.

I'm quite sad that the whole session only took an hour, but at least JJ has gone to collect the car from the village hall car park after packing up his gear. It gives me an extra few minutes cuddling George.

'You really are so lucky, Charlotte,' I gush, kissing the top of his head before handing him back to his mum. 'I always thought our two were laid-back babies, more down to their dad than me, I must admit, but George takes the biscuit. I'll be more than happy to babysit once you're ready to start dating again.' If I'm honest, being around George this afternoon has gone some way to filling the yawning hole in my heart left by not having a much longed- for son with JJ. That's what happens when we leave it later to start having children, there's not so much time left on the maternal clock if things don't go to plan, and mine has long since stopped ticking.

Charlotte has a strange expression on her face as she reclaims her baby. Maybe I shouldn't have mentioned dating; perhaps it's still too soon.

TWENTY-SEVEN

Charlotte

George is asleep within minutes of me putting him in his cot after his evening feed, which is only to be expected after such a busy day. I go up to check on him shortly before I make the call to JJ.

He answers on the second ring.

'Thank you for today...' I start to say, but he interrupts.

'Cut the small talk, Charlotte. I'm out walking our elderly neighbour's dog and I've only got ten minutes before I'm expected home.'

I'd intended to try and break things to JJ gently, but he's made it clear that he wants to get off the phone as quickly as possible. There's no time to be friendly or try to soften the blow.

'You're George's dad,' I say.

'Don't be ridiculous!'

'I'm not being ridiculous. George is your son. I know for a fact because you are the only man I've slept with since my split with Zack.'

There's a small pause before JJ says, 'What happened? Has

his real dad refused to contribute anything to his upkeep so you thought you'd try it on with me because I've got a few quid?'

I bite my lip. I don't recognise this as the man who was fun company over dinner in Mauritius. Obviously, what I've just told him has come as a shock, but does he have to be quite so unpleasant? Am I such a poor judge of character?

'I had no intention of telling you because I didn't want to wreck your marriage, but—'

'But what, Charlotte? You've decided to be a vindictive little cow?' he demands, raising his voice. I can hear a dog start to bark. 'Enough!' he says and the barking stops. 'You know, Tiff has never had a bad word to say about you. It just goes to show how little we really know about the people we consider our friends.'

His words are hurtful, but I can't allow myself to get upset. As Annabel pointed out, this is not about me.

'George is sick,' I blurt out.

'Are you forgetting that I spent the afternoon taking photographs of him? He's the healthiest looking child I've ever seen. There's nothing wrong with him and you know it. If you ask me, you're the one who's sick if you think you can somehow blackmail me into giving you money.'

Something inside me snaps. How dare he accuse me of lying about George being sick.

'I don't want your money,' I say, struggling to keep the anger I'm feeling from my voice. 'In fact, I don't need anything from you, but George does. He was born with a serious kidney condition. He needs a donor kidney and I'm not a match, but as his dad you might be.'

There is silence on the other end of the line.

'JJ? Are you still there?'

When he finally speaks, all trace of anger has gone. 'Would you have told me I had a son if he wasn't sick?'

It was something I'd agonised over but only for a short

while. I kept seeing the wedding ring and imagining the hurt that would be inflicted. 'My decision not to tell the baby's father was made before I knew it was you. I saw the wedding ring on the shelf in your bathroom at the hotel, so I knew you were married. There didn't seem much point in disrupting people's lives once I'd decided to go ahead with the pregnancy.'

'You didn't think the father had a right to know about the child?'

'Selfish as it might seem to you, I knew I had more than enough love to give to make up for an absent dad.'

'But not absent by choice. That's the point I'm making, Charlotte. I don't even know if I am George's dad as you claim, but was it really your right to choose to go ahead and have a child without the father's consent?'

Much as his comment irritates me, now is not the moment to get into a discussion about a woman's right to make choices about her body. There has been a softening in his approach and I want to keep it that way for George's sake.

'I wouldn't have had an abortion if that's what you mean,' I say. 'Once I discovered that I was pregnant my job was to nurture the baby in my womb. My job now is to make sure that I do everything within my power to give him a happy life, which potentially involves you.'

There's another pause before JJ says, 'I'm sorry that George is sick, but I've only got your word for it that I'm his father. I'll do a paternity test and obviously, if it is positive, we'll have to speak again to discuss George's medical care.'

'Thank you,' I say, relief flooding through me.

'I haven't finished. There is a proviso. If the test is negative, I need you to disappear from Tiff's life. I don't care how you do it, what excuse you make, but you'll agree never to see her again. I made a mistake, a huge mistake which I have to live with for the rest of my life,' he says his voice filled with emotion. 'I betrayed Tiff's trust and showed you no respect, Charlotte, for which I'm sorry. But the thought of having you in our lives, seeing you however occasionally would be a constant reminder of letting the love of my life down. Please say you understand?'

'Yes,' I say immediately. I know that he's George's father and I suspect I'm going to lose Tiff as a friend anyway if he chooses to tell her the truth.

'Call me tomorrow morning at 10 to set up the paternity test,' he says before disconnecting the call.

I let go of my phone as though it has scalded me and watch as it falls into George's baby rocker before I sink down onto the sofa. I'm fully aware of the bombshell I've just dropped and the far-reaching damage it could cause if JJ is completely honest with Tiff. But I would make the same decision again if it means a better life for George.

TWENTY-EIGHT

FRIDAY 29 MARCH

The bell over the door of the Buttercup Tearoom tinkles as I push it open and pull George's pram through the narrow opening. Walking from Bray into Maidenhead has lulled him to sleep, but when the motion stops, he will probably wake up, hopefully in his usual good humour. Tiff was right when she said he was laid-back. But for his health problems, these last few weeks would have been perfect.

Following JJ's instructions, sent by text earlier this morning, I manoeuvre the pram between the wooden tables, most of which are unoccupied in the post-lunch lull, heading for one of the two booths towards the rear of the café. He thought they would give us more privacy for our meeting, and in my mind it also reduces the chance of anyone seeing us together.

I'm early, so there is no sign of him. I order myself a home-made cloudy lemonade and check my phone to make sure he hasn't cancelled on me. I have no messages.

Since receiving the result of the paternity test showing what I knew it would – that he is indeed George's father – JJ has been more civil with me but hasn't yet shown any inclination to spend time with his son, which is fine by me. He immediately agreed to go ahead and be tested as a potential kidney donor for George, although he made it clear that he wasn't necessarily agreeing to proceed with the surgery. He said it would be something he'd have to discuss with Tiff should the need arise. I'm assuming he hasn't told Tiff that he's George's dad as she keeps messaging trying to arrange a meet up with Annabel and me for coffee. She's even suggested dinner at their house, saying Melody would be a ready-made babysitter for George. I feel horribly guilty each time I make a pathetic excuse not to see her: I'm too tired, George has the sniffles, Michaela has asked me to help at the shop for a couple of hours. Actually, I am back at work three afternoons a week, but none of those have coincided with Tiff's suggested dates. The list of excuses is endless, but my reasons for not meeting up are getting progressively weaker.

Now that Annabel knows the truth, she is also avoiding committing to social events that could include JJ. She's still furious with him, seeing him as totally to blame for cheating on his wife. She keeps reminding me that he wasn't wearing his wedding band.

'He made his vows, Charlotte, "til death us do part",' she said, the night she came over to Myrtle Cottage and we talked through my reasons for keeping her in the dark. 'It would be like a recovering alcoholic having a sneaky glass of wine or me having a Mars bar when I've given up chocolate for Lent. Once you've broken the promise you've made, be it to yourself or others, where does it end? It's made me wonder if JJ has been the faithful, loving husband Tiff thinks he is throughout their marriage, particularly as he's had so much opportunity with all the travelling.'

'Sorry I'm a bit late,' JJ says, sliding into the booth opposite me and jolting me from my thoughts. 'I couldn't find anywhere to park. I couldn't risk getting a ticket and having to explain what I was doing in Maidenhead when I'm supposed to be in Oxfordshire doing a recce for a shoot tomorrow.'

Despite his obvious irritation at the lack of parking, JJ is much friendlier than he was when I first told him that George was his son.

'Won't that make tomorrow's shoot a bit tricky?'

'I did a whistle-stop tour this morning, so I won't be flying blind tomorrow. Do you want another one of those?' he asks, indicating my glass as the waitress approaches.

'No, I'm fine thanks.'

'And I guess he's too young for anything but you,' JJ says, acknowledging George's presence for the first time, all trace of irritation gone.

'He's only two months, so still mostly me,' I agree. 'Although he does have boiled water in his comforter sometimes.'

As if he knows we're talking about him, George opens his eyes and smiles. It's one of those that is most likely wind, so I reach down to release him from the harness, then sit him on my knee, gently patting his back to encourage the belch while JJ orders himself a flat white. George obliges and then chuckles as though reacting to the noise he's just made.

'He seems like a very contented baby,' JJ remarks once the waitress has left with his order.

'He is, considering what he went through in his first couple of weeks. I don't suppose you want to hold him?' I offer.

JJ shakes his head. 'I don't think that's a good idea,' he says. I might be imagining it, but I think I detect a hint of regret in his voice. 'Look,' he continues, 'I might as well get straight to the point. There was a letter from Guy's Hospital when I called in at my studio yesterday.'

I catch my breath. So much is riding on what JJ says next.

'It's not good news, I'm afraid. I'm even less of a match than you are. And being older, it was always a riskier option unless I was a total match.'

The pressure I feel in my chest is like the manifestation of the crushing disappointment of JJ's news. I can barely breathe.

My hopes were pinned on him being able to give our baby a chance of a near-normal life and now that hope has been cruelly dashed.

'I'm sorry, Charlotte, truly I am,' he says, reaching across the table to pat my hand, which I snatch away as though I've been scalded and, in the process, almost knock over my glass of lemonade. JJ grabs it and steadies it on the table before continuing. 'I know it's not what you wanted to hear, but it seems that the only option for George is to go on a donor register and hope that a suitable match is found.'

The disappointment of JJ not being a match is almost unbearable. I hadn't allowed myself to contemplate any other outcome than a positive one. I move George from sitting on my knee to lying against my chest with his head resting on my shoulder. The aroma of baby lotion fills my nostrils as I breathe in deeply, attempting to calm my pounding heart.

'But that could take years,' I say, my voice barely more than a whisper when I'm eventually in control of my emotions sufficiently to speak. 'George may not have years. Every day his kidneys are working so much harder than they should. What if they don't find a suitable donor in time? I can't bear the thought that one day his kidneys will just stop, and he'll be on dialysis for the rest of his life. It's so...' the lump in my throat almost stops me from finishing my sentence... 'so unfair.'

'Or they could find a donor tomorrow, Charlotte,' he says, compassion evident in his voice. 'I'm sure Mr Kottaridis also told you that they wouldn't want to go ahead with a transplant in George's first year anyway, so it gives them a bit of time to find an unrelated donor.'

It's JJ's use of the word 'unrelated' that resonates. When the transplant option was first discussed, Mr Kottaridis had mentioned parental and sibling suitability. At the time, I'd dismissed the notion of a possible sibling match as I was so sure that I would be able to donate one of my kidneys to help

George, but now it offers a stirring of hope. Although it's far less likely that JJ and Tiff's girls will be a good match for George, it is possible.

'Are you going to be all right?' JJ asks, responding to my silence. 'I can't stay long, but I knew you'd be upset, so I wanted to be with you when I told you.'

'There is another option,' I say, protectively stroking George's back and resting my cheek against his downy head. 'It's an even slimmer chance than either you or me being a perfect donor for our child, but we have to give it a shot.'

I watch his eyes widen as the realisation dawns on him. 'No. You can't mean what I think you do. There is no way I could put my girls through that,' he says, shaking his head.

'Not even to save your son?' I ask, turning George to face his father. 'Doesn't he deserve a chance?'

JJ's expression is difficult to read as he gazes across the table at the son he was unaware of until three and a half weeks ago. 'Have you any idea what you are asking?' he asks, a slight quiver in his voice. 'Quite apart from the emotional trauma of them finding out that their dad has been unfaithful to their mum, there would be physical and psychological trauma too. Let's just say that one, or possibly both of them, was a suitable donor. The decision to give up a kidney at such a young age is huge. They've got their whole lives ahead of them. How will that work if they only have one kidney? Would it potentially shorten their life or leave them less fit to live it as fully as they should?' He shakes his head again and drops his gaze for a moment. 'And if they know about George's issue and refuse to be tested because they are scared and then something happened to him, can you imagine the guilt they would feel?'

I know he's right, but I'm desperate. 'Please, just think about it,' I beg. 'You love your girls, just as I love my son. None of what has happened to George is his fault. You're potentially holding his future in your hands. Your decision could be the difference between him living a normal life or one tied to a machine.'

JJ drops his head into his hands. I can see that he is in torment. The decision he makes now could be the end of his life as he knows it.

Without raising his gaze to look at me or George he says, 'No, I can't do it. There's no way my girls should make that kind of sacrifice because of a mistake I've made. I'm sorry, Charlotte, this is a non-starter.'

'And I'm sorry, JJ,' I reply, 'but this is not your decision to make. You can't disregard the idea without discussing it with the two people who might, just might, give our son the chance that every child deserves.' I take a deep breath. I don't want to say what I'm about to, but now that I have George, I understand how fiercely a mother will fight to protect her child. 'You have to tell Tiff what happened. I know it will be difficult, but imagine how much worse it will be if she hears it from me.'

His head snaps up. 'You wouldn't do that. You're supposed to be her friend.'

The last thing I want to do is hurt Tiff any more than I already inadvertently have, but the dishonesty surrounding George is eating away at our friendship every time I make an excuse not to meet up with her. I care for Tiff, of course I do, but I'll do anything for my son and, as a mother too, I hope she would understand. 'It's precisely because she's my friend that I haven't already told her. I was hoping that you would find the courage to do the right thing by her. Trust is the single most important thing in a relationship, be it a marriage or friendship, and I've already betrayed that. I don't expect she will ever forgive me, but you two might still be able to work things out.'

'I love my wife,' he says, his voice weighed down with sorrow and guilt. 'I can't count how many times I've thought back to that night trying to understand why we did what we did. I wanted to confess the moment I arrived home, but I was too afraid that she might leave me. I thought the right moment would present itself, but it never did. If only I'd just told her straight away. After seeing you at Tiff's party, I knew there would never be a right moment. How much worse can infidelity be than sleeping with a person who your wife believes is a friend?'

'But we weren't aware of that at the time, JJ. We didn't set out to deliberately hurt Tiff. If she can find it in her heart to forgive you for being unfaithful, then your marriage has a chance. She'll need to blame someone, and I'll take that and suffer the consequences if you agree to tell your girls that they have a half-brother who needs their help.'

There is nothing more for me to say. I fiddle with George's perfect little fingers while I wait for his father to speak.

'I wish I'd never laid eyes on you,' he finally says, no trace of anger in his voice, just hopelessness. 'You made the decision to go ahead with a pregnancy without consulting me. You really have no idea of the enormity of this situation.' He seems about to add something, but instead he closes his eyes and inhales deeply.

After a few moments, JJ opens his eyes and without warning he reaches his arms out for George. I pass our baby to him and experience a surge of emotion as JJ holds him up for a moment, examining his little face, before pulling him into his chest and gently rocking backwards and forwards.

In that instant, the reality of our situation bites. Although unplanned, George has made me feel like a whole person from the moment I first held him in my arms. But seeing him cradled by his father highlights what he will be missing growing up without one. JJ was wrong to intimate that I should have considered terminating George's life before it began. But will I be enough for my little boy?

'I'd forgotten how good this feels,' JJ says, almost to himself.

'Giving life to another human being really is the most precious gift.' He is clearly fighting his own internal battle.

'And that's what Melody or Tamsin might be able to do for their little brother,' I say.

JJ nods his head slowly. 'You're right. This little lad shouldn't suffer any more than is necessary. I'll have to think about how and when I'm going to break this news to Tiff and the girls, but you have my word that I will.' He drops a kiss onto George's head just as a waitress approaches our table.

'That is so lovely,' she says. 'It warms my heart to see a family enjoying precious time together. Can I get either of you a refill?'

'No, thanks,' I say, trying to quash the wave of sadness at the whole situation before it engulfs me. 'Just the bill, please.'

JJ hands George back to me and gets to his feet. 'I'll pay.'

Our eyes connect. I think we're both hoping that the price he pays for our night of passion isn't the end of his marriage.

TWENTY-NINE

MOTHERING SUNDAY 31 MARCH

Since George's birth, I've rarely had the luxury of a lie-in, but ironically this morning, when I can't wait to celebrate my first Mothering Sunday as a mother, there hasn't been a sound from my son, who's sleeping peacefully in his cradle.

For years I've allowed myself to imagine how Mothering Sunday would feel as a member of the motherhood club I've been excluded from for so long. The position I find myself in isn't what I would have chosen had I been given a choice, but at last I feel complete.

There have been many times over the past fourteen months where I've wondered whether my split with Zack was an over-reaction, but the feeling of pure love that I experience as I gaze down on George vindicates the decision I made. I have an over-whelming urge to reach into his cot, lift him out and hold him against my chest. I want to feel the beat of his heart against mine, touch his peachy soft skin and breathe in the aroma of baby powder. George is my world, and as his mum I will do whatever it takes to make his world the best it can be.

As I watch the rhythmic rise and fall of his chest my mind drifts back to Friday and the difficult conversation I had with his father. Unsurprisingly, I haven't heard anything from JJ yet. It would be incredibly insensitive of him to break the news of his infidelity to Tiff before her special day with their girls. Whatever Annabel and I think of what he did in Mauritius, there is no doubt in my mind that he loves his wife and wholeheartedly regrets his betrayal. I feel dreadful forcing him to tell Tiff, but George's condition gives me no alternative. My priority has to be him.

I must admit to mixed emotions when JJ was holding his son. Just like Tiff, he looked so at ease. It warmed my heart to see someone else cradling my son with an expression that only a parent has, which made me sad that George wouldn't have a full-time father in his life, if JJ chooses to be part of it at all.

It wasn't until I was on the way home that I recalled what he'd said with a tingle of fear. JJ had seemed to be lost in a memory when he'd mentioned that he and Tiff had always wanted a son, but it wasn't meant to be. An awful thought crept into my mind. What if Tiff was able to forgive JJ, but only on condition that the two of them would raise JJ's son as their own? There's no doubt that they are better placed than I am financially, and he would be in a settled family with his older sisters. I had to stop walking for a few moments to catch my breath, which was coming in shallow gasps as the thought gained momentum. I was eventually able to convince myself that Tiff wouldn't be so cruel. But just before I fell asleep last night the thought appeared again and I was less sure. Would Tiff still consider me a friend once she found out that I had slept with her husband?

A gentle exhalation of breath akin to a sigh escapes George's lips as he begins to stir. Before the thought of a life without him in it can take hold, I push back my duvet cover and reach into his cot. He opens his eyes and I'm treated to a smile as I lift him out.

'Come on, little man,' I say, 'we've got a busy day ahead of us.'

Initially, I declined Annabel's suggestion of meeting up for a walk around the nature reserve this morning, having already made my excuses not to go and visit my mum for the traditional Mother's Day lunch. I say 'traditional'. It's a tradition my sister started after she became a mother, so I've always been an outsider until now. Maybe I'll go next year, but I'm not quite ready for it yet.

I changed my mind about meeting up after a bit of persuasion from Annabel. She assured me it would brighten Finn's day. He lost his mum when he was in his teens, so for him it's always a day tinged with sadness. I said no to lunch, though, as they're going straight on to tea with Annabel's mum this afternoon. George and I were invited but I decided against it for a couple of reasons. Although Annabel and Finn are engaged, they haven't set a wedding date yet and Annabel confided in me that her mum keeps trying to hurry it along as she's desperate to be a grandma. George would only put more pressure on the whole delicate situation. Besides, I want a bit of me and George time today.

Once I've changed and fed George, we head downstairs to get some breakfast before Annabel and Finn arrive. I'm greeted by the sweet aroma of freesias in the bouquet of spring flowers Michaela dropped off on her way home from work last night. I'd been in to Stems to help with some of the Mother's Day arrangements yesterday morning but had to leave her to it from lunchtime. I was so touched when she knocked on my door with the flowers and a card. The envelope is propped up against the vase on my kitchen table waiting to be opened.

I strap George into his highchair and flick the switch on the kettle before reaching for the card and ripping it open. The picture on the front is of a mother duck swimming on a pond with her ducklings following behind. The words inside are heart-warming.

Some people take to motherhood like a duck to water.

It's a sweet message and brings a smile to my face but it's what she has written beneath it that really touches my heart.

YOU are one of those people... George is a very lucky little boy xx

I drop a kiss onto the top of George's head and hand him his rattle to bang on the tray of his highchair, which always makes him giggle in delight. Then I reach for a tissue to mop my eyes.

If Zack had wanted what I wanted instead of denying me the opportunity to become a mother, there wouldn't be George. Despite everything, I wouldn't change him for the world.

THIRTY

SATURDAY 6 APRIL

When I first broached the idea to Annabel, she was adamant
that she wanted no part of it. In fact, she went as far as to say
that she didn't think she could be in the same room as JJ without
slapping his lily-livered face, even after I gave her a blow-by-
blow account of the conversation we had at the Buttercup
Tearoom.

I completely understood her reaction because that was how
I felt when I first received his email on Tuesday...

As I'm sure you can imagine, I've been giving what we talked
about last Friday a great deal of thought. My priority is to try
to break the news as gently as I can to Tiff and for that I need
your help, and possibly that of Annabel too. It may sound
crazy, but I think Tiff would be less likely to go off the deep
end and not hear anything other than the fact that I broke my
wedding vow to her if you and Annabel were present. I know
it makes me sound weak but trust me when I say that I'm
trying to minimise the enormous hurt I'm about to cause.

So, I'm going to suggest to Tiff that she invites the two of
you to ours for dinner this Saturday. Finn is away on a golf

weekend. I know, because I was invited too but have now made my excuses.

There will never be a good way of confessing what I did but, with your help, Tiff may eventually be able to forgive us both.

I know I'm asking a lot, but in the end, it may result in the best outcome for everyone, especially George.

JJ

I read and re-read the email several times. Initially, I did see it as weakness that he wanted Annabel and me with him when he broke the news that would surely break Tiff's heart, but putting myself in his position, I could understand why he had suggested it. Eventually I replied saying that while I would go to theirs for dinner, I couldn't imagine Annabel agreeing, as she's totally cast him as the villain of the piece. He replied to say that Tiff would invite her regardless.

I was at Stems when Tiff's text arrived on Thursday morning and before I could reply to it, Annabel messaged asking what excuse I was going to use this time so that she didn't double up. I asked Michaela if I could take George for a short walk to get him off to sleep and rang Annabel before we got to the end of the road.

'Hi,' she said. 'I'm starting to run out of reasons not to meet up with Tiff.'

'Erm, actually, Annabel, I'm going to accept.'

'Are you mad? How can you even think about being at a dinner table with that man?' she demanded.

'He... he wants to tell Tiff the truth and thinks she might be able to deal with it better if the two of us are there.'

'Are you bloody joking? I was always a bit of a JJ fan, but he's weaker than a milky cup of tea. Why would you even consider it?'

'Because he tested negative as a donor for George as well,' I explained. I hadn't been able to bring myself to tell her before because it would make it too real.

'Oh God, Charlotte, that is just the worst news.' There was quite a pause before she continued. 'But I don't see how that has anything to do with you going to a dinner party thrown by his wife where he tells her he's been unfaithful to her with one of her best friends. You've lost me somewhere.'

'You remember Mr Kottaridis saying that siblings are sometimes a donor match?'

'Yes, but surely they have to share both parents?'

'I checked with him after JJ confirmed that he's not a good match and apparently not. There's a very slim chance that Melody or Tamsin could be a match, but for them to be tested Tiff not only needs to know about JJ being George's dad but also has to give her consent.'

I heard Annabel sigh deeply at the other end of the call.

'What an awful situation,' she eventually said.

'Yes, it is,' I agreed. 'And poor little George is stuck in the middle of it all.'

'Not forgetting Melody and Tamsin,' she replied.

Her words hit the mark. My sole consideration since finding out about George's condition has been for him to have the best possible chance of a normal life, but at what cost to others? Maybe it's too much to expect of Tiff and JJ's girls and we should just wait for a suitable donor? I fall silent wondering if I'm asking too much of others in my effort to get what is best for my boy.

Annabel breaks the silence. 'Look, I get why JJ has to come clean and tell Tiff that he is George's biological father, but I still don't see why we should be present when he tells his wife what a cheating arsehole he's been.'

'He thinks it might temper her reaction, making it more likely she'll agree to Melody and Tamsin being tested.'

'Yeah, right. Or alternatively he thinks she'll be so furious with you that she'll forget to be mad with him. I'm sorry, Charlotte. You know I love you and George and would do almost anything for you, but I refuse to watch you suffer while he gets off lightly. If you want my advice, you should tell him to stick the dinner party where the sun doesn't shine.'

With that, she ended the call. In all the years we've known each other, I think that was the first time Annabel ever hung up on me.

It didn't change my decision though. Annabel had no compelling reason to put herself through what was bound to be an excruciating evening, but I did. George's future.

So to say I'm surprised to see Annabel's car already on the drive of Tiff and JJ's house when I pull onto it in my battered old Mini is an understatement. I have no idea why she changed her mind about coming, I'm just mightily relieved she did.

THIRTY-ONE

The moment Tiff opens her front door to welcome me and George, I notice an elaborate display of white calla lilies in an impressive vase on the round table in the middle of the reception hall. As she takes George's baby bag from me and leads the way through to the kitchen, I spot another beautiful floral arrangement in the fireplace of the lounge as we pass and there's a selection of garden flowers, including tulips and daffodils, in a rustic jug on the kitchen island. Of course, it's entirely possible that Tiff and JJ's home is always full of flowers, but I'm guessing it's more likely that she's made a special effort because she knows how much I love them. What it actually achieves is the realisation that I've arrived at a dinner party empty-handed apart from all the paraphernalia required when travelling with a small baby. And it's not just any old dinner party. Tiff's world is about to come crashing down at some point in the evening making me feel even guiltier about arriving without a small token for the hostess.

Annabel is perched on one of the teal-coloured velvet stools at the kitchen island, but there is no sign of JJ or the girls. I put

George's carry seat on the woodblock worktop and lean in to give Annabel a hug.

'Thanks for coming,' I whisper into her hair.

She tightens her squeeze in response.

'I'm sorry...' I start to say to Tiff in apology for my lack of a gift.

'You're not really late,' Annabel interrupts. 'I was early and it must be tricky running to time with all the stuff you have to bring for George. This was the wine you asked me to get, wasn't it?' She indicates two bottles of expensive-looking Sauvignon Blanc.

'Oh, erm, yes. Thanks for getting it,' I say, playing along. 'I'd have been even later if I'd had to stop at the off-licence on my way.' Just one more thing to add to the ever-increasing list of things to be grateful to Annabel for.

'And I think you were definitely right about coming in separate cars,' Annabel continues, 'in case you need to get George home early. Do you think he might be teething already?'

'Doubtful,' Tiff replies, releasing the buckle on George's car seat and lifting him out before settling him on her hip and placing the baby seat on the floor. 'It'll probably be at least a couple more months before they start to push through. Crikey, Charlotte, what have you been feeding him? He feels double the weight since he had his photos taken.'

She looks totally at ease handling my baby. I doubt she will still feel so comfortable with him when she learns the truth.

'Just me,' I reply brightly. 'But he's a good feeder.'

'Well, you let us know when he needs his next one and we can arrange dinner time around that,' Tiff says in the knowing way that only a mother could.

'Already fed and changed. That's why I'm a bit late.'

'Do you want to eat now then? Everything is ready. I did a slow-cook lamb tagine. It's been in the oven since I dropped the girls off at dance class this morning.'

'Don't tell me they're still there?' I used to go to dance class as a teenager and would often spend my entire Saturday there, mostly to avoid being around my parents if truth be told, but even so, I would be back well before 7 p.m.

'No,' Tiff laughs. 'They've just gone to get something from upstairs, they'll be back in a minute.'

Right on cue, I hear footsteps on the staircase and excited chatter. Moments later, JJ throws open the double doors that lead into the kitchen from the dining room to reveal the girls holding a large object between them. It appears to be a frame of some sort wrapped in bright blue tissue paper and decorated with a gold bow that they are holding out towards me.

'Go on then,' Tiff says excitedly. 'Open it.'

With my feet dragging and studiously avoiding JJ's gaze, I walk through to the dining room and start to tear off the paper. It's immediately clear that the frame holds one of the photographs that JJ took of George and me at the photo session, blown up and finished to look like an oil painting. I'm fighting to hold back tears. Not only is it a beautiful photograph, but it also underlines how kind and thoughtful Tiff is.

'I... I don't know what to say,' I mutter, glancing from JJ to Tiff, who is still cuddling my baby on her hip, and then back to the photograph. 'It's gorgeous. Thank you so much.'

'Do you really like it? I know you said you didn't want any gifts from us, but this picture was too beautiful not to have on display. He is so like you, Charlotte. Such a handsome little chap.' Tiff chucks him under the chin and rubs noses with him. 'You really should consider doing some mother and baby modelling, even if you just use the money to open a savings account for him.'

I catch Annabel's eye. Breaking the news to Tiff is going to be so much harder than I could ever have imagined, but a small part of me wants to blurt it out there and then to get it over and done with.

As though she is reading my mind, Annabel gives a slight shake of her head.

She's right, of course. The plan is for Melody and Tamsin to take George upstairs and babysit him to give the adults a bit of space to sit and chat uninterrupted. Of course, chat is entirely the wrong word, but that was Tiff's word and she's the only one who is blissfully unaware of the dramatic turn the evening is going to take. It's as though a high-speed train is hurtling towards a family car stuck on a level crossing. There is no way of stopping it and there will be no survivors, not even Annabel. Tiff is certain to ask her if she knew, and Annabel won't lie to her. By coming tonight she's risking her twenty-year friendship. I shiver, which doesn't go unnoticed.

'Is it a bit chilly in here?' Tiff asks. 'Do you want JJ to put one of the heaters on? We wouldn't want this little chap to catch a cold.' She gazes down at George with a look of pure adoration that squeezes my heart.

'No, it's fine,' I say. 'We'd all overheat pretty quickly once we start eating the tagine if the aroma of the spices is anything to go by. Shall I take him?' I hold out my arms towards my baby son. 'I don't know about anyone else, but I'm ravenous.'

Tiff hands George over and heads towards the cooker, putting on her oven gloves en route to retrieve the ceramic tagine dish from the oven. It's a good job she has her back to us so misses the look exchanged between JJ, Annabel and me when she says, 'That's what I've always loved about you, Charlotte, your honesty.'

THIRTY-TWO

It's almost nine o'clock by the time Melody and Tamsin carry a sleeping George upstairs to their chill-out room to watch television, leaving us adults to decamp to the lounge. I hated leaving the dessert plates on the dining-room table, but Tiff was insistent, saying there would be plenty of time for her and JJ to clear things up after we'd gone. I'm hoping that's prophetic.

Putting his indiscretion in Mauritius aside, what has been blatantly obvious throughout the evening is how much Tiff and JJ belong together. They laugh at the same things and end each other's sentences, as often happens with people who have been in a loving relationship for a long time. It brought back memories of my relationship with Zack. We were so in tune on so many levels. He would often leave the room and return minutes later with a snack or a drink that I'd been craving without me mentioning it. And yet we were so out of synch on the one thing that mattered most to me, and which eventually broke us apart. I hope that Tiff will find it in her heart to be more forgiving of JJ's dishonesty than I was with Zack. There is so much more at stake.

For one thing, the family that I was never destined to have

with Zack would be torn apart if they split up as a consequence of JJ being unfaithful. Their girls would be stuck in the middle, forced to make choices at a very sensitive stage in their lives when what they really need is stability.

And then, of course, there's George. At the very least, he needs Tiff to overcome her emotions and any animosity she may feel towards me and JJ to give him a chance of a better future.

I've barely been able to eat all day as my stomach has been in knots. The plate that Tiff placed in front of me was piled high with couscous and lamb tagine. With the first forkful, I could pick out cumin, coriander, cinnamon and just the right amount of harissa to give flavour without too much heat. The ground almonds added texture and there was a hint of sweetness from the chunks of apricot, while the lamb itself was completely melt in the mouth. At any other time I would have wolfed down the lot, but my appetite has deserted me. It was almost insulting to leave as much as I did on my plate.

Tiff clearly noticed but chose not to comment, instead presenting me with a much smaller portion of sticky toffee pudding with vanilla ice-cream than she gave to everyone else. It felt wrong to be accepting such lavish hospitality from someone whose life I was about to shatter.

When Tiff headed out to the kitchen to make coffee, Annabel excused herself to go to the loo, presumably to give JJ and me a few minutes to ourselves.

'I'm not sure I can do this,' I say to him, my voice barely above a whisper.

'We have to,' he replies. 'This is the first time we've all been together since I found out that George is my son. We need to tell Tiff the truth tonight or we'd be lying to her face. There'd be no coming back from that and where would that leave George? We don't have a choice, Charlotte.'

All night I've been avoiding eye contact with JJ wherever possible, afraid of what I might see there, but I'm holding his gaze now. There is no sign of the anger or repulsion that I feared. All I can see is sadness. He's right. We must tell Tiff tonight, but broaching the subject will not be easy. How do you tell one of your best friends that you've not only had sex with their husband but you also have a child together? Even the thought of it makes me feel faint.

'Here, let me get that.'

It's Annabel's voice, slightly louder than normal volume, presumably to alert me and JJ to Tiff's imminent arrival. Moments later, she enters their opulent lounge carrying a tray of coffee mugs and a plate of wafer-thin chocolate mints.

'In case anyone is still hungry.' Tiff places the mints in the centre of the marble coffee table.

'I'm stuffed,' Annabel declares, patting her smooth stomach. 'That dinner was delicious.'

'I'm glad you enjoyed it,' Tiff replies.

'It was really tasty,' I agree, 'but I don't seem to have much of an appetite since I had George.'

'That'll be why you've got your figure back so quickly.' Tiff reaches for a mint, sliding it out of the dark paper wrapper and nibbling the corner off it. 'My weight ballooned after having Tamsin. I was not only eating my own meals, but also finishing off anything Melody left on her plate.'

'Ballooned?' Annabel laughs. 'By that, you mean you were only a few pounds under the average weight for your height rather than a stone or two. I wish I had your metabolism. My relationship with the bathroom scales is more intimate than mine and Finn's sometimes.'

Tiff joins in the laughter, but to me, Annabel's comment seems like a first attempt to steer the conversation towards the reason that she and I are here tonight.

I'm not ready yet, so instead focus my attention on the coasters. 'They're pretty,' I say, lifting my mug to reveal the multicoloured bejewelled square underneath.

'From the same trip to Morocco as the tagine recipe,' Tiff replies. 'JJ came home after three weeks away on a shoot with stuffed camel toys for the girls, the coasters and the glazed tagine cooking pot. It's a minor miracle he got it back in one piece. He hadn't realised that the recipe for tonight's dinner was inside, so I made it as a surprise the first time. We all loved it so much that it's now a family favourite.' She smiles indulgently at her husband.

I'm in danger of choking on the sip of coffee I've just taken as my throat constricts. Everything about Tiff's home life seems perfect and I'm about to destroy it with a giant wrecking ball.

'Does he always bring you souvenirs from work trips?' Annabel asks, throwing me a look from beneath her eyelashes.

I know she's right and this must be tackled tonight, but my hands are suddenly so moist with perspiration that I'm forced to replace my mug on the coaster for fear of dropping it.

'Not always, and they're not always so useful are they, darling?' she says, squeezing JJ's forearm. 'I still haven't found a place for the wooden dodo he brought me back from Mauritius. You probably saw them? You press a lever, and it makes a sound like a dodo. Although how anyone can know whether it's accurate or not when they've been extinct for years, I've no idea. It's an ugly-looking thing too. What?' she asks when no one comments. 'Oh no, don't tell me you brought one back as well and you like it? I thought you girls had better taste than that.' She laughs, but it's a nervous laugh, almost as though she knows something is not quite right.

The opportunity has presented itself, but JJ seems unwilling or unable to seize it. I think of George sleeping peacefully in his baby carrier upstairs, minded by Tiff and JJ's two girls, one of whom could hold the key to his future. However much I don't want to destroy their perfect family life, my priority has to be my son.

'No, we didn't bring a dodo back with us,' I say. My voice is calm. 'But I did bring something back that I wasn't aware of at the time.'

Although it's not the most subtle or sensitive way to broach the subject we've come here to talk about, I have to try and start the conversation and JJ is being no help.

'Oh my God, you didn't get asked to carry something for another passenger, did you?' Tiff asks, a horrified look on her face. 'Was it drugs? You're lucky the sniffer dogs at Gatwick didn't find it or you could have ended up in jail.'

I shoot a meaningful look in JJ's direction, but he still doesn't speak so I feel forced to plough on.

'That's not what I meant, Tiff. I... I didn't know at the time, but a man I had sex with on the last night of our holiday got me pregnant.'

'Oh,' she says. 'So, it wasn't an anonymous donor, like you said?'

'No, it wasn't, and I'm sorry I lied about it, but there was a good reason.'

I keep opening the door for JJ, but he's still not forthcoming.

'You didn't need to worry about me being judgemental,' Tiff says. 'We're all adults and your body was probably craving sex after the end of your relationship with Zack.'

This is excruciating. I just want JJ to man up and admit what happened in Mauritius. It would be so much better if the truth came from him rather than me.

'Hold on a minute though,' Tiff says, as what I've just admitted sinks in. 'Have you been in touch with the man? Does he know that he's fathered a child?'

The silence that follows Tiff's question is deafening and seems to last an eternity until finally JJ speaks.

'I do now.'

Three pairs of eyes are on Tiff. There is nothing any of us can add until the realisation of exactly what her husband has said dawns on her. I've often heard the phrase 'her face crumpled', but I've never previously seen it happen with my own eyes. Tiff's expression of understanding and acceptance from moments earlier is frozen in place for a couple of seconds, before her cheeks appear to hollow, and her skin turns ashen grey. I'm not sure what I'm expecting her to do or say, but this total stillness is quite frightening. My heart is thudding in my chest, which feels so tight I can barely breathe.

I need to say something while I still have a chance. I must make her understand that I didn't knowingly sleep with her husband. 'Please believe me when I say I had no idea that the man I got together with on my last night in Mauritius was your husband.' My voice sounds whiny and desperate even to my own ears, but I persist. 'I'd never met JJ and was completely unaware that his real name is Justin. But even if I'd known, I would never have put two and two together, because what are the chances of us meeting in those circumstances?'

Tiff still doesn't speak. She's staring at JJ as if he's a stranger. He has dropped his head to rest in his hands.

'I... I was mortified when I found out,' I add.

Tiff turns her gaze on me. Her voice is unsettlingly calm when she asks, 'I'm assuming that was at my party?'

'Yes,' I admit.

'So, let me get this straight, Charlotte.' Her tone is still neutral, but the way she used my name punctuates her point. 'Since last June, you've known that you slept with my husband and were carrying his baby, but you chose not to tell me?'

Put like that it sounds cold and calculated, which is not how it was at all. My priority since discovering JJ's identity has been to cause Tiff the least amount of pain. It would be bad enough to find out that your husband has been unfaithful but totally devastating to discover that it was with someone you consider to be a friend.

'How could I tell you, Tiff? What would I have said? It was a horrible situation to find myself in. When I thought I'd miscarried my baby, I allowed myself to think it was the best thing for everyone. But George had other ideas. He clung onto life, and I had no right to deny him that. That's why I didn't try to contact JJ and tell him I was pregnant. I was certain he would have tried to persuade me to have a termination and I couldn't do that to George. I decided that nothing would be gained by telling the truth, but so much could be lost.' I glance over in JJ's direction. His head is still bowed. He must be regretting ever having requested sharing my table in the beach restaurant. 'I'm not proud of the way George was conceived. I'd had too much to drink, and as you pointed out, my body was desperate for sex. There were never any feelings involved, it was purely physical.'

'But sex with a married man?' Tiff says, a slightly sharper edge creeping into her voice. 'I thought better of you than that, Charlotte. If it hadn't been my husband, it would have been someone else's. You ignored that detail in your own desire to get laid, giving no thought to the lives that could be devastated by your selfishness. So long as you got what you wanted, you didn't care about hurting anyone else.'

I want to tell her that I didn't know JJ was married, that, as far as I knew, we were two single people having fun. But if I tell her he wasn't wearing his wedding band the chance of them being able to reconcile might disappear, so I drop my gaze and stay silent.

At my lack of response, Tiff turns her attention to Annabel. 'And what about you, Annabel? How long have you known that my husband cheated on me with our friend? If you tell me you've known about this all along and chose to keep it secret, I don't think I can cope.'

The hurt and hope in Tiff's voice is there for us all to hear. It's far more upsetting than if she'd started shouting or even crying.

'I didn't know until a few weeks ago,' Annabel says quietly. 'Charlotte didn't tell me because she knew I would tell you. For what it's worth, I genuinely believe she was trying to do what she thought was best for you and JJ and George.'

Tiff's shoulders relax and she nods her head slightly, clearly relieved that the betrayal hasn't included Annabel.

'But Charlotte confessing this tonight has nothing to do with me persuading her to tell you the truth, although I probably would have done eventually. There's a more pressing issue,' Annabel says, reaching for Tiff's hand and giving it a squeeze. 'George is sick. He has a medical condition that can best be helped by a blood relative and, unfortunately, Charlotte isn't a suitable match.'

'You never said that there was anything wrong with George,' Tiff says, returning her attention to me. 'Something else you chose to keep from me.'

'I'm so sorry, Tiff. I know how all this must look, but it really wasn't my intention to keep his illness secret. It was just so much more difficult because I knew JJ was his father.'

Slowly, she nods her head. Her voice when she speaks is filled with a mother's compassion. 'What's wrong with George?'

I'm relieved that she cares enough to ask, giving me hope that she might at least consider the possibility that her girls could help their half-brother.

'He has massively reduced kidney function. It was touch-and-go for the first forty-eight hours of his life, but, as we've already established, George is a fighter. The trouble is,' I say, breathing deeply to keep my emotions in check, 'this is a battle he can't win without help. To live a long and full life, he's going to need a kidney transplant from a compatible donor. I had hoped that would be me, but...' I can't finish my sentence.

'But you're not a close enough match,' Tiff says finishing my sentence. 'So, that's why you're telling me all this. As his next closest relative, you want JJ to donate one of his kidneys to George.'

'Not quite.' JJ finally raises his head to make eye contact

with his wife. 'I had tests done to check for compatibility and I'm not a close enough match either.'

Before Tiff can respond, a noise over by the door attracts our attention. We all turn in unison. Standing in the doorway with a wide-awake George settled on her hip, mirroring what she saw her mother do earlier, is Melody.

'Tammy was tired, so she went to bed and then this little guy woke up.' She smiles down at George while fiddling with his chubby little fingers. 'I thought I should bring him down in case he needed feeding or something. Was that the right thing to do?'

A quick glance around the four of us tells me that I'm not the only one who is wondering whether Melody heard any of our conversation.

Tiff recovers first. 'Absolutely,' she says, smiling reassuringly at her eldest daughter. 'And perfect timing as Charlotte and Annabel were just saying they need to leave.'

While I would have preferred to finish the conversation now that the lid is off Pandora's Box, I have to respect Tiff's wishes and save my questions for another time. I'm on my feet and across the room in moments to relieve Melody of her charge.

'He's such a good baby,' she says, kissing the top of his head before handing him over. 'I'll happily babysit for him if you and Mum and Annabel want a girls' night out.'

The chances of that happening are slim to impossible after what Tiff has just learned, but at least it seems unlikely that Melody overheard anything, which is a relief.

'He's so cute,' she continues, seemingly oblivious to the tension in the room. 'It kind of makes me wish that Mum and Dad had had another one.'

Her words have me cringing. Having been reluctant to leave a few moments earlier, I now can't wait to get away from Tiff and JJ's.

'Thanks for the offer,' I say, grateful that my back is to the two of them.

'I'll fetch his baby carrier,' Melody says, racing back up the stairs, while Annabel heads into the kitchen to gather George's things.

My hands are shaking as I fasten the straps securely around George in his carrier and head towards the front door, where JJ, Tiff and Melody are waiting to bid us goodnight. I'm acutely aware that Tiff and JJ haven't spoken to each other since their eldest daughter appeared in the doorway holding my baby, but I don't think Melody has noticed as she's been so preoccupied with George.

'Thank you for a lovely evening,' I mumble as my cheek connects with Tiff's in an air kiss. Her body is stiff and unyielding.

'The tagine was divine,' I hear Annabel say as I hurry across the drive towards my car, gravel crunching loudly underfoot.

I'm shaking so much now, I'm struggling to fasten the seat belt around George's baby carrier when Annabel catches up with me.

'Are you sure you're all right to drive? I can leave my car here and come back for it tomorrow.'

'Why are you being so kind to me?' I ask, my voice shaking as badly as my hands. 'I've shattered three lives. I don't deserve kindness.'

'You made a mistake – well, a few, if truth be told,' she says, wrapping her arms around me and pulling me into a hug. 'But none of it was planned or malicious. If you hadn't fallen pregnant, it might have been awkward being around JJ, but I'm pretty sure that neither of you would have seen any benefit in telling Tiff. That's the thing you must remember.' She holds me at arm's length so that she can look into my eyes. 'He's the one who broke his wedding vows when he cheated on his wife. You weren't in a relationship, and he wasn't wearing a wedding band. How were you supposed to know he was married?'

I shrug.

'Listen to me. Whatever happens between Tiff and JJ now is not your fault. Do you understand?'

I nod. I hear what she's saying, but I'm not sure I can accept that she's right.

I slide into the driver's seat and glance at my son, blissfully unaware of the drama he is at the centre of. In spite of everything, I can't imagine my life without him in it. I feel my throat contract as the thought I've had a few times since discovering that JJ was not a suitable donor match for George forces its way to the forefront of my mind. What if the only way Tiff will agree for their girls to be tested is if she and JJ take on the responsibility of raising George as their own? Both have expressed that they would dearly have loved a son. Would I be able to give up my beautiful boy to them? It might be the sacrifice I have to make to give him his best shot at life. But is the price too high to pay?

Brushing the back of my left hand across my cheek to wipe away the tear that's trickling down it, I pull the driver's door closed with my right, then press the button to lower the window.

'Thank you for being my friend, Annabel. I wouldn't have been able to cope with any of this if it hadn't been for you.'

'You're stronger than you think,' she says. 'Go home and get some sleep and I'll pop over to check on you in the morning.'

As I pull my Mini out of the driveway, I can see Tiff standing in the doorway watching us leave. I can only imagine how completely betrayed she must be feeling. What Zack kept from me was bad enough, but that was just between the two of us. Tiff has got to come to terms not only with her husband's infidelity, but also her two best friends sharing a secret that they withheld from her. However confident and self-assured she may appear to be, we all have a vulnerable side, a soft underbelly that once breached is difficult to recover from. I hope with all my heart that she will reach out to JJ and Annabel for support even if she turns her back on me. In fairness, it's no more than I deserve.

THIRTY-THREE

Tiff

Watching my two best friends from my vantage point on the front doorstep, I experience a pang of jealousy as Annabel puts her arms around Charlotte and pulls her into a hug.

It was a massive relief to find out that Annabel hasn't been keeping this secret from me for the best part of a year, but I can see how the whole situation has her backed into a corner. She's been Charlotte's mainstay since the break-up with Zack and even more so throughout the pregnancy. Annabel's always been closer to Charlotte than I have, which I put down to them being a similar age and neither of them having children. But what if it's more than that? What if she simply prefers Charlotte to me? If I decide to cut Charlotte out of my life, will I also need to be prepared to lose Annabel? Just as I finally have the freedom to spend more time with them now that my girls are older, will the opportunity be snatched away from me? It really all depends on what I do next...

My main consideration should be my husband cheating on me. The fact that it was with one of my best friends is almost irrelevant. JJ has been travelling away for work since I've known him, and I've never even considered that he would be unfaithful to me, despite being surrounded by some of the world's most beautiful-looking people. But what if I was wrong to trust him so implicitly? What if his night of passion with Charlotte was just the latest in a long line of indiscretions and our entire marriage has been a sham? Just the idea has me reaching for the door frame for support.

No, I think, shaking my head to clear my thoughts, I refuse to believe it. JJ and I made our vows on our wedding day and from that moment I truly believe we've been faithful to each other. Well, aside from Charlotte, of course.

I'd only known him for six weeks when we got married, but I'd never felt that way about anyone in my life and he told me that he felt the same. There was just a tiny nagging doubt in my mind the night before our wedding. Was it all happening too quickly? Was I certain I wanted to spend the rest of my life with this man?

'Do you need a hand clearing up, Mum?' Melody's voice startles me.

I close and lock the front door and plaster a smile on my face before turning to face my daughter, who was born exactly nine months after our wedding day.

'No, you go up. Your dad and I can manage,' I say. 'Thanks for looking after George.'

'No worries, I enjoyed being trusted with him. See you in the morning.' She blows me a kiss, which I pretend to catch and hold against my heart. It's something we've done since she was a toddler, and I dropped her off at nursery school for the first time. When the door closed behind her, I stood listening for several minutes to make sure she wasn't crying out for me before I pushed Tamsin's pram along the little footpath back to the car, tears streaming down my cheeks. When I picked Melody up at lunchtime, even before she excitedly started to tell me how her morning had been, she asked, 'Have you still got my kiss, Mummy?'

I'm smiling at the memory when I notice JJ standing in the kitchen doorway.

'Do you want to talk now, or do you want to sleep on it? I can go in the spare room if that's what you want,' he says.

He sounds like a man who has the weight of the world on his shoulders. Maybe it's not the weight of the entire world, but what he has to say will have an impact on my world and that of the girls. I'm so shocked and disappointed that we even need to have this conversation, but I am willing to give him a chance to explain.

'We may as well get it over with,' I reply, trying to keep my voice neutral. 'I don't suppose either of us would get much sleep anyway.'

He follows me through to the lounge and we sit down opposite each other with the coffee table between us. It's a few moments before he starts to speak, which allows me time to examine the face of the man I've loved unconditionally for the past seventeen years. Whatever happens in the next hours and days, our relationship will never be quite the same again and this makes me terribly sad.

'I've loved you from the moment I first laid eyes on you,' JJ begins. 'Crazy, isn't it. I've been surrounded by beautiful women all my working life and I'm not going to insult you by suggesting that I never fancied any of them or took it a step further, but you were different. I quickly realised that it was more than a mere physical attraction. It was as though we'd been waiting to find each other.'

He pauses. Maybe he's expecting me to confirm that I felt the same way, but I stay silent, fearful of breaking down if I try to speak.

'Since we made our vows on that cliff top in South Africa,' he continues, 'I've never looked at another woman in a sexual way. Yes, I could appreciate their beauty, but I had no desire to sleep with them, even if they came on to me. I just wasn't interested in any of them. Why would I want a Porsche when I had a Ferrari at home?'

His analogy brings forth a watery smile. JJ has always wanted a flashy sports car but never owned one because it would have been impractical for all his photographic equipment.

'So, what changed on that night in Mauritius?' I manage to say.

'I've asked myself that same question so many times.' He shakes his head with a look of bewilderment on his face. 'There's no denying that Charlotte is a stunning woman, but it was as though she didn't believe it. There was a vulnerability and fragility to her that made me want to look after her. God,' he says, obviously reacting to my raised eyebrows, 'putting it like that makes me sound like a pervert. That's not what I meant at all. She'd had a lot to drink and in part I felt responsible. I just wanted to walk her back to her room so that she got there safely. And then...' He stops.

'And then, what?' I probe. I need to know what made my husband cross a line that he assures me he'd never crossed previously even if hearing it may destroy me.

'I... I don't know, Tiff. She asked me to make her a coffee to help her to sober up and I noticed her shiver. I put my jacket around her shoulders and the next minute things just spiralled out of control. I can't lie to you, I knew exactly what I was doing, but, in that moment, I just couldn't stop myself. I lost my self-control,' he says, a sob catching in his throat. 'I would give anything for it not to have happened, but it did, and I wish I'd been man enough to tell you about it the moment I got home.'

And there it is. That's the main issue with all of this. I'm not sure I'll ever be able to wholly trust my husband again.

'I'm so, so sorry,' he starts to say. 'I know that doesn't even come close—'

I raise my hand to stop him speaking. 'But what is it you are sorry for, JJ? Being unfaithful or being forced to tell me that you were? Please answer me honestly. Would you have told me that you broke our marriage vows if you hadn't been forced into it?'

The silence that follows hangs heavy in the air.

After a few moments, he raises his eyes to connect with mine. 'I don't know,' he admits. 'I knew what I'd done was wrong, but I also knew it didn't change the way I feel about you, and I was so afraid of losing you. I should have told you the minute I got home, but once the moment was gone, I simply didn't have the courage.'

Although his answer is non-committal, at least he has been truthful when he could have lied.

'If there's anyone else you need to tell me about, JJ, it should be now,' I say, trying to keep my voice calm and steady. 'I won't give you another opportunity. This is your only chance to come clean.'

I'm expecting him to speak straight away, to assure me that this was an isolated incident, but he doesn't. My heart is thudding against my ribs. The longer the silence extends, the more my imagination races. Has my whole marriage been a complete lie?

In a voice so quiet that I can barely hear him, he eventually says, 'There is no one else, but in the interest of honesty, there is something else you should know. Charlotte didn't know she was sleeping with a married man.'

The vice-like grip on my heart relaxes slightly.

'She must have noticed your wedding band,' I say, my eyes dropping to JJ's left hand.

'I... I wasn't wearing it,' he mutters.

My head snaps up. I'd just started to accept that his night of passion in Mauritius was a terrible mistake, but maybe I'm too gullible. Why would a married man not be wearing his wedding ring unless he was looking to get laid? 'Wow. You almost had me believing you, JJ. You must take me for a proper fool. I suppose you're going to come up with some half-arsed excuse for taking it off that you'll expect me to accept. I'm trusting, but not stupid. That really does shine a different light on things.'

He's up from his seat and around my side of the coffee table in a flash, reaching for my hands, but I push him away.

'I know what you're thinking, but you're wrong. I didn't leave it off deliberately.'

I snort. 'Really? Most decent women wouldn't sleep with a married man. Hold on a minute. Why didn't Charlotte mention that you weren't wearing a wedding ring when I accused her earlier?'

'Probably because she's a better friend than you give her credit for,' he says, dropping to his haunches in front of me. 'She only saw my ring in the bathroom where I'd left it after cleaning tar off it from the beach shots I'd taken that morning. I can only assume that she realised how it would seem to you and decided our marriage was more important to try to save than your rela-tionship with her.'

I'm trying to think back to earlier in the evening. Just how cruel and accusatory was I to Charlotte? If what JJ is saying is true, she couldn't have known he was married and so did abso-lutely nothing wrong. She's been a free agent since her split with Zack.

I glance at my watch, wondering if it's too late to call her now. It's past midnight, and anyway, I think it's a conversation that needs to be had in person rather than over the phone. It will have to wait until the morning.

I refocus my attention on JJ. I want to believe him. He's often said he wished he had gone for a plain band instead of having diamonds set into it because it's a nuisance when stuff gets stuck in them, but is that just a convenient excuse? He's watching me with the look of a puppy who has pissed on the carpet, unsure how his apology will be received. Will he be given another chance, or turfed out in the cold? We all make mistakes, as I know only too well. I would give anything to change what happened the night before our wedding, but what's done is done and no amount of regret can alter it. For a moment, I consider telling JJ what I've kept from him for seventeen years. Instead, I pat the sofa cushion at my side and watch as he half rises before settling on to it.

'I really am sorry, Tiff,' he says. I believe him. He has a look of genuine regret in his eyes.

'I know,' I say, resting my hand on his knee. 'It won't be easy, but we're strong enough to get past this, aren't we?'

'Oh, God, Tiff. I love you so much. I'll never do anything to hurt you again, I promise.' He places his hand tentatively over mine.

I don't snatch my hand away. The warmth and moisture of my husband's damp palms are a sign of how anxious he is feeling. After a couple of minutes, I turn my hand over and clasp his tightly. I love my husband. We're good together. If this is an isolated incident, as I fervently hope it is, we can work things out. None of us is perfect. Everyone deserves a second chance, don't they?

'We need to talk about George and how we can best help him,' I eventually say, 'but I'd rather sleep on things first, if that's all right with you?'

'Spare room for me?' he asks.

I take a moment to consider his suggestion. If I didn't have a huge secret of my own maybe that would have been my preference. But as things stand, when I eventually find the courage to confess, I'll need his forgiveness as much as he needs mine.

'Our room,' I reply. 'We can't change the past, what's important are the decisions we make now for all of us and our futures.'

THIRTY-FOUR
SUNDAY 7 APRIL

Charlotte

Maybe George isn't as blissfully unaware of the situation as I initially thought. He's normally a very good baby, sleeping through until the dawn chorus, but last night he was awake every couple of hours and, more unusually for him, he was crying. My first thought was that his kidneys might be playing up, but after a wet nappy, followed by a soiled one at the next change, I concluded that either he had started teething unusually early, or he's tuned in to my mood. The latter is highly likely as I clung on to him for a long time before settling him into his cot. The thought that forced its way to the front of my mind as I sat in my car on the driveway of Tiff and JJ's house last night is refusing to go away.

Much as the idea of living my life without him in it is overwhelmingly sad, he is, and always has been, my main consideration. Growing up with Tiff and JJ, he would be at the heart of a loving family who are much better placed than me to give him what he needs. As a single mum, I'm not only money-poor but also time-poor as I need to work to make ends meet. It was always going to be tough even if George had been a completely healthy baby, but he's not. There will be doctor's appointments and hospital visits, and potentially major surgery and recovery. How will I manage, even with the help Annabel has assured me she will give? And once she and Finn are married and start their own family, will she really have enough time for me and mine? But without George in it, my life would be pointless. I wouldn't want to carry on.

All these thoughts were running through my mind as I lay trying to sleep between George's wakeful periods last night. The one thing he would never be short of from me is love, but I'm not sure that will be enough. Of course, it could all be hypothetical as Tiff and JJ's marriage may not survive his infidelity. On the other hand, I'm sure Tiff would grow to love George as much as if she were his birth mother. It could be the very thing that saves their marriage. But I'm not so sure I'd survive without my beautiful boy. Looking down at him now, full from his breakfast feed, his chubby hand resting possessively on my bare breast, I cannot imagine a future without him.

It feels like only moments later that we are both woken by my mobile ringing, which starts George crying. I lift him against my chest to soothe him after pulling my sweatshirt down to cover myself and reach for my phone, still fuddled from sleep. A glance at the clock shows that the two of us have been cuddled up on the comfy chair in the corner of my bedroom for a little under an hour as it's still only half past eight. Annabel must be worried about me to be calling so early. In truth, I was pretty distraught when I left Tiff and JJ's last night.

My attention is on George, whose cries are starting to subside as I answer the phone, saying, 'Hi Annabel. I'm sorry to have got you up so early. We're fine, really.' This is said to reassure her, even though I'm anything but.

There's a slight pause before the reply. 'It's not Annabel, it's your mother.'

I'm immediately wide awake. It's unusual for my mother to ring me at all, even though her attitude towards me has softened since George's birth, but at this time on a Sunday morning, it's unheard of.

'Mum? What's wrong? Are you okay?' I try to keep the panic from my voice.

'I'm fine,' she replies. 'I've been up since half past six because your father had an early tee-off time, so I thought I'd get a few calls in while he's out. You sound a bit on edge. Is everything all right with George?'

'Yes. We had a disturbed night and just dozed off, so the phone woke us, and George was none too pleased. He's settling now though,' I say, gazing down at my baby, who I've manoeuvred into the crook of my arm.

'I hope you're not mollycoddling him, Charlotte. I know it must be difficult with there only being you, but you mustn't give in to him all the time. You need to set the boundaries early or you'll cause problems for yourself as he gets older.'

My mother hasn't been on the phone for more than a minute and she's already criticising the way I'm bringing up my son. I bite the inside of my cheek until I taste blood to stop me from telling her to mind her own business.

'Anyway, I haven't rung to tell you how to raise your child, you'll be pleased to hear. I'm sure you'll have remembered it's your father's seventieth birthday in August and it falls on a Sunday. We're planning a bit of a lunchtime do at the golf club and I need to get an idea of numbers. You will be able to make it, won't you?'

It's less a question, more a statement of fact. Much as the prospect doesn't exactly fill me with joy, I can hardly refuse to help my dad celebrate his entry into a new decade. 'Of course we'll be there.'

'We?' she asks.

There is undeniable hope in her question. Perhaps she thinks I've got a new man in my life.

'Me and George,' I clarify.

'Oh, right. I wondered if maybe you and Zack were going to give things another go? I hope you replied to his letter?'

My grip tightens around my phone. 'What are you talking about?' I demand.

'Well, after he sent me the Christmas card saying how sorry he was that things hadn't worked out with you two, I sent him one back telling him how disappointed I was with his behaviour in not telling you about the vasectomy and how it had devastated you because having children was so important to you. I admit I laid it on a bit thick,' she says, an element of satisfaction in her tone, 'but I thought he needed to be told how selfish he'd been in letting you hold on to hope all those years.'

'Mum! How could you go behind my back to contact Zack? I told you that in confidence.'

I eventually confided in my mum when I was in my third trimester. She'd come up on the train from Poole for a visit, which is one of the most motherly things she has ever done. My hormones must have been running amok because the whole story of my five years of trying unsuccessfully for a baby with Zack came pouring out of me. When I told her that he'd had the snip before he and I got together, there was no major reaction, merely a tut. No wonder I underestimated how upset about it she was.

'Well, at least it provoked some sort of recognition of how badly he treated you. He told me he sent the letter to the flower shop to arrive on what was your anniversary.'

I'm confused and furious at the same time. I can't believe my mother has interfered in this way. I'm speechless.

'Don't tell me you just ignored it, Charlotte,' she says after a couple of moments of silence. 'That wasn't very kind of you after he had the decency to apologise.'

Through gritted teeth, I manage to say, 'Zack may have told you that he wrote to apologise to me, but he must have been lying because I've not had any contact with him since he came to the shop a month after our split. I know you'll find that hard to accept because you've always had a soft spot for him. In fact, I've long suspected you liked him more than me.'

'Don't be ridiculous, Charlotte...' she starts to say, but I cut her short.

'I can't talk to you about this now, Mum. It's not okay to interfere in my life whatever your motivation was. I'm hanging up to stop me saying what I really want to.'

I sit staring at my phone. I'm shocked that my mum would communicate with Zack behind my back, however well-intentioned it may have been. And what was all this talk of him sending me a letter? If something arrived at the shop for me while I was off for George's birth, I'm certain Michaela would have told me. Nevertheless, I dash off a quick text message just for my own peace of mind.

Hi Michaela, sorry to disturb you on a Sunday, and no urgency to reply, but I just got off the phone with my mum and she said I should have received a letter at the shop around the time that I was off having George. I'm sure you would have mentioned it, so it probably got lost in the post. By the way, I'll be okay to open the shop tomorrow morning on my own. I need to start getting back into my old routine. Charlotte x

I hit send and then carefully lay George in his cradle, a gift from my mum and dad. I want to have a shower before breakfast and Annabel's expected arrival at some point this morning, although no amount of showering will be able to wash away the tremendous guilt I feel after last night. All things considered, Tiff was remarkably calm, but it's the thought of what happens next that terrifies me.

THIRTY-FIVE

George has had his mid-morning feed and I've just finished my toast when the doorbell rings.

'You be a good boy while I let your auntie Annabel in,' I say to George as I squeeze past his highchair and head out into the hall. I've had no response to the text message I sent to Michaela earlier, but it's a lovely sunny morning so she's probably out for a walk with her kids and her mum.

'You didn't need to come around, I'm okay,' I'm saying as I open my front door.

For the second time in a couple of hours, I've mistakenly assumed Annabel is checking up on me.

'Can I come in?' Tiff asks before the door is even fully open. She has dark circles under her eyes, suggesting that George and I are not the only ones who didn't get much sleep.

'Tiff,' I say, my mouth feeling suddenly dry. 'Sorry, I thought it was Annabel. She said she'd call in this morning.' I'm talking out of nervousness rather than the need to explain. Possibly the last person I expected to see on my doorstep this morning was Tiff and I can't help wondering why she's here. 'Can I get you a tea or coffee?'

'Please,' she says, without elaborating on which.

I hold the door open for her and follow her into the kitchen. Before I move past her to flick the switch on the kettle, I unclip George's safety harness and lift him out of his highchair. Tiff has perched on a kitchen chair, and I sit down opposite her with George on my lap. He is staring at her, seemingly mesmerised.

'I'm so sorry, Tiff,' I say. It's completely inadequate in the circumstances, but I can't think of anything more appropriate.

She moves her hand in a dismissive gesture. 'What's done is done. Nothing can change what has happened in the past, however much we may want it to.'

Her behaviour is strange. I wouldn't be so calm if I'd found out that Zack had been unfaithful to me during our relationship. Even last night, when she'd just learned of JJ's infidelity and that he was the father of my child, Tiff was less angry, more shocked. She didn't scream and shout as I'm sure I would have done if our positions had been reversed. She just seemed overwhelmingly sad.

When she continues, Tiff isn't looking at me, she's looking at my baby. 'You know it's funny. Looking at George now, knowing he's JJ's son, I can see a strong resemblance around his eyes and nose. I totally missed it when I wasn't expecting to see it. It set me wondering if Callum would have looked that way if he'd survived.'

I'm confused. I have no idea who Callum is.

Realising my confusion, Tiff continues, 'Of course. You don't know about Callum. Nobody does, not even our girls. JJ and I decided to keep it between the two of us when we lost him.'

My heart is thumping so loudly that I wouldn't be surprised if Tiff could hear it. If I'm understanding her correctly, she and JJ suffered a miscarriage, and the baby would have been a boy. As if the loss of her child wasn't devastating enough, I've resurrected all those feelings of grief because my son is there to remind her of what she might have had. I feel sick to the pit of my stomach.

'Things felt different right from the start of the pregnancy,' Tiff continues, her voice trance-like as she relives the memory. 'I never had morning sickness with either of the girls, but I couldn't face anything to eat or drink before midday for the first few weeks. The doctor warned that it might be a bit trickier because of my age, so I took things very easy. In the end, it didn't make any difference.'

It's incredibly upsetting to hear Tiff speak like this. She's usually so confident and positive, but she sounds crushed and defeated and, in a way, I'm responsible.

'JJ and I didn't tell the girls about the baby straight away, or anyone else for that matter, because we knew there was the risk of miscarriage at my age. We decided that we'd wait until twenty weeks because he would have had a chance of surviving if he came early. I was eighteen weeks pregnant when I lost him.'

Her shoulders have sagged forward with the effort of recounting what must have been the worst moment of her life. Why do things have to be so unfair? I'm struggling to find any meaningful words to comfort her.

'You never truly get over it, you know,' she continues, dragging her eyes away from George to meet mine. 'You bury it deep in your heart because life has to go on and you have two other children. But each special date that we never got to spend with Callum – his first Christmas, the anniversary of his due date, even what would have been his first day at school last September – twists the dagger a little bit more of everything you've been denied.'

'Oh, Tiff,' I say, finally finding my voice. 'I wish you'd told me and Annabel. We would have been there for you.'

The half-smile that touches her lips does nothing to ease the sadness in her eyes. 'You were also part of the reason that we didn't tell people we were expecting. I knew how desperately you wanted a baby. It felt unkind to flaunt our good fortune in your face.'

I bite down on my lip to stop the tears amassing at the back of my eyes from falling. Tiff's consideration for me and my feelings makes me feel even guiltier.

'Not telling anyone turned out to be a blessing in disguise. At least when we lost him, I didn't have to listen to the platitudes of well-meaning people who couldn't possibly understand what I was going through unless they'd experienced it themselves. I felt such a... a failure, Charlotte,' she says, her voice faltering again. 'I let Callum down by not giving him a safe place to develop and grow and I don't suppose I'll ever be able to forgive myself.'

I want to tell her that I understand; that I have terrible feelings of guilt about George's health problems because I was drinking early in the pregnancy. But even that is not the same. I have my beautiful boy, despite his medical issues, and all she has is memories of her tiny stillborn child and thoughts of what might have been.

'It wasn't your fault, Tiff. There may have been something wrong that he couldn't have survived even if you'd carried him to full term. Nature is sometimes cruel to be kind. That's what I tried to comfort myself with when I thought I'd lost George.'

'That would have been a tragedy.' Her eyes rest back on George, who is reaching out towards her with one of his chubby hands and making a gurgling noise. 'He's a gorgeous little lad and deserves the best shot at life.'

Hope floods my heart. Has JJ been able to persuade Tiff to allow their girls to be tested to see if they are a positive match?

'As you can imagine, it got quite emotional after you and Annabel left last night.' She reaches into her handbag for a tissue as if to underline how fragile she's still feeling.

'Do you want to talk about it?' I ask nervously.

'That's why I'm here. We've got a lot to talk about,' she says, her eyes fully connecting with mine for the first time. 'Do you want me to take George?'

It was a heart-stopping moment until I realised Tiff was nodding her head in the direction of the kettle which had just come to the boil. She was offering to hold him while I made the hot drinks.

'Oh, right,' I said, getting to my feet and handing George to her. 'I'll bring the teas through to the lounge.'

Now, I'm in the doorway to my lounge, a mug of tea in each hand, watching my friend as she looks out of the bay window while cuddling my baby son. She's swaying from side to side as she softly sings to him, her lips brushing the top of his downy head. It seems the most normal scene in the world and yet it is anything but.

'You're a natural with babies,' I say, placing the mugs on the small walnut table and sinking down onto my sofa.

'I wasn't always.' She turns to face me. 'It was thrust on me so quickly after the wedding. I improved with practice and, of course, I had JJ who was an amazing dad even when the girls were tiny babies. But you seem to have taken to it like a duck to water.' Her eyes flick to the Mother's Day card from Michaela which is still lined up on the wooden mantelpiece along with those from my parents, my sister, Annabel and Tiff herself. 'It's such a shame that you had to wait so long to become what you were clearly born to be... a mother.'

Tiff's words touch me to my core. All this must be so difficult for her to deal with. I'm about to respond when there is another knock at the door.

'Annabel?' Tiff asks.

'Probably,' I reply, getting to my feet. 'Although I've been wrong twice this morning already, so there are no guarantees.'

'I hope it is,' Tiff says as I head into the hall. 'There's something I need to talk to you girls about.'

I'm wondering what that could possibly be as I undo the catch on the front door to let Annabel in.

THIRTY-SIX

Tiff

Annabel can't hide her look of surprise when she walks into the lounge of Myrtle Cottage. I heard Charlotte say that I was here and could imagine the raised eyebrows, but Annabel clearly wasn't prepared for me to be cuddling my husband's baby son.

'Tiff,' she says, recovering her composure. 'I'm not going to lie; I wasn't expecting to see you here this morning.'

I've always admired Annabel's honesty, which is why I was so relieved to discover that she hadn't known long before me about JJ being George's dad.

'I'm kind of surprised to be here,' I admit.

'You... you haven't left JJ, have you?'

'No. It wasn't an easy conversation after you and Charlotte left last night, as I'm sure you can imagine, but I accepted what he told me was true and I think our relationship is strong enough to get through this. It might even make us appreciate what we have more and not be so inclined to take each other for granted.' What I don't add is that JJ had dropped off to sleep fairly quickly while I lay in bed turning things over in my mind.

'Oh, God,' Annabel gushes. 'That is such a relief to hear. While JJ is not my favourite person at the moment, watching you two last night made me realise that you are possibly the most perfectly matched couple I know. If *you* can't work things out, what kind of a chance does anyone else have?'

Although she hasn't said it in as many words, I know Annabel is thinking of herself and Finn. She was unsure about accepting his proposal in the first place and is probably now panicking that at the first sign of a problem their relationship would falter.

'Nobody's perfect, Annabel,' I say. 'In fact, there's something I want to run by the two of you which will show you both just how imperfect I am.'

'Is it about your girls getting tested?' Charlotte asks from the doorway to the kitchen. 'Are you going to try to prevent it?'

Her face is pale and tense. I didn't notice her there, but she must have heard the final part of my sentence.

'Obviously, we do need to have that conversation,' I reply. JJ had tentatively broached the question of our girls being tested as we lay in bed together last night, but I was feeling too raw and emotional to talk about it. It was yet another reason for my insomnia.

An expression I can't quite read flits across Annabel's face before she asks, 'And you're sure you want me here? Isn't it something you and Charlotte need to discuss in private?'

'I don't want any more secrets in my life. Not between us, nor me and JJ.' I notice Charlotte flinch, but now isn't the moment to go back on the decision I reached just before dawn. 'It isn't directly about George and my girls, but it could affect all of them.'

Charlotte puts the coffee she has just made for Annabel on the walnut table next to our untouched mugs of tea. She sits down next to her, and I must confess it's a little unnerving to have both pairs of eyes scrutinising me, wondering what I'm about to say. I hug George a little closer to my chest. It's amazing how many people have become engulfed in the drama directly linked to his birth. And it's not over yet.

'Do you remember how surprised you both were when I told you JJ and I got married just six weeks after we met?'

'Shocked might be a better choice of word,' Annabel says.

Charlotte just nods, probably wondering what on earth that has to do with George and the current situation we all find ourselves in.

'I think I fell in love with JJ within hours of our first meeting,' I say, allowing myself to briefly relive the moment. 'When he introduced himself at the getting-to-know-you drinks the night before the shoot started, I felt an immediate attraction. All us models travelled as a group, arriving earlier that afternoon, but, as usual, the crew had already been there several days doing a recce. Unlike some of the girls I didn't bother with a full face of make-up, just going for a sweep of lip gloss and mascara. JJ leaned in, grinned and whispered that he preferred girls with the confidence to go *au naturel* and that was it, I was smitten. Looks and a sense of humour – a lethal combination. From that moment, we couldn't get enough of each other. Within days, we were already talking about spending the rest of our lives together. It was a wonderful avalanche of love and desire, and I was completely swept along by its power.'

I pause for a moment. Charlotte's cheeks are flushed, suggesting how uncomfortable she feels, but I need my friends to know how out of control it all felt in order for them to have a chance of understanding what I'm about to say.

'With a few hours to go until our wedding, I started worrying that everything was moving too quickly. I was on this crazy rollercoaster ride spinning faster and faster and I began to feel sick with fear that I was making a huge mistake, even though in my heart of hearts I believed JJ was my *one,* my *true love.*'

I take a breath to steady my nerves. I've never told a soul what I'm about to share with my friends.

'Because every other aspect of our wedding was so unconventional, we thought it would be funny to do something a little more traditional, so we agreed not to see each other the night before. He went out with members of the creative team, and I went on a bar crawl with the other models on the shoot. I was pretty wasted by the time we got back to the hotel, but I'm not trying to use that as an excuse.'

Charlotte drops her gaze for a moment. She said something similar the previous evening when she was telling me about Mauritius.

Annabel's eyes widen in disbelief as she says, 'Are you telling us you slept with one of the models? Blimey, you should almost be applauded for finding one that was heterosexual. I can't tell you how many times I was disappointed to discover that my handsome "boyfriend" on a shoot had no interest in me whatsoever.'

'Does JJ know?' Charlotte asks, ignoring Annabel's flippant comments.

'No,' I admit, shaking my head. 'I was disgusted with myself the next morning but convinced myself that it happened before we made our vows, so I wasn't being unfaithful. It's ridiculous really; although I hadn't said a bunch of words, my heart should already have been committed.' If I'm honest with myself it was. I knew I'd done wrong sleeping with Marco but made up the excuse about it happening before we were married to ease my guilty conscience.

'Are you thinking of telling him now?' Charlotte persists. 'Is that what you wanted to ask us, whether we think you should own up and start over with a clean slate?'

Before I can respond, Annabel says, 'I'm not so sure that's a good idea. Weren't you most hurt by the fact that JJ hadn't been honest with you straight away? You've kept this from him your entire married life.'

I move George against my chest so that I can rock him gently back and forth. 'I know, but as things have turned out, I'm left with very little choice.'

'Oh my God,' Charlotte says, understanding showing on her face. 'You mean me asking if the girls can be tested to see if they are a suitable donor match for George. Is there a possibility that JJ isn't Melody's biological father?'

'Shit,' Annabel chimes in. 'I hadn't thought of that. I just assumed you'd have used a condom.'

'I hadn't planned on having sex with anyone that night and, as I've already said, I was pretty drunk. This is probably sounding horribly familiar,' I say, addressing Charlotte. 'If you were wondering why I didn't go off the deep end last night when you told me about you and JJ in Mauritius, it's because I'd been there and done it. I was more angry with you for sleeping with a married man, but JJ explained that he hadn't been wearing his ring, so you couldn't have known he was someone else's husband.'

'He told you?' Charlotte says.

'Yes. And he pointed out that you hadn't said anything because you didn't want to damage our chances of staying together. You really were trying to minimise the impact of what happened. I should have had more faith in you,' I say, our eyes meeting in mutual understanding.

'Did he say why he wasn't wearing his ring?' Annabel asks.

'He'd taken it off to clean it and forgotten to put it back on.'

Annabel raises her eyebrows, clearly not convinced.

'It's the diamonds; I have the same problem. They're constantly getting stuff trapped in the setting,' I explain.

'I'll remember that when Finn and I get around to choosing,' Annabel scoffs.

'To get back to my question,' Charlotte interrupts. '*Is* there a chance that Melody isn't JJ's daughter?'

'A slim one,' I admit. 'She was born nine months after our wedding, so it's impossible to be a hundred per cent certain either way and I've always tried to ignore any nagging doubt.' That was one of the thoughts that kept me awake for most of the previous night. What if Melody isn't JJ's daughter? Will she insist on meeting her biological father even though he's never featured in her upbringing?

'Has Melody never had any blood tests?' Charlotte persists.

'She's O positive – we all are. It's the most common blood group so doesn't prove anything. We could have continued in blissful ignorance, but that's not an option now.' I sigh.

'I'm so sorry for the awful situation I've put you in, Tiff,' Charlotte says, dropping her head into her hands.

'I'm not going to lie, Charlotte, I don't really want either of my girls to give up one of their kidneys, even for this gorgeous little boy.' I rub my hand up and down his back and rest my cheek against his head, his downy hair tickling my skin. 'It would have an impact on their health and their ability to live life to the full. But what sort of a person would I be to deny them the right to decide? Even if it reveals that Melody isn't JJ's.'

Annabel comes over and lifts George out of my arms to hand him to his mother, before wrapping her arms around me in a very tight hug. 'This is one heck of a mess, Tiff,' she says, her voice slightly muffled as she talks into my hair. 'Maybe the truth was always going to be discovered one day. At least this way, you can tell JJ what happened before you speak to the girls about George and how he might need their help. If it turns out Melody is JJ's daughter, there's no need for her to know about something that happened before she was conceived. That's for you and JJ to come to terms with and hopefully move on from, but whatever happens I'm proud of you for the way you're handling everything.'

I'm taking strength from Annabel's firm hold and her wise words. I've felt weak and wronged, and helpless and guilty in equal measure, since Charlotte dropped her bombshell last night. Was it really only last night? It seems so much longer. I almost told JJ about the night before our wedding then, but it didn't feel like the right time. I've kept the secret for so long, I couldn't see that another twenty-four hours would make any difference. I wanted to try to gauge his reaction by telling my friends, but now there seems an urgency to tell him.

'I need to go,' I say, disentangling myself from Annabel's hug. 'The sooner all of this is out in the open, the better.' I have no idea whether my marriage will survive this new revelation, but my decision has now been made with a little help from my friends.

THIRTY-SEVEN

When I get back from Charlotte's, I go straight upstairs to our bedroom, claiming a headache. I can't face JJ fussing around me because of the guilt he's feeling when I have a guilty secret of my own. He'll also be overly jolly with the girls, knowing what we're going to have to tell them on Friday. We decided to get through the first week of the school Easter holidays to give the girls some time to relax and enjoy themselves before we have our family talk. They are likely to be shocked and upset, so they'll need time to react and ask all the questions they want to before the school summer term starts just after Easter.

I must have eventually managed to drop off to sleep, despite the turmoil in my head, because I'm awoken much later by the girls saying goodnight to their dad. A few minutes after that, I hear his tread on the stairs. He comes into our room and straight over to my side, where he switches the lamp on before perching on the edge of the bed and reaching for my hand.

'This is going to be harder for you than you imagined,' he says, his voice loaded with remorse. 'It's a massive thing to expect you to accept, Tiff, and if you'd rather I move out for a couple of days while you get your head around it, I completely understand. I can fake a last-minute job and stay over at my studio so that the girls are kept out of it until we're ready to tell them. It doesn't have to be Friday, you know. If you need more time, just say.'

His consideration for me and our girls is oozing from every pore. It makes what happened with Charlotte seem even more out of character. I wonder if he will still be as compassionate after what I am about to say. But I must tell him. This final secret needs to be out in the open, whatever the consequences might be.

'I stand by everything I said last night about trying to move forward,' I begin. 'But to move forward there can be no more secrets between us.'

'I've told you everything,' he says. 'I swear I have.'

'I wasn't talking about you.'

I've manoeuvred myself into an upright position so that I can look him in the eyes when I tell him the awful truth. His expression is one of bewilderment.

'Something happened very early on in our relationship. Something I'm not proud of and should have told you about at the time,' I say, battling the dryness in my mouth.

'It doesn't matter.' He touches my lips with his fingers in an effort to stop me speaking. 'That's the past and we need to concentrate on our future.'

I gently remove his hand, intertwining my fingers with his in the process. 'What if I told you that it might impact our future?'

'I don't see how it possibly could. It's all water under the bridge, and whatever it is isn't important anymore.' He sounds edgy, as though he really doesn't want to hear what I have to say, but I have no choice.

'Just listen to me, JJ,' I implore him.

He gives a slight shrug and I take it as the green light.

'Marrying you six weeks after we met seemed to be the most natural thing in the world. We were so in love. It was as though destiny had thrown us together. But the night before our wedding, I suddenly got cold feet. I'd been so certain that we were doing the right thing and then a niggling doubt forced its way into my head,' I say, holding his gaze and trying to remain calm. 'With the benefit of hindsight, it was probably the pre-wedding nerves that every bride and groom experience, but most don't do what I did.'

He's looking at me with such intensity, it's as though he can see into my soul. 'I don't want you to tell me what you did, Tiff, really I don't. Once I know, I'll know for the rest of my life and that might be too big a burden to carry. I'm not as strong as you. Let's just leave it that something happened, I don't need the specifics,' he beseeches.

'You eventually told me about you and Charlotte,' I say.

'But only because I was forced to. If it hadn't been for George, I would have done everything in my power to protect you from the damage. I'll carry the guilt of hurting you to my grave and it's much heavier than having a guilty secret. Trust me, and keep whatever it is to yourself.'

How I wish I could, but it isn't possible, and it isn't fair. I take a breath.

'I had sex with Marco the night before our wedding,' I blurt out.

JJ doesn't speak immediately, allowing the words to settle. His face is impassive, so I have no idea what he is thinking.

'Do you feel better for telling me?' he eventually asks.

I ignore his question and say, 'That's not the worst of it. I don't know, in fact have never known for sure, if you or Marco is Melody's father.'

He jolts backwards as though struck by a lightning bolt, releasing my hand as he does so.

'You see now why I had to tell you,' I whisper. 'If Melody

wants to be tested to see if she's a match for George, it might reveal that she's no blood relation to him at all.'

JJ is nodding his head slowly, weighing up what he's going to say next.

When he speaks, his voice is heavy with emotion. 'So, I've gained a child that I didn't want but have now accepted and, as a consequence, I might be about to lose my precious girl? I know I deserve to be punished for what I did, but this?'

'You won't lose Melody, JJ, she loves you. You're the person who picked her up and cuddled her after a fall and played snap with her tirelessly until she won. It was you who stood freezing on the touchline throughout her lacrosse games and shouted out in jubilation when she won her first dance medal. Whatever her DNA might say, you'll always be her dad.'

'That will be for her to decide,' he says, getting up heavily from the bed and walking over to the window as though he has lead weights in his shoes. He stands looking out onto our garden, probably remembering games of cricket and leapfrog accompanied by shrieks of laughter. His shoulders are moving up and down. I know he's crying, but I feel powerless to help. 'What if she feels compelled to trace her biological father? Where would that leave me, Tiff?'

I'm out of bed and across the room in an instant, turning him to face me and enveloping him in my arms. Although this has come to a head because of baby George's illness, it has always been a ticking timebomb. 'We'll cross that bridge if we get to it,' I say, pushing him to arm's length so that I can look into his eyes. 'For now, there's no reason to put unnecessary doubt in Melody's mind about who her father is. They're both going to have enough to deal with when we tell them about George.'

'Do you think you made the right decision?' JJ asks, twisting my hair around his fingers as he has done hundreds of times before.

'I don't know,' I reply, leaning my head against his chest. 'Part of me has always wanted to tell you, but I tried to convince myself that what you didn't know couldn't hurt you, and the last thing I ever wanted to do was to hurt you. But now I've seen first-hand how secrets and lies can threaten the happiness of those we hold closest to our hearts. Yes, the truth hurts, but how much worse would any of these secrets have been if they'd been uncovered rather than told. In a weird way, we should thank Charlotte for making us face our mistakes and start afresh with the slate wiped clean, whatever the consequences.'

I'm hoping us both admitting that we've made mistakes will make our relationship unbreakable. But at the moment there is a fragility there has never been before, and things are set to become increasingly difficult when we have to sit down with our girls and explain about George.

'That's not what I meant,' JJ says. 'I meant do you think you made the right decision in marrying me?'

'Do you really need to ask?' I tilt my head to look up at the man I've loved from the moment I saw him. 'You are my soulmate. The man I didn't know I was looking for until I found you.'

He smiles before his lips close on mine with the tenderest of kisses.

THIRTY-EIGHT
MONDAY 8 APRIL

Charlotte

It felt good arriving at Stems this morning at half past seven and punching in the code to the key box in order to open the shop. It's the first time since George's birth that I've done it, so it was a bit of an experiment to see whether it is going to be manageable on a regular basis.

There was a lot to get organised before we left Myrtle Cottage for the twenty-minute walk into Maidenhead: his buggy laden with bottles and nappies and all the other paraphernalia required for a few hours in the life of a ten-week-old baby.

George has been as well-behaved as usual, which was more than I dared hope as he's been stuck in his buggy for most of the morning while I dealt with customer's orders and started making up arrangements for delivery and collection later. At 11 a.m., I flipped the sign on the door to closed and stuck a hand-written note on the outside saying BACK IN FIFTEEN MINUTES, while I fed George and changed his nappy in the room at the back of the shop. I kept him on my hip for a while afterwards when I was serving customers who'd selected ready-made bunches of flowers. It was easy enough to drop them into plastic bags and operate the till one-handed, but now he's back in his buggy as I've some more orders to complete before Michaela is due in at 2 p.m. George is happily kicking out at the row of brightly coloured plastic animals strung across the front of his buggy, slightly out of reach of his chubby, grasping hands when the bell above the door tinkles.

'You're early,' I say, smiling at my boss.

'I wondered if you might need an extra pair of hands on your first solo morning, but it seems you've got everything firmly under control.' Michaela indicates the dozen or so arrangements I've already completed standing in the row of metal buckets behind the counter. 'How has George been?' she asks, dropping to her haunches and tickling his feet.

His giggles fill the shop.

'He's been a little angel,' I say, my voice filled with pride. 'I'm very lucky to have such a well-behaved baby.'

'There's an element of luck, for sure, but you should also give yourself credit because he's clearly very contented. Babies and young children are far more sensitive to their surroundings than some people realise. We had lots of tears and tantrums from the kids whenever my ex and I were arguing, which towards the end of our marriage was almost daily.'

Michaela mentioning her ex reminds me of the text I sent her yesterday about the letter from Zack. With all the drama surrounding Tiff and her revelations, it had completely slipped my mind.

'Did you get my message yesterday?' I ask, finishing the arrangement I've been working on and standing it in a free bucket.

'I don't think so.' Michaela reaches into her crossbody bag for her phone. 'Oh, shit. I'm sorry, Charlotte. I had it on silent when we were at church and must have forgotten to switch the sound back on.' Her eyes scan my message. 'To answer your question about a letter, there was one that arrived for you. I remember it as I thought it might be a new baby card from one of our regulars, so I popped it through your letterbox at home. I hope that was the right thing to do?'

I don't want to draw attention to the fact that I haven't received it, so I just say, 'Oh, the card? I got confused when Mum said it was a letter. Shall I put the kettle on?'

The rest of the afternoon dragged a bit. Monday is always the quietest day of the week in Stems, which is why I used to work it on my own to give Michaela a day off. We agreed that I would stay until 4 p.m. so I could get home in time for George's normal routine of playmat, bath, feed and bed at 7 p.m.

It's only after I've settled him in his cot that I go in search of the missing letter. When I arrived home from the hospital, there was a pile of post behind the door as I'd been away for a couple of weeks. I picked everything up and put it on the Victorian hallstand to deal with later. There was no letter from Zack amongst it, but I'm now wondering if it had somehow slipped down the back of the hallstand. Using the torch on my phone, I shine light behind it and can see some papers. Trying not to think about the spiders that might be lurking there too, I reach my hand in and retrieve them. There are a couple of flyers from the local pizza place, a communication from the Conservative candidate in a local election that pre-dated me moving into Myrtle Cottage, and a square white envelope addressed to Stems in Zack's handwriting. My breath catches in my throat in a gasp. This must be the card Michaela referred to earlier. My mother was right after all; Zack did write to me.

I carry the items through to the kitchen, where I put the junk mail in the recycling bin and prop Zack's letter up against the vase of perfumed narcissus on the table, the aroma vying for prominence with the jacket potato that has been baking while I attended to George. I was intending to have it for my dinner, but I've now lost my appetite. I turn the oven off, pour myself a glass of tonic water and sit down in front of the slightly dusty white envelope. I take a sip of the tonic, which would have been greatly improved by a double measure of gin, and reach for Zack's letter.

I say letter, but Michaela was right; it's actually a card – though not a new baby card. The picture on the front brings a lump to my throat. It's an unassuming blue ceramic vase containing daffodils. They were the flowers Zack bought for me on our first Valentine's Day together. We'd only known each other two weeks and he thought red roses would have been too full on. It was early in the season for daffodils, so they were still in bud when he handed them over, but when they bloomed a couple of days later, they were a double trumpet variety and had the most beautiful smell. It was always daffodils for me on Valentine's Day thereafter.

I open up the card which has no message, just the words I WILL ALWAYS LOVE YOU in Zack's writing. A folded square of writing paper falls onto the surface of the table. It takes me a few minutes before I can unfold it with shaking hands.

Charlotte,

I don't really know how to start or what to say, except that I am so so sorry for everything.

I came to Stems to beg your forgiveness for treating you so thoughtlessly and to plead with you to come home, but you seemed to have moved on, so there didn't seem to be much point. Here I am, a year after you left, still lost without my soulmate and unable to move forward with my life. I will never get past my feelings for you and the enormous wrong I did you by not being honest from the start.

I can't lie and say that I didn't know how much you longed to be a mother, but please believe me when I say I had no idea how all-consuming your yearning was. The hurt you must have suffered each month as a direct result of me not being honest with you is almost unimaginable and something I will never forgive myself for inflicting.

You deserved – and still deserve – better than me, but if there is a tiny corner of your heart that misses me even a hundredth as much as I miss you, I would be willing to do anything to have you back in my life. And yes, I truly mean anything. You deserve to be happy, Charlotte, and I can only pray that you will consider trying to regain the happiness we once shared.

I won't contact you again if I don't hear from you, because I wouldn't want to jeopardise the new life you may have forged for yourself, but I just wanted you to know that you were the best thing that ever happened to me, and you are completely irreplaceable.

With all my heart forever,

Zack x

I read the words over and over with eyes that are trying to blink away tears but failing miserably. I'm not even sure why I'm crying. This is a declaration of undying love. It should make me happy, but instead it makes me realise what I had and chose to give up instead of staying and trying to work things through. If I had, would I have been able to make Zack understand how integral to my happiness becoming a mother was? Maybe I only assumed that he realised the utter devastation I felt each month when my period came. Did I ever let him truly see the depths of my feelings or did I hide them away because I thought it was my fault that I couldn't become pregnant? If I'd told him how desperately I wanted to become a mother, how I needed it to feel complete, would he have told me about his vasectomy sooner and could we have tried to find a solution?

There's no doubt in my mind that Zack should have told me the truth. Withholding something so important was selfish, not to mention dishonest. But I'm now questioning whether he was the only one who wasn't completely honest. I certainly wasn't when he visited me in Stems. I made him believe that I didn't love him anymore and had moved on. Perhaps that was because I'd been trying so hard to convince myself when I knew I still had feelings for him.

I glance down at the start of the final paragraph again.

I won't contact you again if I don't hear back from you...

I release the letter from my grasp and rest my head in my hands. It's been over two months since he sent this letter. Whatever excuse I give for not replying sooner is going to sound fake. And besides, fate intervened in the most dramatic of ways; I am now a mother. I have what I always wanted, and Zack did not. A child.

I thought I'd managed to suppress all my feelings for Zack but the pang I feel in my chest would suggest otherwise. No matter. It's too late for us; we're not meant to be together.

THIRTY-NINE

FRIDAY 12 APRIL

Tiff

I think Melody and Tamsin sensed something was not quite right when I picked them up from dance class earlier and suggested takeaway pizza for tonight's dinner. JJ and I have always tried to steer them in the direction of a healthy lifestyle with plenty of sporting activities and a balanced diet, so pizza, or in fact any type of takeaway, is a rare treat normally reserved for special occasions.

Although we all dived in with gusto after the delivery driver arrived, there is still enough food on our dining-room table to feed another family of four. This is in part due to me over-compensating for what is about to happen by ordering a whole pizza each when we normally share three between the four of us, but also because both JJ and I have been picking at our food.

'I think you may have over-ordered, Mum,' Melody says, leaning back in her chair with her hands on her stomach. 'I'm as stuffed as that pizza crust.'

'Me too,' Tamsin agrees. 'There's no way I can tackle the

Ben and Jerry's for dessert. What are we celebrating anyway? You don't normally let us pig out like this.'

JJ stops fiddling with the stringy melted mozzarella and takes a deep breath.

'Your mum and I need to talk to you about something,' he says, clearly making an effort to keep his voice calm despite the adrenalin that must be coursing through his veins in anticipation of what he is about to reveal.

Although we've tried all week to keep things between the two of us as normal as possible, the atmosphere in the house has at times been strained. I've caught JJ with a faraway expression on his face a couple of times. When I've asked if he's okay, he's merely shrugged. And I've been distracted by what might happen if Melody does turn out to be Marco's child. Despite my assurances to JJ, the only person who knows how she'll react is Melody herself. I can't bear the thought that she may turn her back on JJ, or possibly me for sleeping with Marco in the first place.

'You're not getting a divorce, are you?' Tamsin laughs. When neither of us speaks, she exchanges a worried look with her sister and says, 'You're not, are you? That was meant to be a joke.'

'No, Tammy, your dad and I are not getting divorced, but we have had a little blip in our marriage.' Despite sticking to the script in terms of how we wanted to approach this with the girls, I feel myself flinch at saying the words out loud.

'What's going on, Mum?' Melody asks.

I turn to JJ; this needs to come from him.

'I've let your mum down,' he says. 'In fact, I've let us all down, myself included. I... I had a liaison when I was away on one of my work trips.'

The girls are blinking as though trapped in the bright headlights of a car. Neither of them knows how to react. Why would they? This is not the sort of thing they could ever have imagined hearing from the father they adore and who adores them in return.

The oversized clock on the wall ticks on ponderously, its sound loud and echoey in our otherwise silent dining room.

'I have no excuse,' JJ continues. 'I love your mum more than anything in the world, but I drank more than I should and that affected my judgement.'

Everything JJ is saying is measured and without blame, just as we agreed it should be. When the girls find out that the liaison was with Charlotte, we need them to be able to accept that adults make mistakes too if there is to be any kind of relationship between them and their half-brother.

'Why are you telling us this, Dad?' Melody asks, sounding pained and confused. 'Isn't this something for you and Mum to sort out between the two of you? I don't understand why you think we need to know.'

'You're right, Mel,' JJ responds. 'If circumstances were different, we wouldn't burden the two of you with this, but... there was a consequence to my actions. The woman became pregnant and has now had our baby.'

Tamsin gasps.

'For fuck's sake, Dad,' Melody shouts. 'Have you never heard of condoms?'

For some reason, quite possibly hysteria, I find it extremely funny hearing our daughter saying this to her dad. I'm struggling to suppress a bubble of laughter one minute, but the next I'm fighting back tears at the absurdity of the situation.

'Language, Melody,' JJ says, throwing me a look, demanding support I can't offer as I'm still hovering between laughing and crying. 'But you make a very valid point about condoms and I'm sure your mum has stressed the importance of using them, and not only to protect against an unwanted pregnancy.'

'Ugh, gross,' Melody says.

'The fact is,' JJ continues, 'I didn't use one because I'm

married to your mum, and we don't need to use them anymore, so I didn't have any. Not only was what I did reprehensible, it was also irresponsible and I'm going to have to work very hard to regain your mum's trust.'

Tamsin has slid out of the blue velvet chair and come around to my side of the table. She puts her arms around me and nuzzles into my neck. I hold her tightly for a moment and then push her away to make eye contact with her when I speak.

'I know this must be very upsetting for you and Mel, as it is for me too, but I believe your dad when he says it was a one-off mistake which he wholeheartedly regrets.'

Melody makes a 'pah' sound and rolls her eyes.

'Of course, we'd all rather it hadn't happened,' I continue, 'but it has, and now there is another little person to consider, who is a complete innocent in all this.'

'How can you be so calm about it, Mum?' Melody demands. 'Dad cheated on you! It's not okay however he tries to paint it.'

'Nobody is trying to suggest it's okay, Mel,' I counter. 'The fact is, we can't change what has happened however much we might want to.'

'But how do you know he hasn't done it before?' she continues in a raised and angry voice. 'And how do you know he won't do it again?' She bangs her hand on the table and glares at JJ, her eyes blazing.

'Because he told me it won't and I believe him,' I say simply.

'Well, more fool you then,' Melody says, chair legs scraping against the tiled floor as she gets to her feet. 'I'm going to my room. I can't bear to be in the same room as a cheat and a gullible fool.'

'Mel, come back,' I say, but my plea falls on deaf ears. I suppose her reaction was only to be expected, and a normal way for a teenager to react, but I harboured a hope that it wouldn't be quite as bad.

'I'll go, Mum,' Tamsin says, following her sister out of the room.

'Well, that went well,' JJ says, dropping his head into his hands.

'It wasn't unexpected. You can't throw a stone into a pond and there not be ripples.' An image of JJ teaching our girls how to skim pebbles on Worthing beach fills my mind. Whatever else, he's always been an amazing dad. 'I'll give her a few minutes to calm down and then I'll go and fetch her back,' I say, wondering how on earth she will react when she finds out who her dad's indiscretion was with.

'Mel,' I say, tapping on her bedroom door. 'Can I come in?'

Thirty minutes have passed since she stormed out of the dining room and if I know my daughter as well as I think I do, the anger will have given way to tears.

When there is no reply, I press down on the door handle and open the door. The room is in darkness, but I can just make out the outline of Mel's body under the duvet on her bed.

'Go away,' she mumbles.

I can tell from her voice that, as expected, she's been crying. I've always struggled when the girls have been upset, wanting to ease their pain by loading it on my shoulders, and it saddens me to think that there is more to inflict on them.

'You know I'm not going to do that,' I say, crossing the room and sitting on the edge of her bed.

'How could he do that to you, Mum?' she asks, still talking into the pillow she is hugging. The anger is gone, replaced by sadness and bewilderment.

'I've asked myself that question over and over, Mel, but the only person who truly knows the answer is your dad. I'm not going to try to tell you that you must forgive him, because that has to come from your heart. But what I will say is that he's made a mistake, a huge one, but he never meant for any of us to get caught up in it.'

She rolls over onto her back and I can see the glisten of tears on her cheeks as they catch the light from the landing. 'Is he going to leave us and go to live with his new family?'

Melody is so grown up in so many ways, it's easy to forget that at fifteen she's still a child.

'If that's what you are most afraid of then you can stop worrying, Mel. That's not going to happen.'

'How do you know? He might be having a mid-life crisis that he thinks a younger woman and a new baby will solve.'

'You need to come back downstairs, sweetheart. As shocked as you are by your dad's confession, I'm afraid there's more to it and we might as well get it all out there so we can start to deal with it.'

Melody pushes her duvet back as though it's filled with bricks rather than feathers and sits up. I wrap my arms around her and hold her in a tight hug for a few moments before we both make our way back downstairs and into the lounge, where Tamsin and her dad are sitting next to each other on one of the sofas. I'm not sure why Tamsin seems to be handling this awful situation better than her older sister, but she is. I suppose I should be grateful for the small mercy that I'm not having to deal with two traumatised children... at least not yet. Who knows how Tamsin will react when the truth about George comes out.

'Mel, I'm so sorry...' JJ starts to say, but Melody interrupts.

'Mum says there's more,' she says, cutting him dead.

JJ catches my eye and I nod. There is no point in holding anything back.

'Yes, well, the reason you girls had to know about all this is because the baby is sick and there is a chance that one of you might be able to help.'

'Sick in what way, Dad?' Tamsin asks.

'His kidneys aren't working properly,' JJ answers. 'He's doing well at the moment, but at some point in the future, they might... well, to be honest, they will stop working altogether, so he's going to need medical intervention.' As he finishes speaking, JJ's face is pale and strained.

Since learning about George's medical condition, I've tried to put myself in Charlotte's position. Being a single parent of a healthy child must be daunting but coping with one with such a major medical issue is almost impossible to comprehend. No wonder Charlotte is grasping at every available straw. I would do exactly the same for my girls if the situation was reversed.

The girls exchange an anxious look, and both turn to me for reassurance.

'What your dad is trying to say is that if a suitable donor can't be found, then George will be on dialysis from the moment his kidneys fail.'

It's a millisecond before I realise what I've said. I now have three pairs of eyes staring at me, two in total shock and the other in horror. Melody is the first to react.

'George, as in Auntie Charlotte's baby?'

I can feel the heat rising in my cheeks. Unintentionally, I've pulled the pin and lobbed a grenade into an already explosive situation.

FORTY

SATURDAY 13 APRIL

Charlotte

I'm pulling the bedroom door closed when I feel my mobile phone start to vibrate in my pocket. I always turn the sound off when I'm trying to settle George down for the night as invariably someone calls just as his eyelids are drooping and it then takes another fifteen minutes or so to lull him back to sleep.

Much as I love spending time with my baby son, being a lone parent is both challenging and exhausting at times, so the few hours I get in the evening help to recharge my batteries. I always start off with good intentions. Once I've had my dinner and loaded the dishwasher, I mean to read a few chapters of my latest book or watch TV, but nine times out of ten, I doze off a few minutes after I've sat down on the sofa because I'm so shattered. When I wake up an hour or so later, it's an immense effort to drag myself up to bed. At least I'll be staying awake tonight as Annabel and Tiff are coming round to talk over what happened the previous evening when she and JJ told their girls that George is their half-brother. Understandably, Tiff sounded tense earlier when she called to suggest meeting up and as I reach into my pocket for my phone, I'm wondering if it's her ringing to cancel. A glance at the phone screen tells me it's not.

When I reach the bottom of the stairs, I click the green phone icon, although I don't actually speak until I'm safely in the kitchen with the door closed so that my voice won't disturb George.

'Hi, Mum,' I say, holding the phone to my ear with my left hand while opening the oven door with my right and sliding the glass dish containing the hastily cobbled together pasta bake into the oven. 'I was just putting George to bed, I couldn't speak until I was out of earshot.'

'I'm so looking forward to seeing him tomorrow,' she says. 'That's why I'm ringing. You are still coming for lunch, aren't you?'

I haven't been down to see my parents in Poole since Christmas, when I was so pregnant I found myself empathising with the overstuffed turkey. Mum's been up to Bray a couple of times, but my dad hasn't met George yet. I had the annual invitation to the Mother's Day lunch last Sunday, but I suggested tomorrow as an alternative.

'Yes, of course. Annabel's lending me her car because she doesn't trust my old Mini to make it all the way there and back. In fact, I can't stay on long because she and Tiff are bringing it over tonight, staying for supper, and then Tiff is dropping Annabel back home.'

'It's nice that you're all still such good friends,' she says.

Mum's comment merely serves to highlight that the dynamic in our friendship has changed irrevocably. Despite our heart-to-heart last Sunday, things can never be the same as they were between Tiff and me which makes me sad. Given time, and with lots of encouragement from Annabel, I hope we'll remain friends.

'Are they both married now or is it still just Tiffany?'

To an outsider, Mum's comment might seem innocent enough, but I know exactly where she is heading with all this.

'Just Tiff at the moment,' I reply, keeping my voice conversational. 'It probably won't be too long before Annabel and Finn tie the knot though. It doesn't seem two minutes since they got engaged, but it's actually over a year.'

'Time always flies when you're busy. Are you still managing to juggle work and parenting?'

'Oh, you know, I'm coping,' I say.

I know what's coming next. Mum's attitude towards me has softened since George was born, but she still disapproves of me having a baby without being in a stable relationship, as does my dad. The lunch tomorrow is a massive step towards him accepting his grandson and it wouldn't be happening but for my mum's persistence. Dad has been untypically slow at following Mum's lead where his new grandson is concerned, but I'm hoping that will change once he's met him.

'It would have been so much easier if you had someone to share the load,' she continues.

By someone, my mother means Zack. Even though she was obviously very upset with him, she clearly still has a soft spot for him. I need to get her off the phone before she mentions his name and I get tetchy with her.

'I didn't actually plan it that way, as you know, but now I can't imagine my life without George. I can honestly say that motherhood is the best thing that's ever happened to me. And you've got to admit, George is one cute little boy.' By steering the conversation back to her grandson, there's a chance of our phone call ending on a positive note. 'He's started on little bits of solid food now, so you can have the pleasure of giving him his mashed banana tomorrow if you like?'

'That brings back memories,' Mum says. 'Roxanne was a fan, but you never liked it. I used to end up wearing more than you swallowed if I recall.'

I don't think she'll ever realise how much she favours my sister over me. At least with George being an only child, it's something he'll never experience.

'Don't worry, George can't get enough of it.' Before she can respond, I continue, 'Look, Mum, I'm going to have to go. Annabel and Tiff will be here any minute and I don't want them ringing the bell and disturbing George. I should be at yours about midday if there's not too much traffic.'

I just hear her say, 'We'll see you both tomorrow then,' before I end the call. And it's in the nick of time. As I walk down the hall to leave my front door ajar for my friends, I see their shadowy outlines approaching.

The pasta bake was average, and that's being kind. I usually make a tomato sauce from scratch but was pushed for time so had to resort to a bottle of sauce. I'd normally feel embarrassed by the amount of food left on everyone's plate, mine included, but that's not the main purpose of tonight and we all know it. At least the shop-bought tiramisu is going down well.

We've been skirting around the reason that Tiff asked for the get-together with small talk, but the subject needs to be broached. Eventually, Annabel picks up the reins.

'So,' she says, 'how did the girls take the news?'

I still have some dessert left in my bowl so I'm able to focus on that rather than making eye contact with Tiff.

'They took the news about their half-brother better than finding out their dad had cheated on their mum,' Tiff says. Her tone is direct rather than accusatory. 'Melody was really upset and angry with JJ and marched off to her room. She's at an age where she's noticing boys and thinking about relationships. The idea that her dad, who has always been the perfect man in her eyes, isn't quite as perfect as she thought really floored her.

Weirdly, it was almost less of a shock to learn that they were related to George.'

'They must hate me,' I say, looking across the table to Tiff, who has been unbelievably calm all evening. 'And I don't blame them.'

'Well, I'm not going to lie. You're not their favourite person at the moment, but JJ and I made it very clear that you had no idea who he was when the two of you... you know.'

I can feel myself colouring up. I do know, and I'm mortified at the memory whenever I'm in Tiff's presence. I'm amazed and relieved by the way she seems to have taken it all in her stride.

'He was insistent that you shouldn't be blamed in any way and tried to focus their attention on the fact that they have a baby brother who isn't very well.'

This time last week, Annabel and I were at Tiff and JJ's and their girls were playing with George, totally oblivious to the fact that he was their brother. They're bound to behave differently towards him from now on, but in what way? I wonder whether their sibling bond will make them closer, or if they'll reject him for the strain he's unwittingly caused in their parents' marriage. And if they do, what will that mean for George's future?

'They've both learnt about the human body in biology so understood the function of the kidneys without us having to go into detail,' Tiff continues.

I'm gripping the table to stop my hands shaking. What Tiff says next could have huge ramifications for both George and me.

'They both said they want to be tested.'

For a second, I have the urge to scream and shout and shower Tiff with thanks, but of course I don't because none of that is appropriate. My joy is tempered by knowing how concerned Tiff must be feeling for her girls. If one of them did prove to be the perfect match there would be a huge decision to make once they knew all the facts and potential side effects. If they then didn't feel able to go ahead with the transplant, the impact that might have on their mental health if something happened to George doesn't bear thinking about. Not for the first time the guilt I feel for disrupting so many lives is weighing heavy on my shoulders, but I didn't have much choice.

'You must be very proud of them,' Annabel says, reaching across the table to squeeze Tiff's hand.

'Proud, but at the same time terrified. I've done some online research and it's a long process of tests and preparation before the surgery can go ahead as you will already know, Charlotte,' she says. She must be waiting for my reaction to the news that her girls are willing to be tested, but I don't know how to communicate the gratitude I'm feeling, so I stay quiet while she continues, 'And, of course, there are no guarantees that George's body would accept the donor kidney. Melody or Tamsin could go through all that trauma, putting themselves at risk, and it could all be for nothing.'

'But what an amazing attitude they have that they are both willing to try,' Annabel says. I'm so grateful that she has put into words what I'm struggling to express. 'You and JJ are responsible for that. You've brought them up to be considerate towards others.'

'I can only hope to be half the mother you are to your girls,' I finally manage to say in recognition of the huge sacrifice I've forced Tiff to make. Her happy settled life has been put in jeopardy because of me. As a mother myself, I now understand the overwhelming desire to put your own child's needs first, and yet I'm expecting her to give priority to her husband's son and, in the process, possibly discover that JJ isn't Melody's biological father. There are so many 'if onlys' running through my head right now. If only I hadn't gone to Mauritius with Annabel; if only she hadn't got sick on the last night of our holiday; if only I hadn't slept with a handsome stranger; if only I hadn't been so desperate for a child that I decided to keep the baby that resulted. I've never thought of myself as a selfish person, but that's exactly what I am, and my selfishness is having far-reaching consequences that I could never have imagined.

I'm so lost in these thoughts that the touch on my hand startles me.

'I'm not blaming you, Charlotte,' Tiff says, squeezing my hand. 'I would have done exactly the same if I'd been in your shoes.'

'Me too,' Annabel agrees, reaching for my other hand. 'We're in this together.'

In that moment, I feel so loved and so grateful to have these two women in my life.

It's only later while I'm thinking of all the things I need to prepare for the trip to Poole tomorrow that the enormity of facing the future alone settles back on my shoulders. It's a weight so heavy that I'm forced to sit down. Unquestionably, I have two of the best friends a person could wish for, but it doesn't stop the overwhelming feelings of loneliness when they're not around. I don't want this to be my life forever. I miss having someone to talk to and cuddle up with on the sofa. I miss lazing in bed on a Sunday morning after making love and going for long walks followed by a pub lunch. The truth is, I miss Zack.

For the hundredth time since finding his letter on Monday evening, I reach for my kitchen notepad and a pen, only this time, instead of staring at the sheet of blank paper not knowing what to say, I start to write.

FORTY-ONE

THURSDAY 18 APRIL

To say I feel nervous is a huge understatement. I chose this spot for our meeting this morning because it's where I usually sit to watch nature. It's where the cares of the day and my complicated life disappear for a short while before I must return to reality. The sound of birdsong is as melodic as ever and that, plus the gentle lapping of the lake against the shore, is normally guaranteed to calm any doubts or anxieties I might be feeling, but not today.

From the moment I received Zack's text message yesterday, just one short sentence saying, *We need to talk,* I've been wondering if I did the right thing in writing to him and telling him all about my life since we split up. I laid my feelings out on the pages of paper, six by the time I'd finished scribbling, telling him all about Mauritius and falling pregnant and George's subsequent diagnosis. It was incredibly cathartic unburdening my soul in that way, but when I'd finished, I had serious doubts about whether I should send the letter to Zack or not. Without reading back what I had written, I folded the sheets of paper and squeezed them into an envelope before propping the letter up on the coat stand in the hall.

Throughout Sunday, the white of the envelope against the dark wood of the hallstand taunted me each time I walked past it, forcing me to ask myself the same question over and over. Is it really Zack that I want back in my life or am I reaching out to him because I have no one else, and I don't want to spend the rest of my life alone? I still wasn't completely sure about my answer to that question when I slipped the letter into the postbox on Monday morning on my walk into Stems, but having seen Tiff and JJ be so forgiving towards each other certainly made me re-examine my feelings towards Zack.

'Hello, Charlotte.'

Just the sound of his voice after so much time apart turns my insides to jelly. I feel exactly as I did on our first date all those years ago, a mixture of nerves and excitement. I decide against getting up as I don't trust my legs not to buckle at the knees. I can't even look at him, so instead I pat the space on the bench next to me.

'So, you found it okay?' I say, stating the obvious in my nervousness. 'I was worried you might be lost when it got to quarter past eleven and you still weren't here. You're never late.' My biggest fear wasn't that Zack was lost; I was afraid that he might have changed his mind about coming.

He sits down next to me, leaving a space so that our legs are not touching but close enough for me to smell his Paul Smith cologne. I first bought it for him for Christmas in 2012 and it pleases me to think that he's chosen to wear it today, knowing it's one of my favourites.

I'm still not ready to turn and look at him because I'm afraid that if I do, I won't be able to think clearly and say what I want to say.

'I wasn't late. I was actually here before you, but I wanted to watch you for a while,' he says, sounding as nervous as I feel. 'I wanted to be sure that I still feel the same way about you after all this time.'

'And?' I ask, finally turning to look at him. The past fifteen months seem to melt away. It's as though Zack and I have come out for a walk to a local beauty spot and are enjoying the peace, the quiet and the view before returning home together. I give my head a shake, attempting to clear the thought from my mind. We are no longer a couple. Everything is different.

'And, like I said in my letter, you are the best thing that ever happened to me. Nobody could ever replace you in my heart and I wouldn't want them to.'

The small hope I've been harbouring that Zack and I might have a future together is starting to grow. But, right on cue, George cries out as though to remind me that the very thing that forced us apart in the first place, my yearning to be a mother, is still a major obstacle in any plan to reconcile. I'm not prepared to give up on the idea that easily though. Reaching down, I release the buckle of George's harness and lift him up onto my knee.

'This is my son,' I say to Zack.

Zack reaches for George's chubby little fist and pumps it up and down lightly. 'Pleased to meet you, George. You look exactly like your mummy.'

George gives one of his cutest chuckles and kicks his feet enthusiastically.

'I think he likes you,' I say, resisting the urge to ask Zack if he'd like to hold my baby. After all, it was his reluctance to father another child that has brought us to the situation we are currently in. It was difficult telling him about George in my letter, but I wanted to be honest. Much as it would have hurt if he'd decided against meeting up because I have an eleven-week-old baby, it would have been even more heartbreaking for me to experience the feelings I currently am only for him to walk out of my life on finding out that I am a mother.

'But he clearly adores you, as do I,' Zack says. 'Look, Charlotte, there's no point in beating around the bush. I made the biggest mistake of my life not being honest with you about my vasectomy and my reasons for having it. I was so wounded when Paula took my boys back to live in Australia, I vowed that I would never risk being put in that position again. I can see now that it might appear selfish on my part, but it was self-preservation. Paula and I were too young when we tied the knot and had our boys much too early in our marriage. We barely knew each other before there were two other people to take into consideration. We never stood a chance, really, so we had to decide what was best for them. My lifestyle at the time – gigging away from home a lot, sleeping during the day because of finishing in the early hours of the morning when I was home – wouldn't have worked. Paula only settled in England to be with me, so I could hardly argue when she said she wanted to return home.' He's been staring down at his hands but now glances up at me. 'It took me a while to find love again, but I did when I met you and it was proper grown-up love, not infatuation leading to rash decisions. But I was scared. I thought if you knew about my vasectomy you wouldn't give our love a proper chance; I couldn't risk it,' he says, his shoulders slumping forward. 'I couldn't bear the thought of you not being in my life.'

I hear what he's saying and understand it to a degree, but there is a little voice nagging at the back of my mind.

'I've had a lot of time to think over the past fifteen months, Zack,' I say. 'At first, I was so totally devastated that you'd kept such a huge secret from me that I didn't realise which aspect of your deception hurt me the most. I kept thinking that if you'd told me, we could have talked about other ways to become parents if you didn't want to or couldn't have a reversal. There are sperm donor banks, we could even have looked into adoption if I'd known that it was never going to happen naturally. And then I realised what had upset me the most. You told me you didn't want to have children with me because you couldn't bear the thought of losing them like you lost your first two.'

'I know it seems selfish, Charlotte. When I arrived home from school and you were gone, I broke down and cried, knowing that letting you slip through my fingers was the worst mistake I've ever made. Of course, I was aware that you longed to have a baby, but I didn't realise how incomplete you felt as a person. Now, watching you with George, I can see you were always destined to be a mother and my selfishness stopped that from happening while we were together. I'm so sorry, truly I am, but I'm here now and I'll do anything to try to undo the wrongs of the past if you'll let me be a part of yours and George's life.'

Zack is saying all the things I wanted to hear him say when I lay awake for hours last night trying to imagine a best-case scenario of our meeting this morning. He says he wants to be with me, and he would like to be present in George's life. I reach across the small gap between us on the bench and take hold of his hand. 'Thank you for accepting that what you did was wrong,' I say, the touch of his skin sending shivers through me, which I need to ignore if I'm to remain focused. 'It means a lot to hear you say it, but...' I take a deep breath, '...you're still missing the reason I was so utterly crushed by your actions.'

He turns his head towards mine, a puzzled expression on his face.

'It was your lack of faith in our ability to weather any stormy water in our relationship and grow old and grey together,' I say. 'If you'd honestly believed that we'd stay together for the rest of our lives, you wouldn't have worried about being separated from any children we might have had. That's what hurt me the most at the time and what concerns me the most about a possible future. How much do you truly believe in us?'

FORTY-TWO

TWO YEARS LATER

George looks so cute in his matching linen trousers and waistcoat over a short-sleeved white shirt. At his neck is a sea-foam green tie, held in position by a piece of elastic and made from the same silky fabric as my dress. I have no doubt that he'll be a perfect little page boy, especially as he'll be looked after by his half-sisters Melody and Tamsin, who he adores. They're both in the room next door with their mum, having their hair and make-up done by Kerry, a make-up artist we know well from our modelling days. She's very much in demand for covers and full-page spreads in glossy magazines, so rarely does weddings unless she knows the happy couple.

Looking at George, no one would have any idea what a stressful couple of weeks he's endured. We've been back and forth to the hospital for tests since the call came through telling us that a kidney donor match had been found after a tragic accident. A seven-year-old girl had broken her neck in a fall from a piece of playground apparatus. Despite their devastation, her parents took the decision to allow her organs to live on in others. Following tests, it was discovered that she was a closer match for

George than any of his blood relatives had been, and because the girl was so young the kidneys would be in better condition than from an older donor. Of course, his body might not accept a new kidney, but it has given us hope at the end of a long tunnel of despair.

It was the call we'd all been waiting for since receiving the news almost two years ago that neither of his half-sisters was a suitable match, but at least the DNA test had proved categorically that Melody was JJ's daughter. Inevitably, it raised questions about whether it was right to reveal that JJ was George's dad, but I think we've all come to recognise that honesty is the best policy even when the truth hurts. If anything, the stress of Melody and Tamsin undergoing all the tests, followed by disappointment when the results showed that neither was a compatible donor for their half-brother, has brought them even closer as a family unit. And although he doesn't live with them, there is so much love for George from all of them. It's as though they have a new addition to the family, which in a way they do. Of course, George will never replace Callum, but it's been cathartic for Tiff having a baby around. And because we're all so conscious about honesty in our relationships now, JJ and Tiff told their girls about the little brother they lost, and they now celebrate his birthday on what would have been his due date.

There's a knock at the door and Tiff appears in the same style of sea-foam green silk dress that I'm wearing. Her long hair has been softly curled and gathered into a loose ponytail with flowers scattered through the length. At fifty-two, Tiff makes a striking bridesmaid. She refused the title 'Matron of Honour' on behalf of both of us, saying it made us sound old. Melody and Tamsin are wearing the same colour dresses as us too but in a different style and George will complete the entourage.

'Kerry's ready for you now,' Tiff says, making a beeline for George. 'My turn with the handsomest man at this wedding,' she adds, grabbing him under his armpits and swinging him high in the air.

'You might regret that,' I say, heading for the door. 'He's just finished a big glass of orange squash.'

Two hours later, we are gathered in the porch of the pretty twelfth-century church waiting for the swell of organ music which is our cue to start down the aisle. The sweet fragrance of rose and gardenia from the bridal bouquet, and bridesmaid's posies fills the small space replacing the slight mustiness we'd noticed on Tuesday evening at the rehearsal.

Like a naughty child, I risk a peek through the velvet curtains that separate us from the body of the church. The pews are filled with friends and family decked out in their finery. At the end of the aisle, in front of the altar, Finn and Zack, now firm friends, are standing side by side, with JJ off to one side ready to capture everything on camera. It hasn't been an easy two years for him, but he's worked hard at trying to rebuild his relationships with us, Tiff's friends. He also whisked Tiff away to the Maldives for a second honeymoon after they renewed their vows.

I turn back to gaze at the bride whose empire-line dress in ivory silk and lace is doing a great job of disguising her swollen belly. There's only a couple of months before Annabel's mother will finally be blessed with the grandchild she has been craving.

My throat tightens with emotion as the first notes of the bridal march sound.

'Ready?' I ask, gently squeezing Annabel's bare shoulder before Tiff lifts the bridal veil forwards to cover our friend's happy, smiling face.

'As I'll ever be,' Annabel replies, an unaccustomed nervousness in her voice.

We start down the aisle, which brings back memories of my own wedding eighteen months ago.

Zack proposed to me a month after our meeting at the nature reserve. He said he wanted to show me just how much he believed in us. I said yes... because I believe in us too.

A LETTER FROM JULIA

Thank you so much for choosing to read *The Dilemma*. If you enjoyed it and want to keep up to date with all my latest releases, please sign up at the following link. Your email address will never be shared and you can unsubscribe at any time.

www.bookouture.com/julia-roberts

Like most authors, I'm often asked where I get the ideas for my books. *The Dilemma* has quite a few 'real life' moments in it, particularly George's illness, which is based around something that happened to my friend David's son at birth. Obviously, I checked with David that he was happy for me to incorporate elements of his son Jude's story in *The Dilemma*. Not only was he completely okay with it, as he believes it can raise awareness that giving birth is not always straightforward, he was able to give me some of the technical information about Meconium Aspiration Syndrome which I used alongside research. David has recently undergone an operation to donate one of his kidneys to his son. Both he and Jude are currently recovering, and I wish them well for the future.

I'm sure you'll agree that Charlotte had more than one dilemma to deal with in the book, the first being Zack's lack of honesty. Poor Charlotte was desperate to be a mother, but did she overreact by ending her ten-year relationship so abruptly without giving Zack a chance to explain his feelings?

And what about Tiff? Would you be able to trust your

partner again if they strayed? Would you believe that it was a one-off? And would you be able to forgive your friend for sleeping with your husband, even though Charlotte was unaware that Justin and JJ were one and the same? Will their friendship ever truly recover?

There are other issues I've left open ended for you to draw your own conclusions. Charlotte and Zack are back together, but will they try for a family of their own or will they be content to focus on George and shower him with the love and attention he's going to need?

I hope *The Dilemma* has given you food for thought. If you'd been Charlotte and discovered that you'd inadvertently slept with the husband of one of your best friends, would you have owned up as soon as you found out? Or would you have done what Charlotte did and kept it secret to protect your friend from getting hurt? And once Charlotte realised she was pregnant, should she have told the father straightaway or was she right to make the decision to keep their baby without his knowledge?

If you loved *The Dilemma*, I'd be most grateful if you would take a few minutes to write a review. Not only is your feedback important to me, it can make a real difference in helping new readers discover my books for the first time.

Thanks,

Julia Roberts

KEEP IN TOUCH WITH JULIA

I love hearing from my readers – you can get in touch on my Facebook page, through Twitter, Instagram, Goodreads or my website.

www.juliarobertsauthor.com

 facebook.com/JuliaRobertsTV

 twitter.com/JuliaRobertsTV

 instagram.com/juliagroberts

ACKNOWLEDGEMENTS

This is where I say a huge thank you to all the members of 'Team Julia' for their work on *The Dilemma*.

As with my previous Bookouture books, my editor is Ruth Tross. I say it after every book, but she truly has the patience of a saint and never more so than with this one. I had a few medical issues last year, thankfully all now resolved, but it was a little optimistic of me to think that my brain would be working completely normally after surgery to remove a tumour on the pituitary gland. It turns out that it takes a few months to be firing on all cylinders again, but Ruth never pressurised me when I was unable to make my due dates. At every stage of edits, she challenges, compliments and encourages. I feel very fortunate to have her as my editor.

I like the title *The Dilemma*... simple but powerful. And as for the cover, designed by Alice Moore, I absolutely LOVE it, as I might have mentioned to Ruth on more than one occasion. Funnily enough, when it was first revealed by the Bookouture publicity team, headed up by Kim Nash, I had lots of people asking if the woman on the cover was me. It's not, but I can see why they thought it might be.

I'd also like to give a special mention to Sarah Hardy for the work puts in to organise blog tours and make suggestions on how best to spread the word prior to and post publication.

I always thank my family for the part they play in each new book. They are the ones who see the hours spent at the computer throughout each stage of the process and that was particularly the case here as we all went on a family holiday together when I was at the line-edit stage. Every day I would disappear for a couple (or more) hours to work on the book, which no one questioned. My daughter and her stepdaughter Amber, who is sixteen, thought it sounded intriguing when I gave them a brief outline of the plot – which encouraged me to forego sunbathing by the pool in favour of working to perfect the book.

I was hoping that now it's just me and my husband Chris in the house, there would be less drama and fewer distractions. That's only the case if I leave my phone in a different room, if you get my drift! But if I do that, I won't be able to see the messages from Chris when my dinner is ready, or my bath run. I know, I know... I'm very lucky to have him, even though I still don't always show it.

Finally, I want to thank you for choosing to read *The Dilemma*. It hasn't been the easiest book to write, but at one point during the process I remarked to Chris that it's a book I would like to read – I do hope you agree.

Printed in Great Britain
by Amazon